allad of

aYa

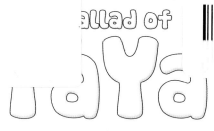

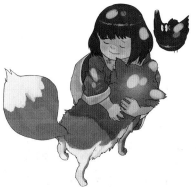

Book 9: Sonata

Written by

Jean-Marie **Omont**   Patrick **Marty**   Charlotte **Girard**

Illustrated by
Golo **Zhao**

Created and Edited by

Patrick **Marty** and Charlotte **Girard**

Translation and Layout by Mike Kennedy

MAGNETIC™

www.magnetic-press.com

YAYA MANAGED TO ESCAPE FROM THE WICKED GANGSTER ZHU!
AFTER A FIERCE CHASE ACROSS THE DECK OF A STEAM LINER
DURING A TERRIBLE STORM, ZHU WAS KNOCKED OVERBOARD,
LEAVING YAYA FREE TO RETURN TO SHANGHAI SAFELY. BUT WHEN
SHE GOT THERE, SHE FOUND THE CITY IS STILL UNDER MILITARY
CONTROL. FORTUNATELY, YAYA IS RECOGNIZED BY HER FORMER
CHAUFFEUR, CHANG, WHO NOW WORKS FOR THE GOVERNMENT!
UNFORTUNATELY, HOWEVER, HE HAS BAD NEWS...
HER PARENTS HAVE BEEN MISSING SINCE
HER DISAPPEARANCE!

TUDUO ALSO FOUND HIS WAY BACK TO SHANGHAI WITH
THE HOPE OF GATHERING HIS LITTLE BROTHER XIAO AND
MAYBE FINDING A NEW HOME WITH YAYA'S FAMILY...

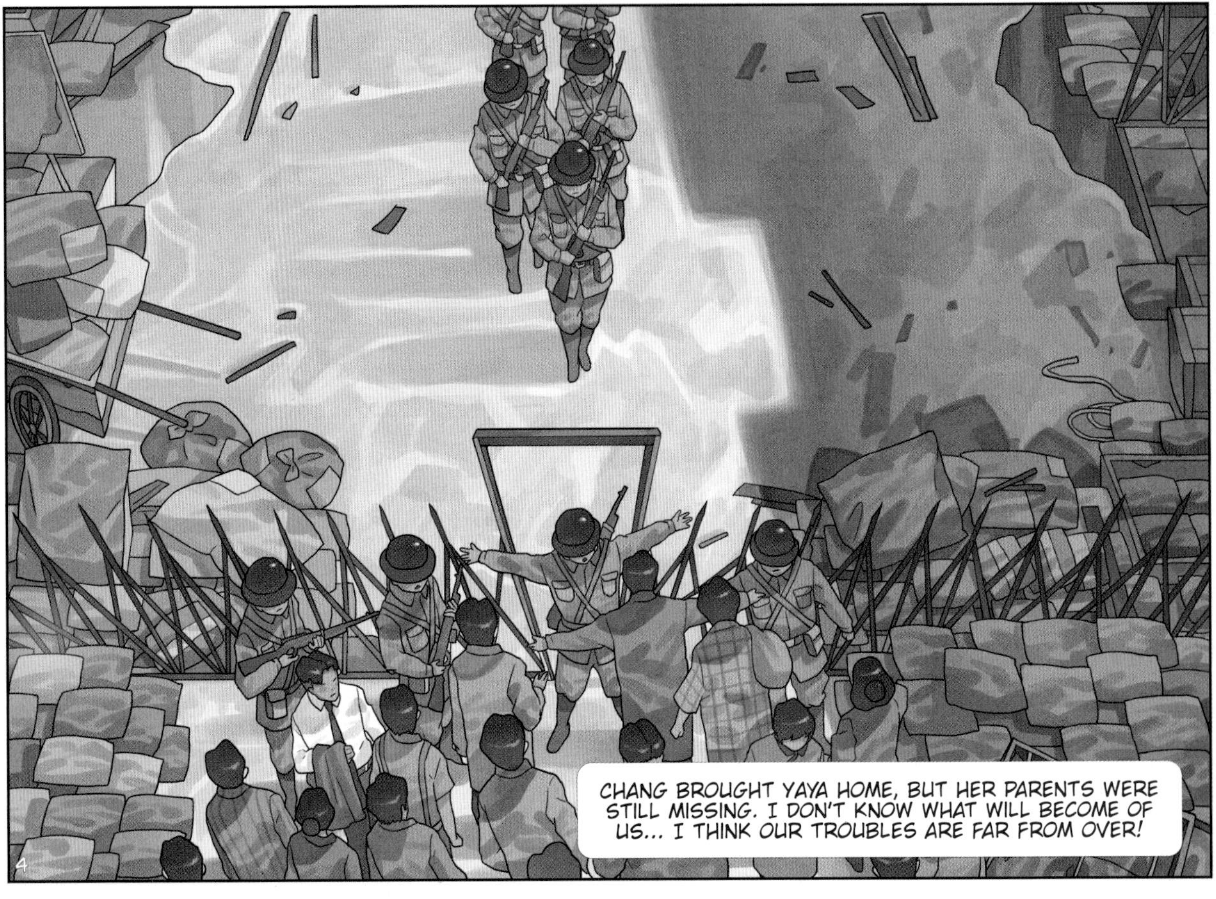
CHANG BROUGHT YAYA HOME, BUT HER PARENTS WERE STILL MISSING. I DON'T KNOW WHAT WILL BECOME OF US... I THINK OUR TROUBLES ARE FAR FROM OVER!

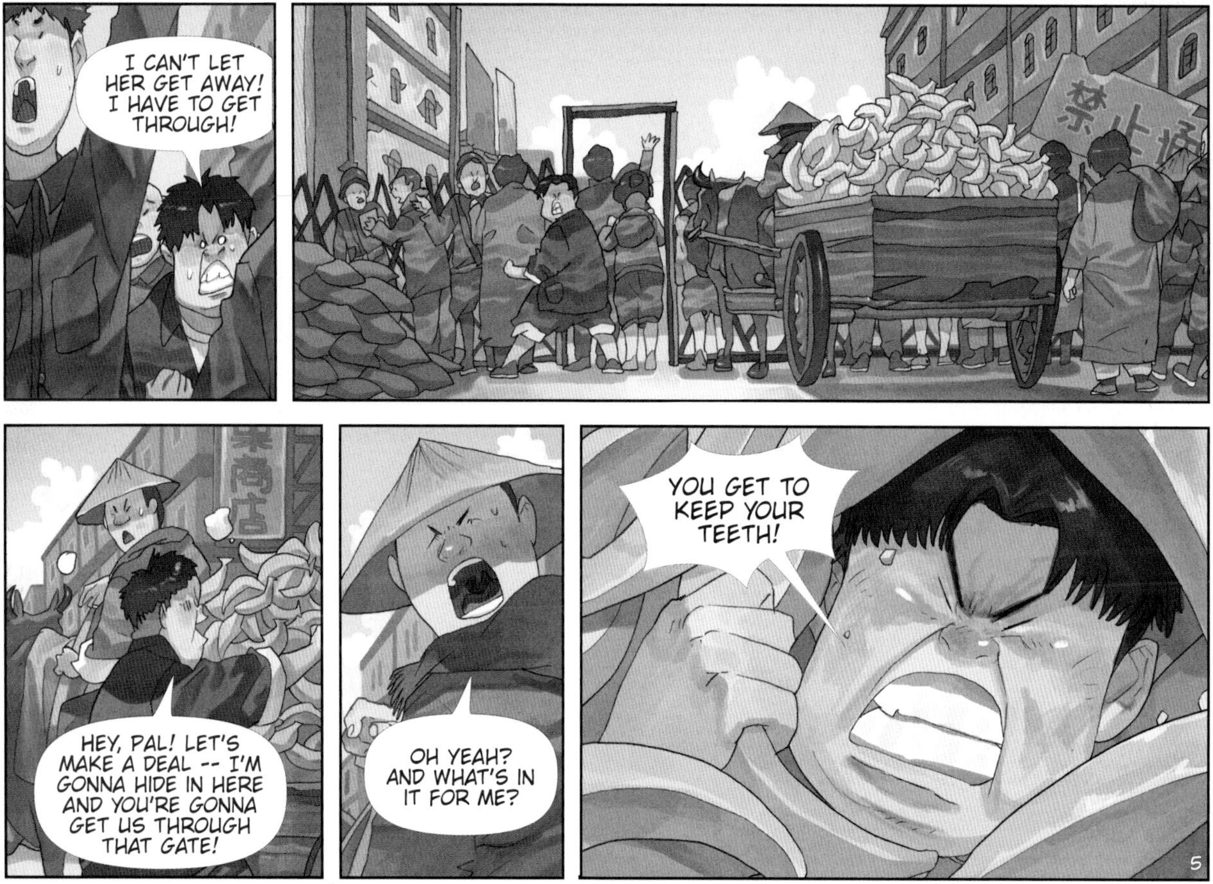

I CAN'T LET HER GET AWAY! I HAVE TO GET THROUGH!
HEY, PAL! LET'S MAKE A DEAL -- I'M GONNA HIDE IN HERE AND YOU'RE GONNA GET US THROUGH THAT GATE!
OH YEAH? AND WHAT'S IN IT FOR ME?
YOU GET TO KEEP YOUR TEETH!

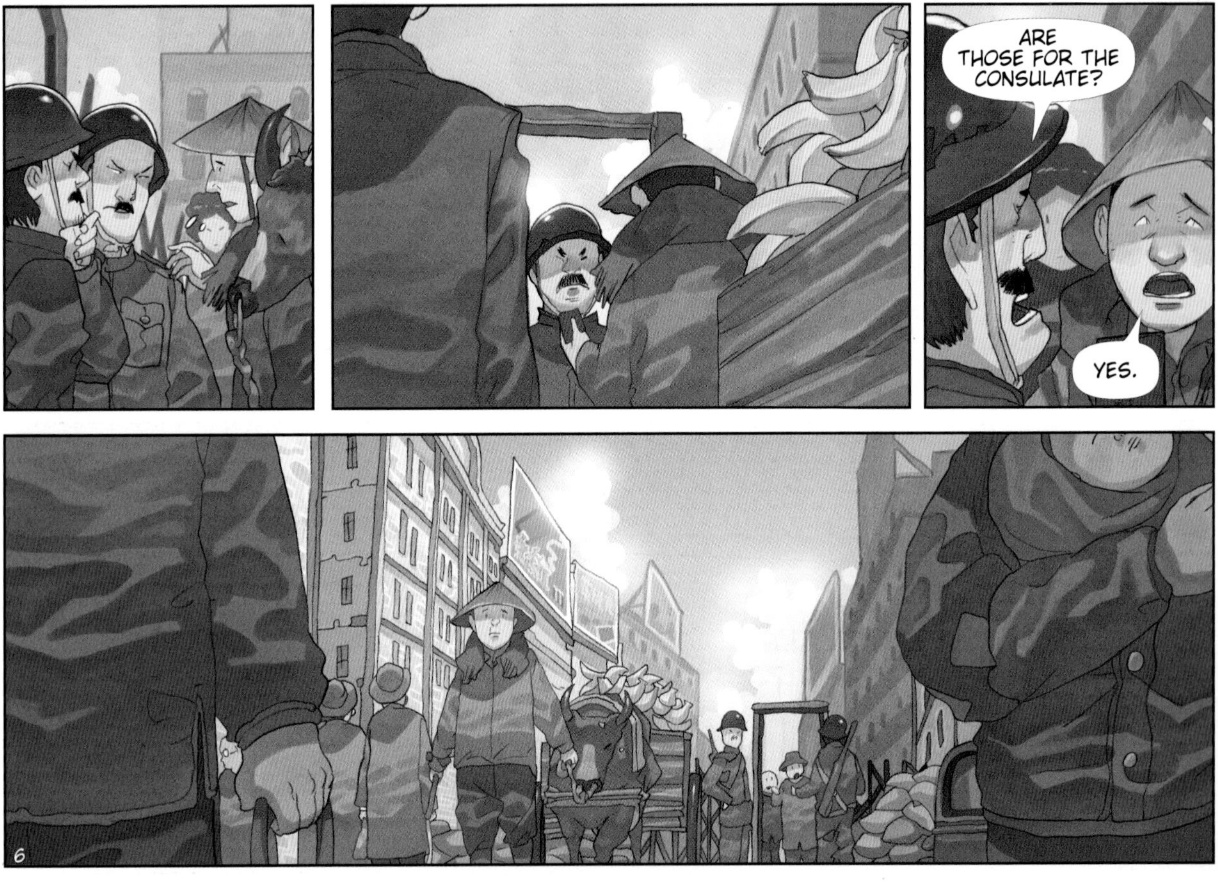
ARE THOSE FOR THE CONSULATE?
YES.

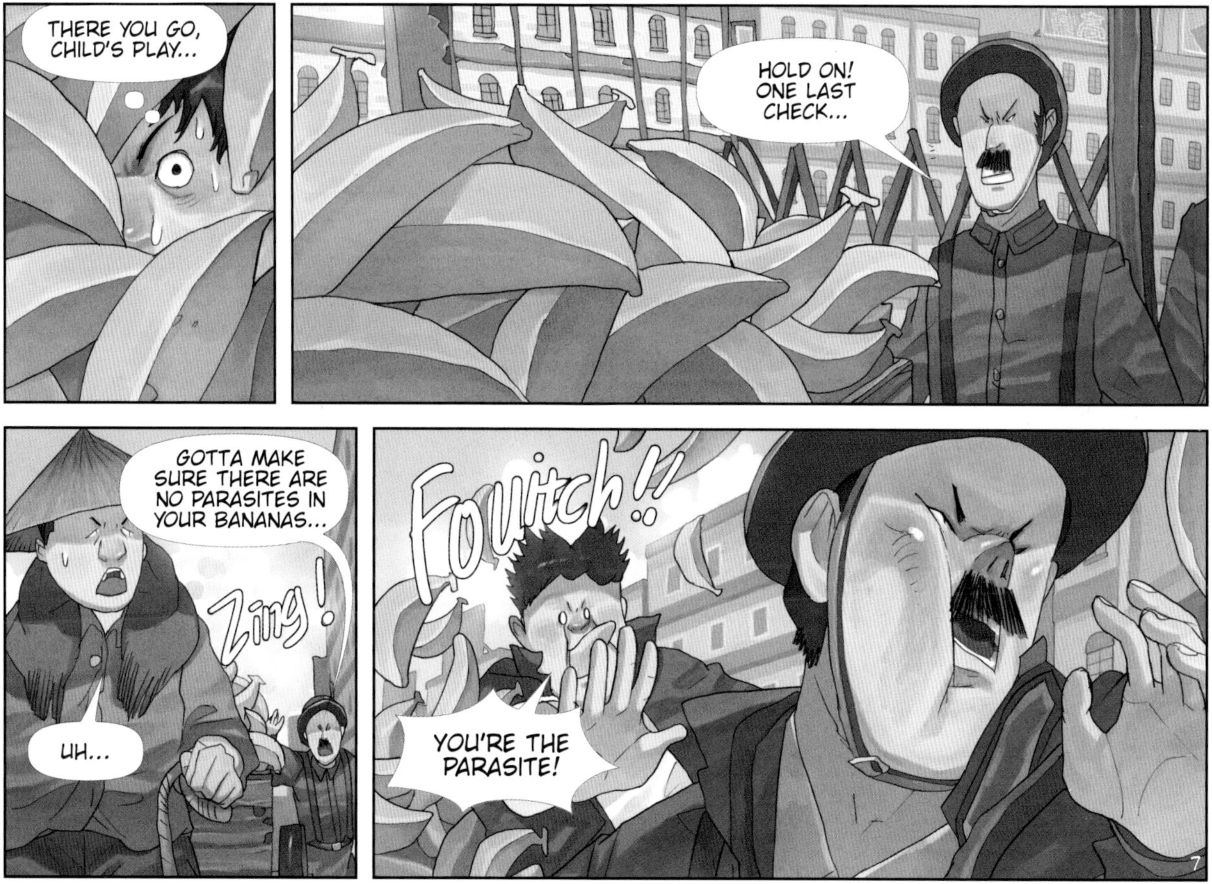
THERE YOU GO, CHILD'S PLAY...
HOLD ON! ONE LAST CHECK...
GOTTA MAKE SURE THERE ARE NO PARASITES IN YOUR BANANAS...
Zing!
UH...
Fouitch!!
YOU'RE THE PARASITE!

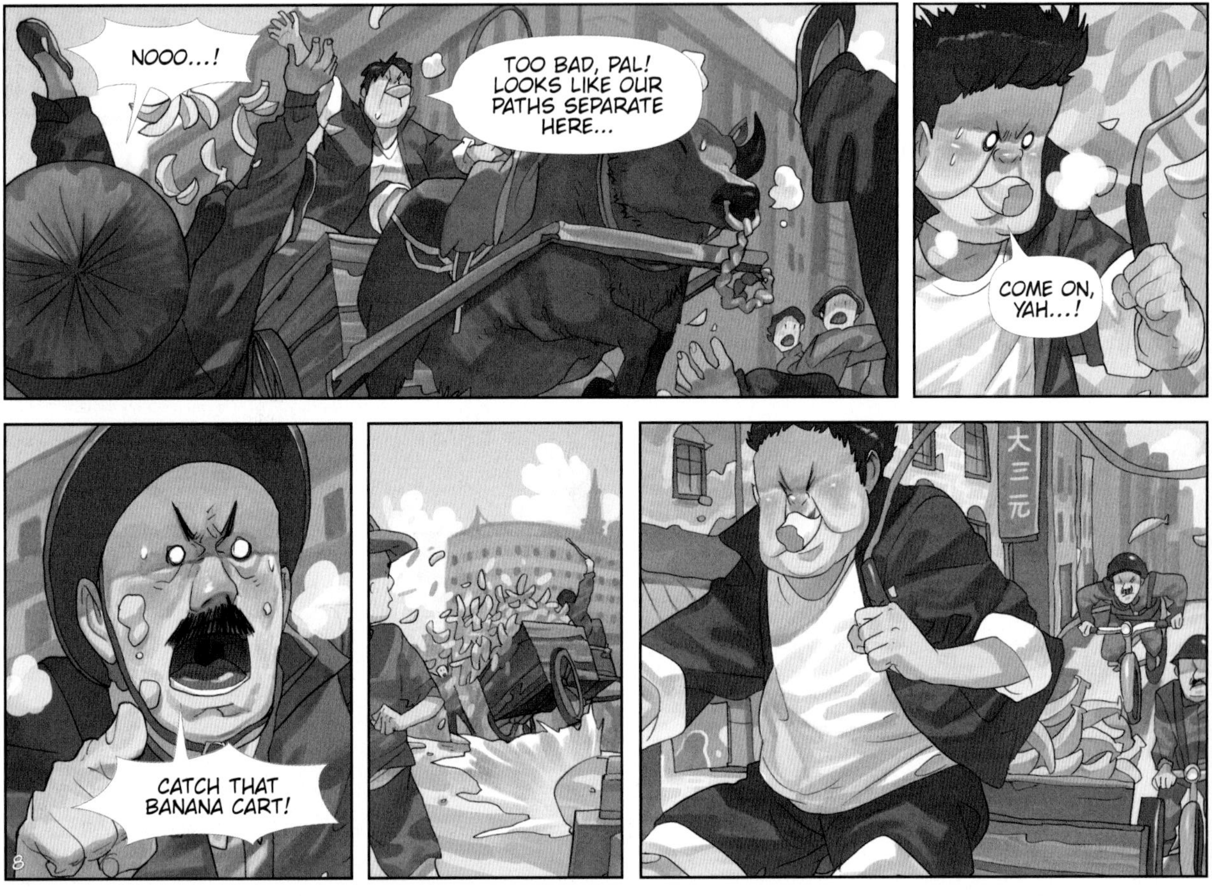
NOOO...!
TOO BAD, PAL! LOOKS LIKE OUR PATHS SEPARATE HERE...
COME ON, YAH...!
CATCH THAT BANANA CART!
大三元

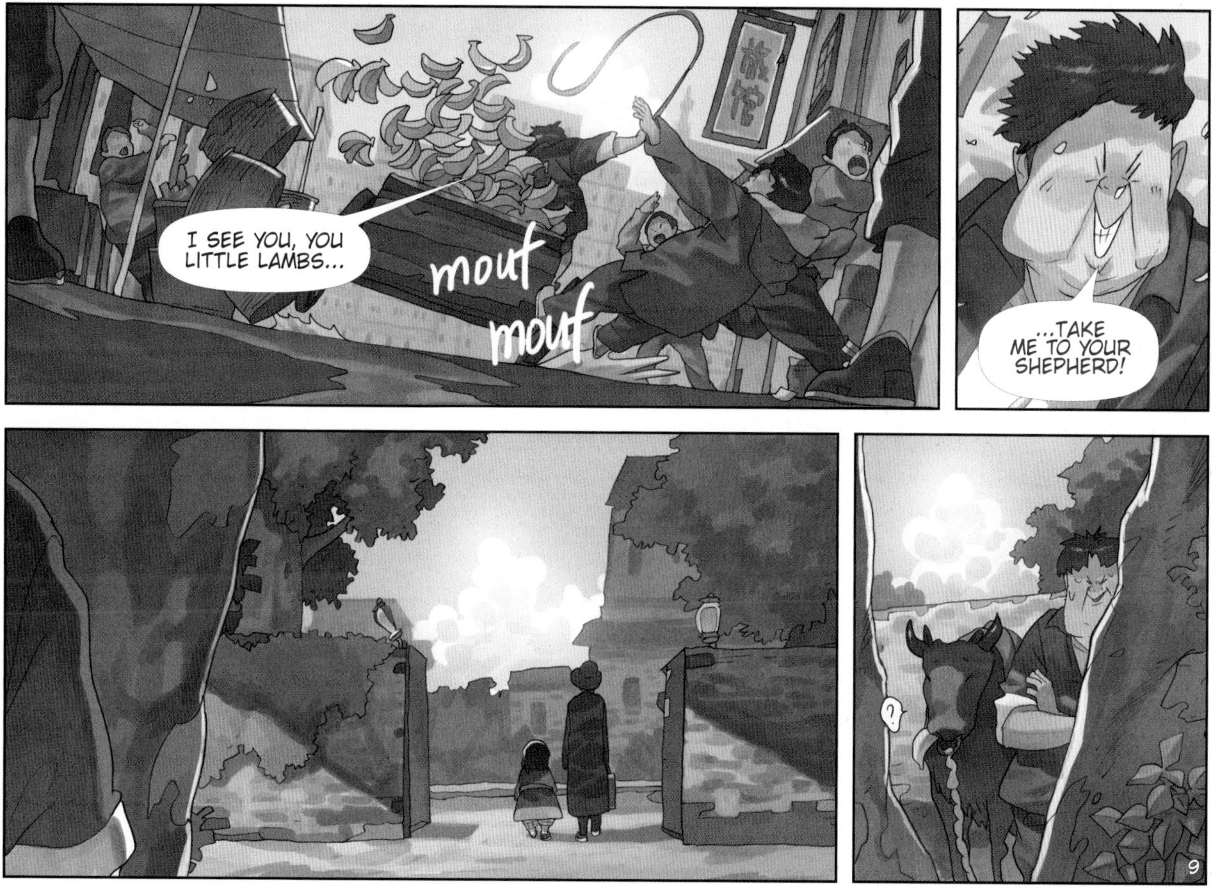
I SEE YOU, YOU LITTLE LAMBS...
mouf
mouf
...TAKE ME TO YOUR SHEPHERD!
?

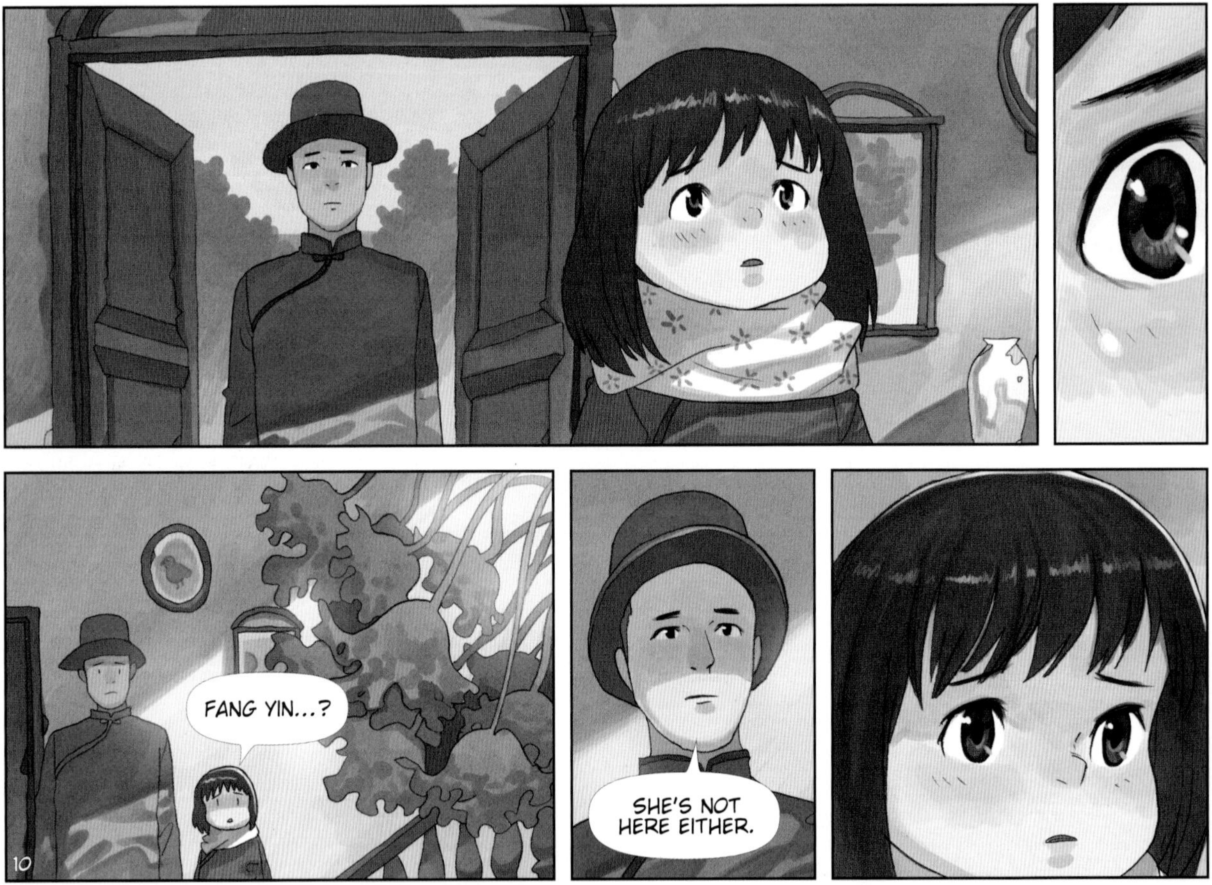
FANG YIN...?
SHE'S NOT HERE EITHER.

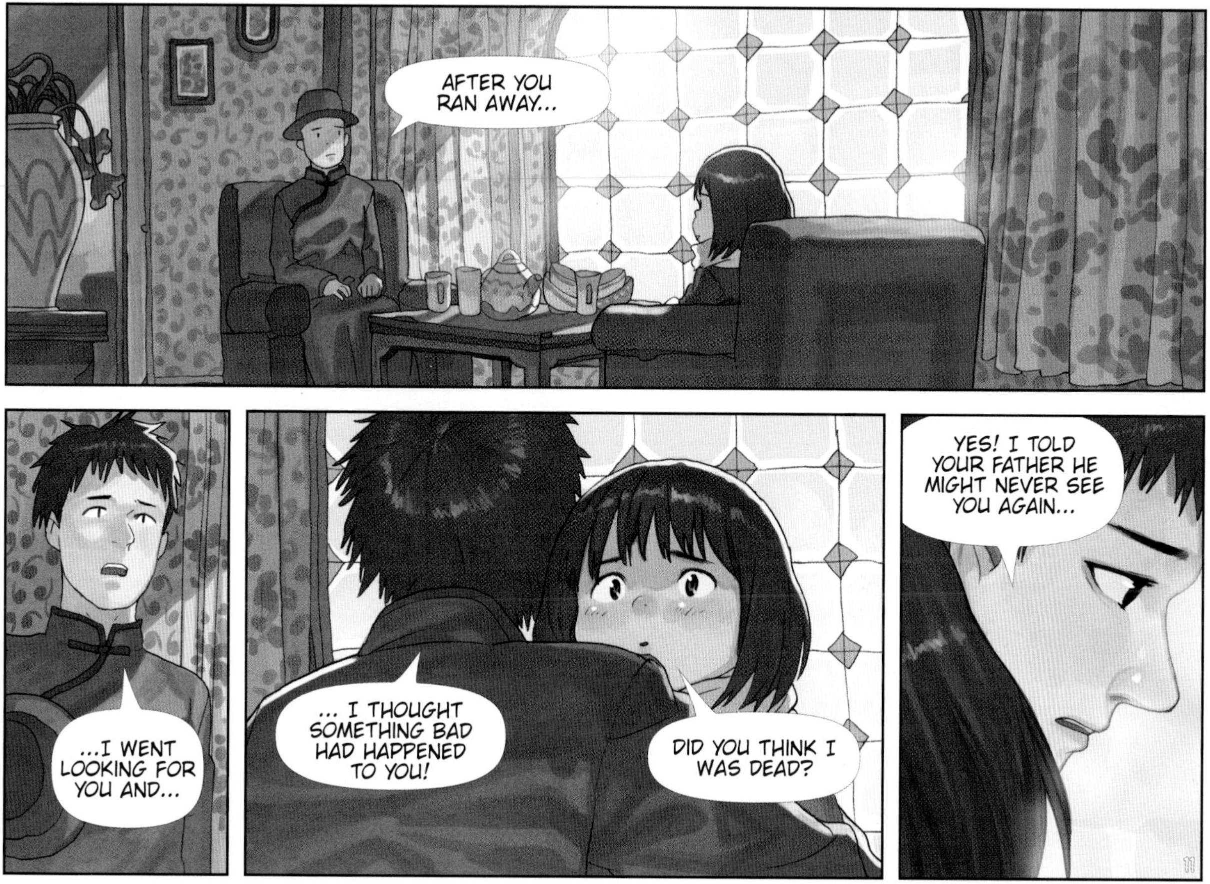
AFTER YOU RAN AWAY...
...I WENT LOOKING FOR YOU AND...
... I THOUGHT SOMETHING BAD HAD HAPPENED TO YOU!
DID YOU THINK I WAS DEAD?
YES! I TOLD YOUR FATHER HE MIGHT NEVER SEE YOU AGAIN...

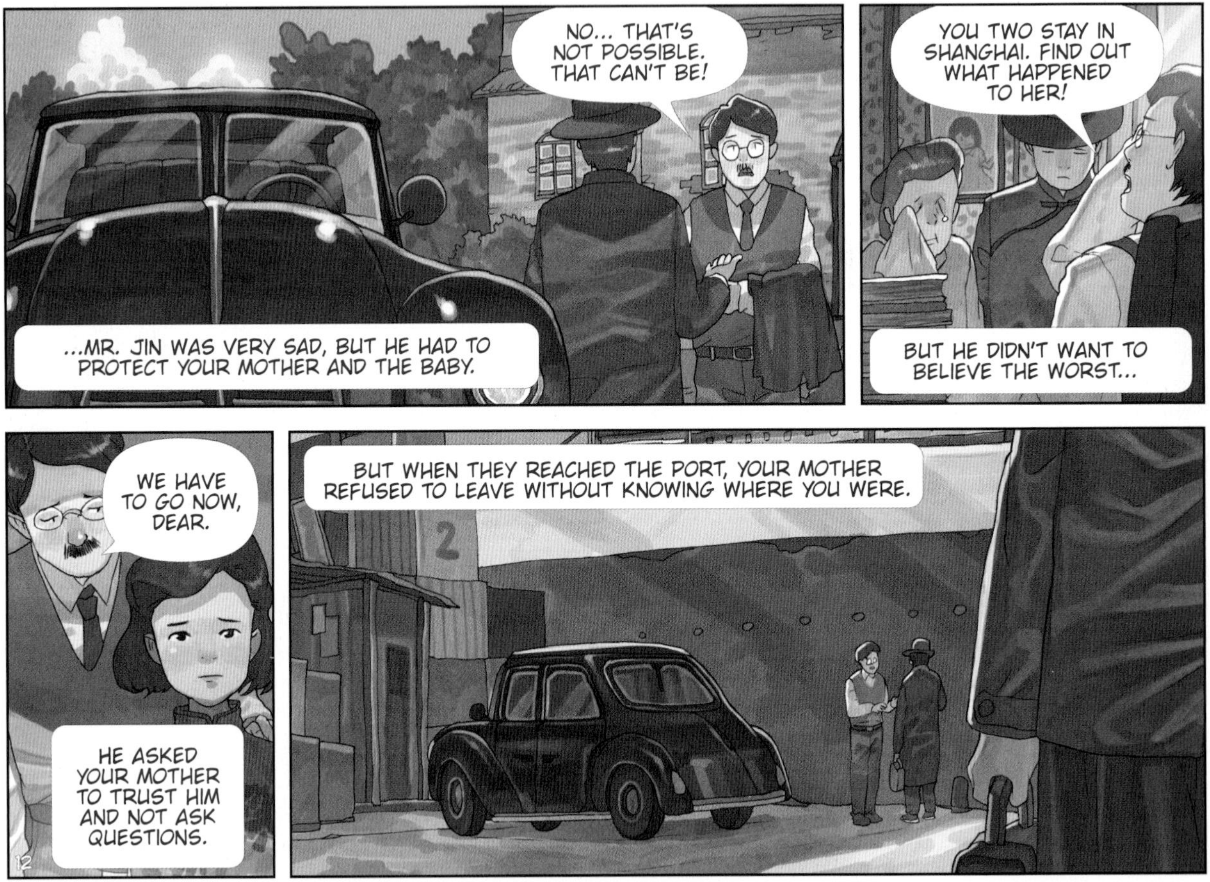
NO... THAT'S NOT POSSIBLE. THAT CAN'T BE!
...MR. JIN WAS VERY SAD, BUT HE HAD TO PROTECT YOUR MOTHER AND THE BABY.
YOU TWO STAY IN SHANGHAI. FIND OUT WHAT HAPPENED TO HER!
BUT HE DIDN'T WANT TO BELIEVE THE WORST...
WE HAVE TO GO NOW, DEAR.
HE ASKED YOUR MOTHER TO TRUST HIM AND NOT ASK QUESTIONS.
BUT WHEN THEY REACHED THE PORT, YOUR MOTHER REFUSED TO LEAVE WITHOUT KNOWING WHERE YOU WERE.
2

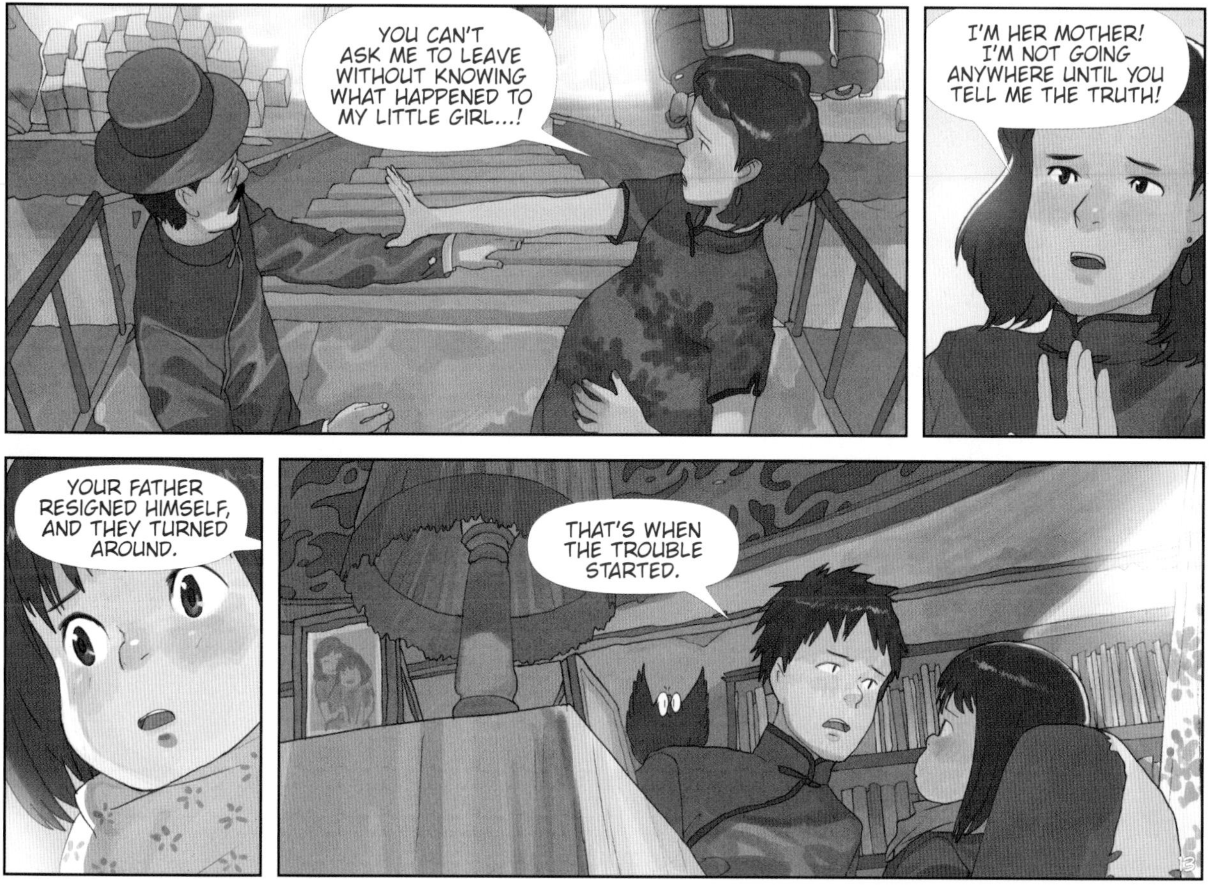
YOU CAN'T ASK ME TO LEAVE WITHOUT KNOWING WHAT HAPPENED TO MY LITTLE GIRL...!
I'M HER MOTHER! I'M NOT GOING ANYWHERE UNTIL YOU TELL ME THE TRUTH!
YOUR FATHER RESIGNED HIMSELF, AND THEY TURNED AROUND.
THAT'S WHEN THE TROUBLE STARTED.
13

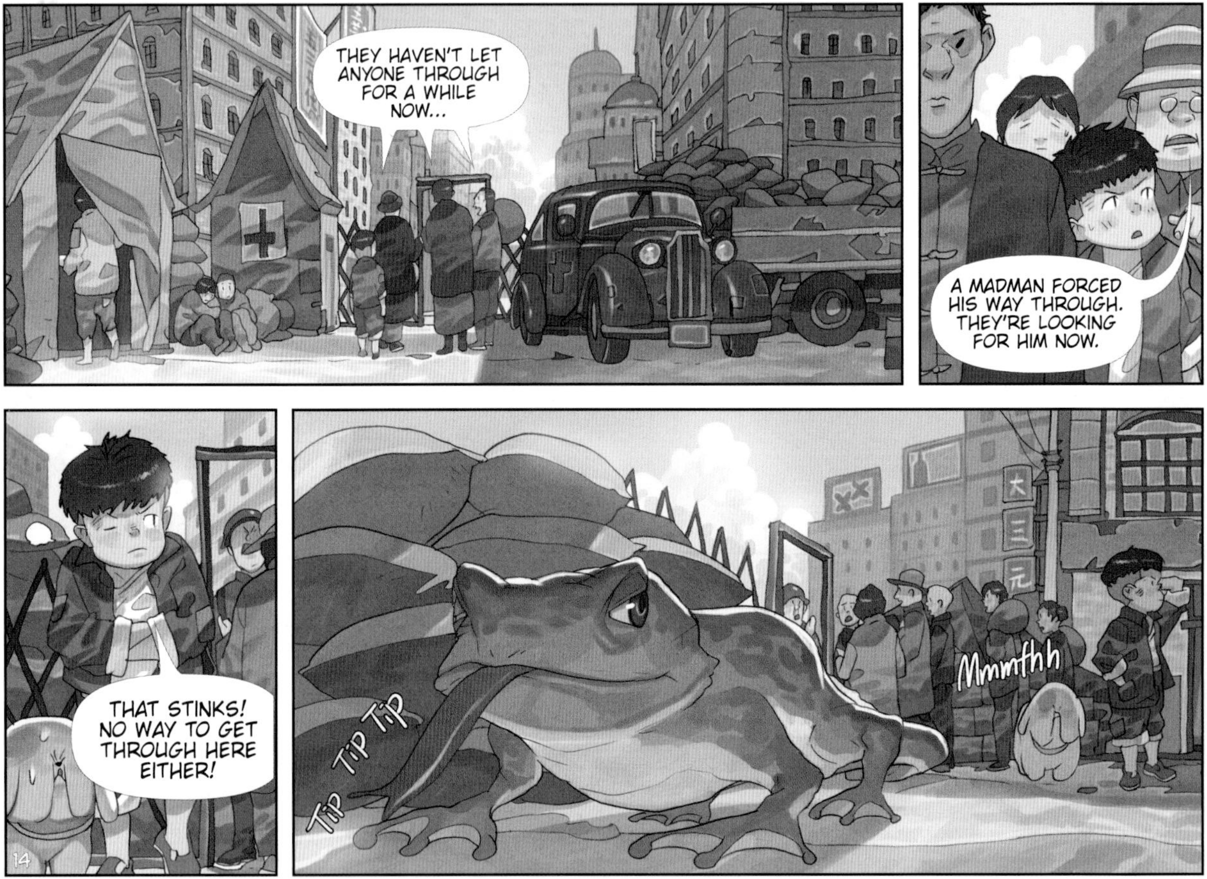
THEY HAVEN'T LET ANYONE THROUGH FOR A WHILE NOW...
A MADMAN FORCED HIS WAY THROUGH. THEY'RE LOOKING FOR HIM NOW.
THAT STINKS! NO WAY TO GET THROUGH HERE EITHER!
TIP TIP TIP
Mmmfhh

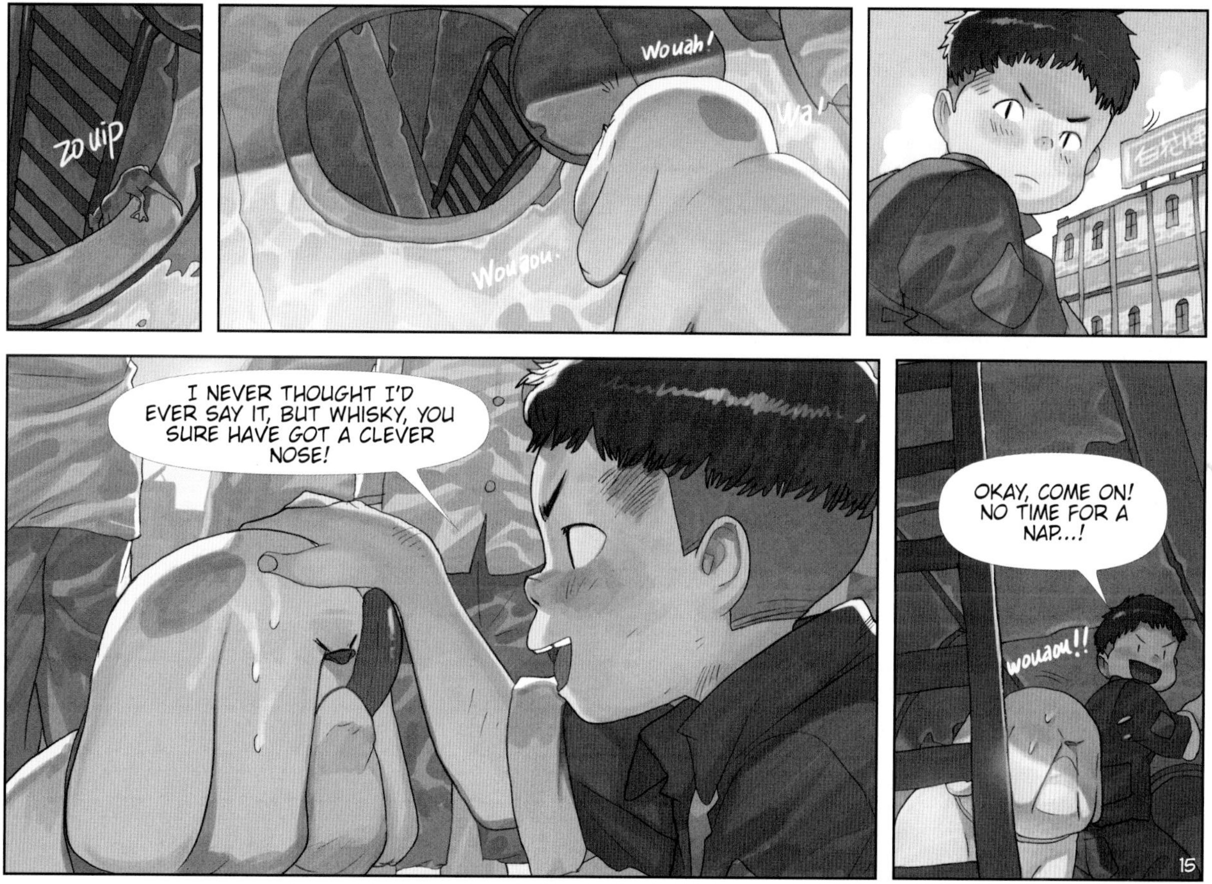

zouip
Wouah!
Wa!
Wouaou.
I NEVER THOUGHT I'D EVER SAY IT, BUT WHISKY, YOU SURE HAVE GOT A CLEVER NOSE!
OKAY, COME ON! NO TIME FOR A NAP...!
wouaou!!

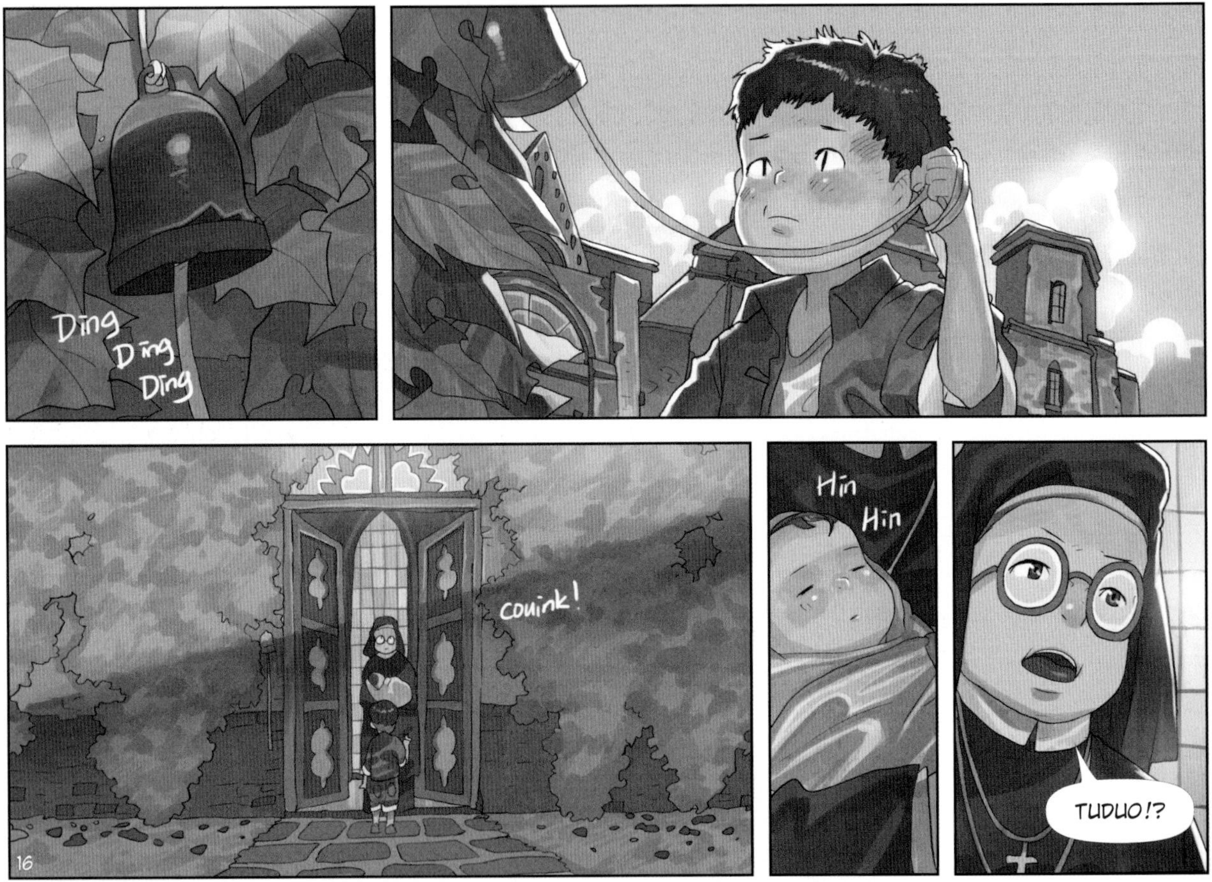
Ding
Ding
Ding
couink!
Hin
Hin
TUDUO!?

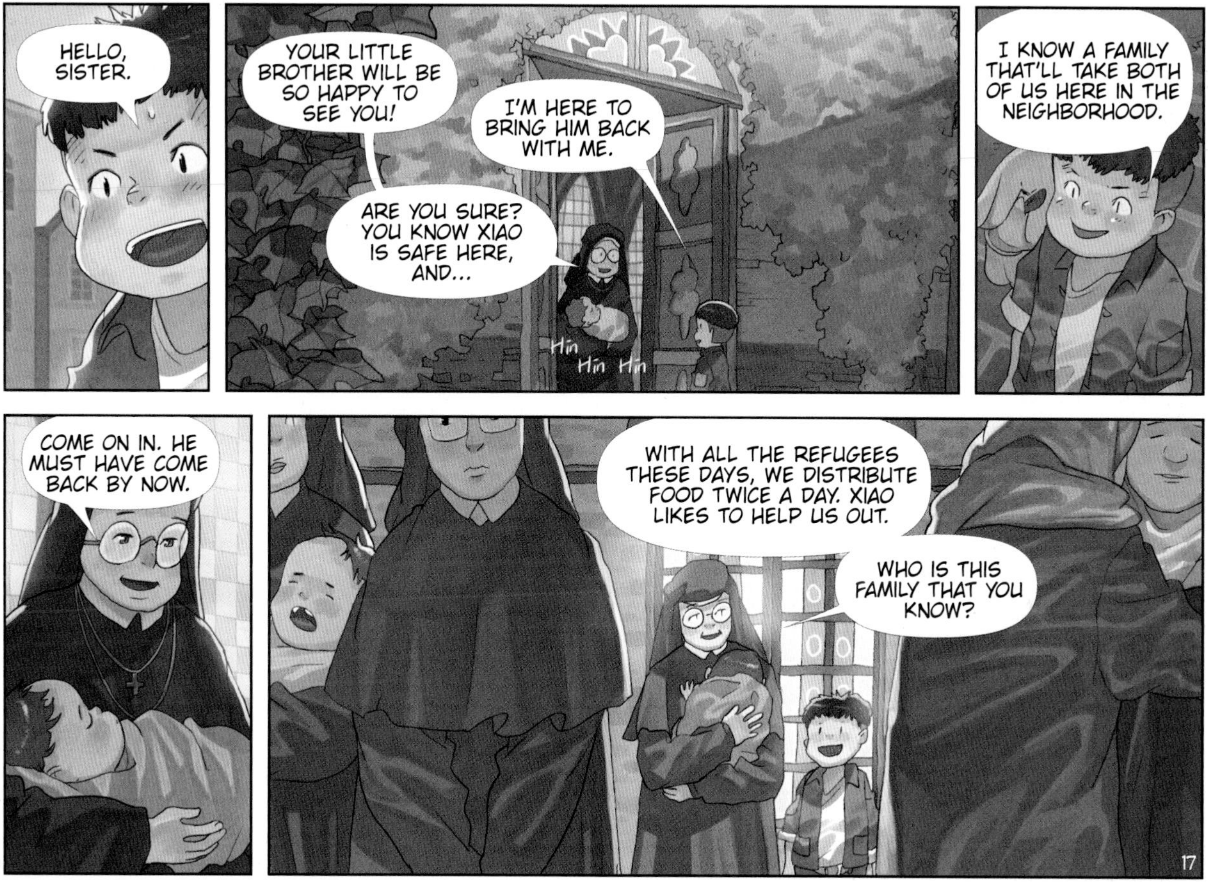
HELLO, SISTER.
YOUR LITTLE BROTHER WILL BE SO HAPPY TO SEE YOU!
I'M HERE TO BRING HIM BACK WITH ME.
ARE YOU SURE? YOU KNOW XIAO IS SAFE HERE, AND...
Hin Hin Hin
I KNOW A FAMILY THAT'LL TAKE BOTH OF US HERE IN THE NEIGHBORHOOD.
COME ON IN. HE MUST HAVE COME BACK BY NOW.
WITH ALL THE REFUGEES THESE DAYS, WE DISTRIBUTE FOOD TWICE A DAY. XIAO LIKES TO HELP US OUT.
WHO IS THIS FAMILY THAT YOU KNOW?

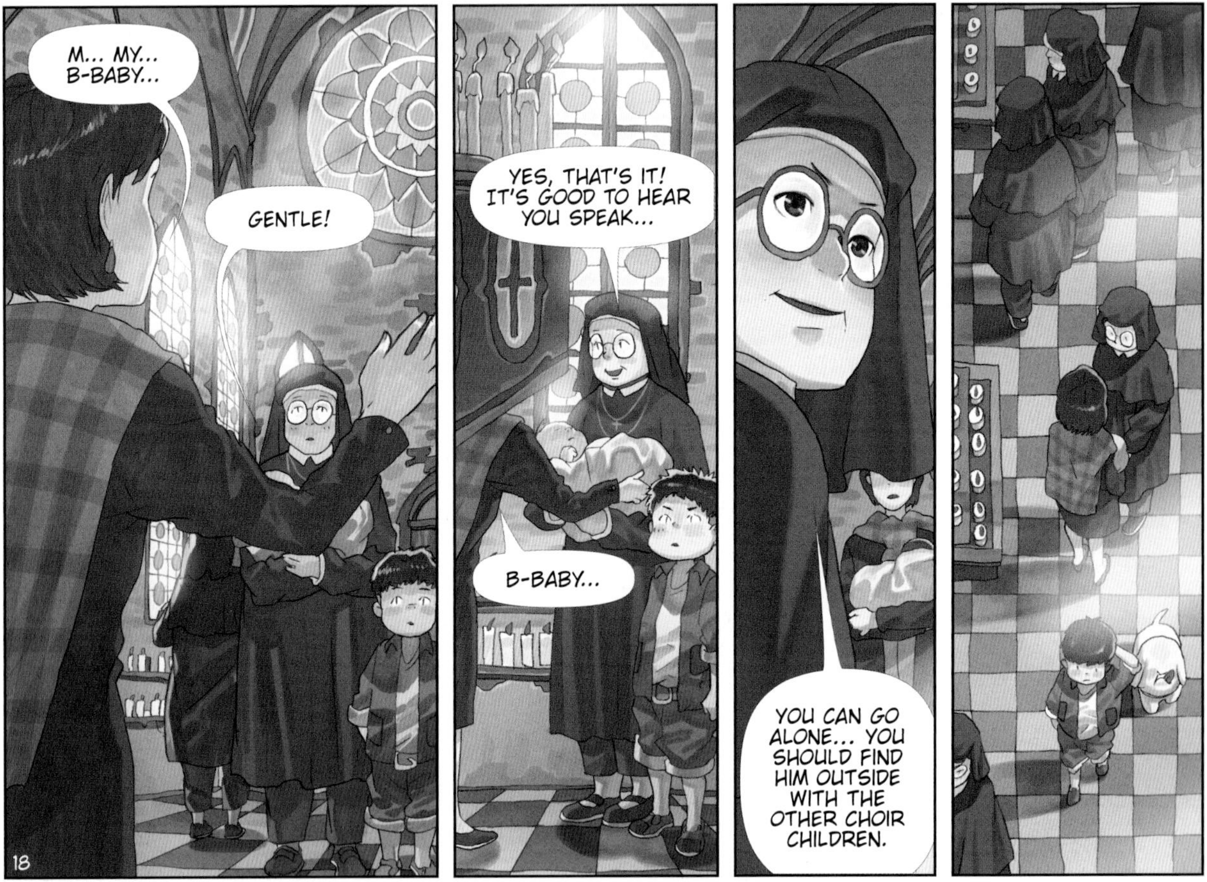
M... MY... B-BABY...
GENTLE!
YES, THAT'S IT! IT'S GOOD TO HEAR YOU SPEAK...
B-BABY...
YOU CAN GO ALONE... YOU SHOULD FIND HIM OUTSIDE WITH THE OTHER CHOIR CHILDREN.

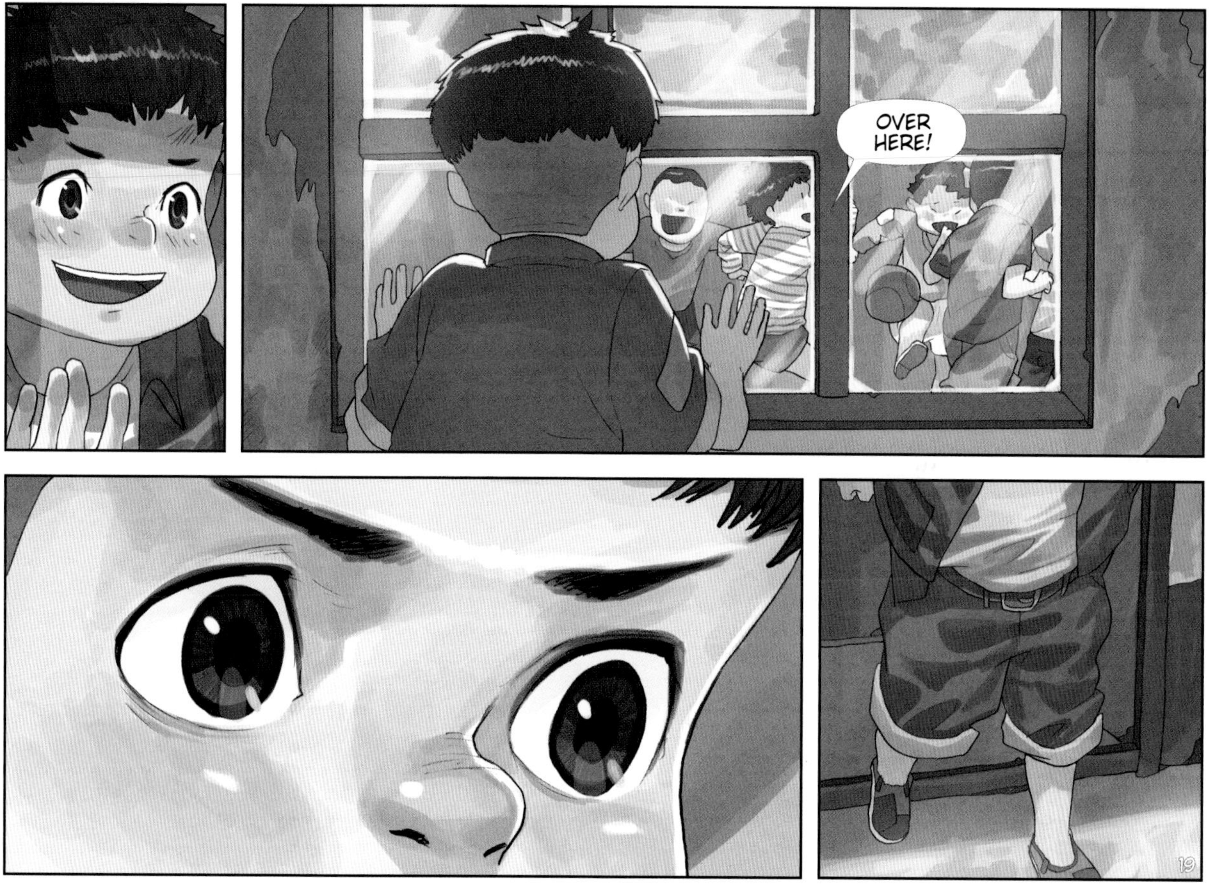
OVER HERE!

HEY! NO FAIR!

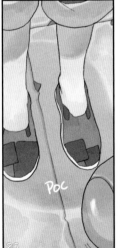

POC

HEY! EXCUSE ME...

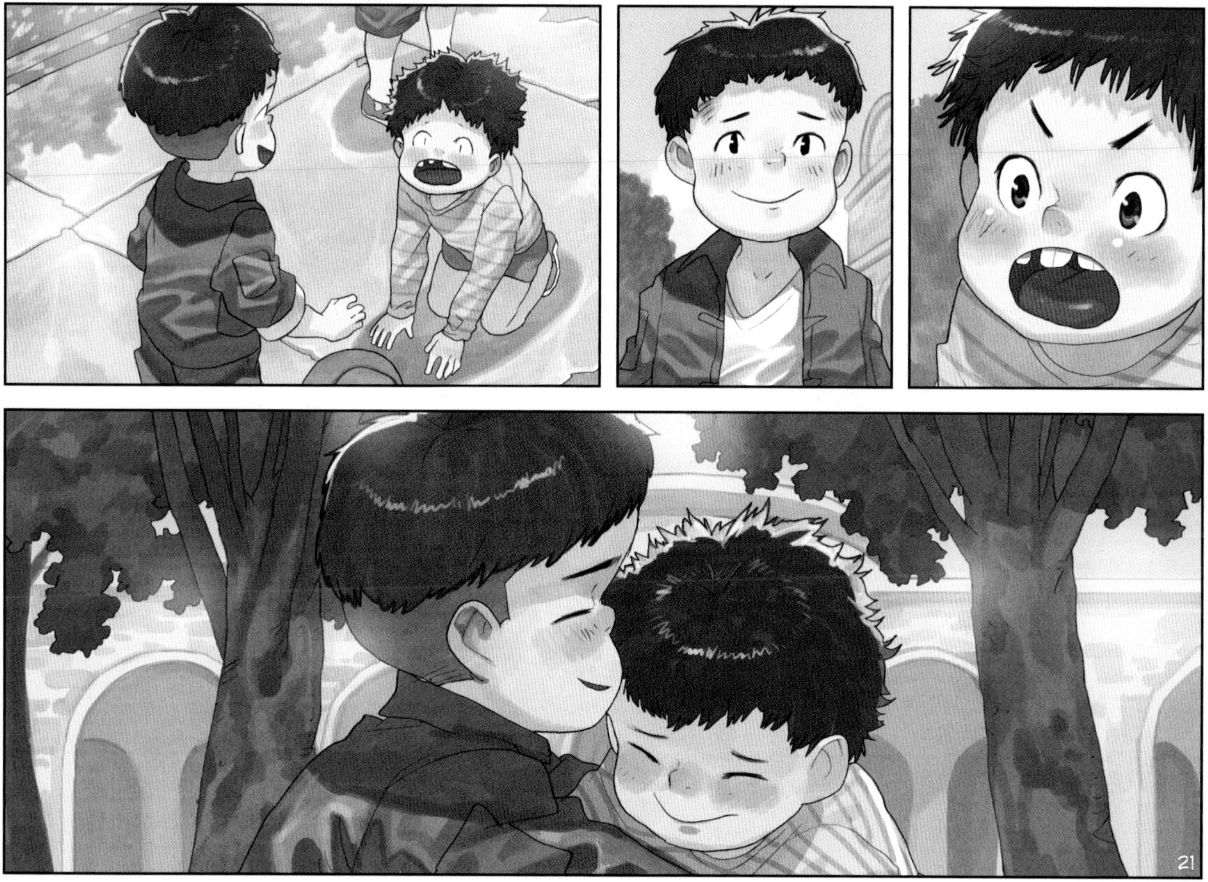

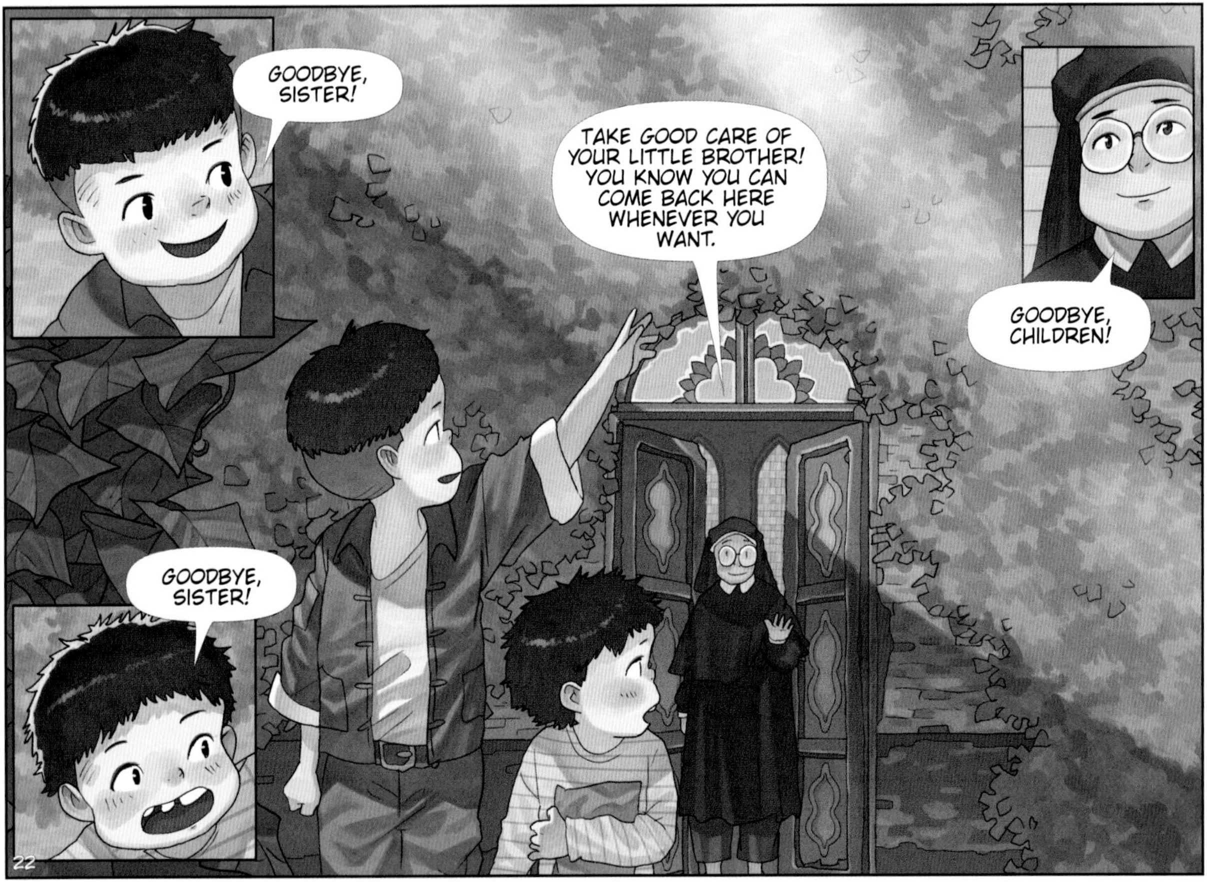
GOODBYE, SISTER!
TAKE GOOD CARE OF YOUR LITTLE BROTHER! YOU KNOW YOU CAN COME BACK HERE WHENEVER YOU WANT.
GOODBYE, CHILDREN!
GOODBYE, SISTER!

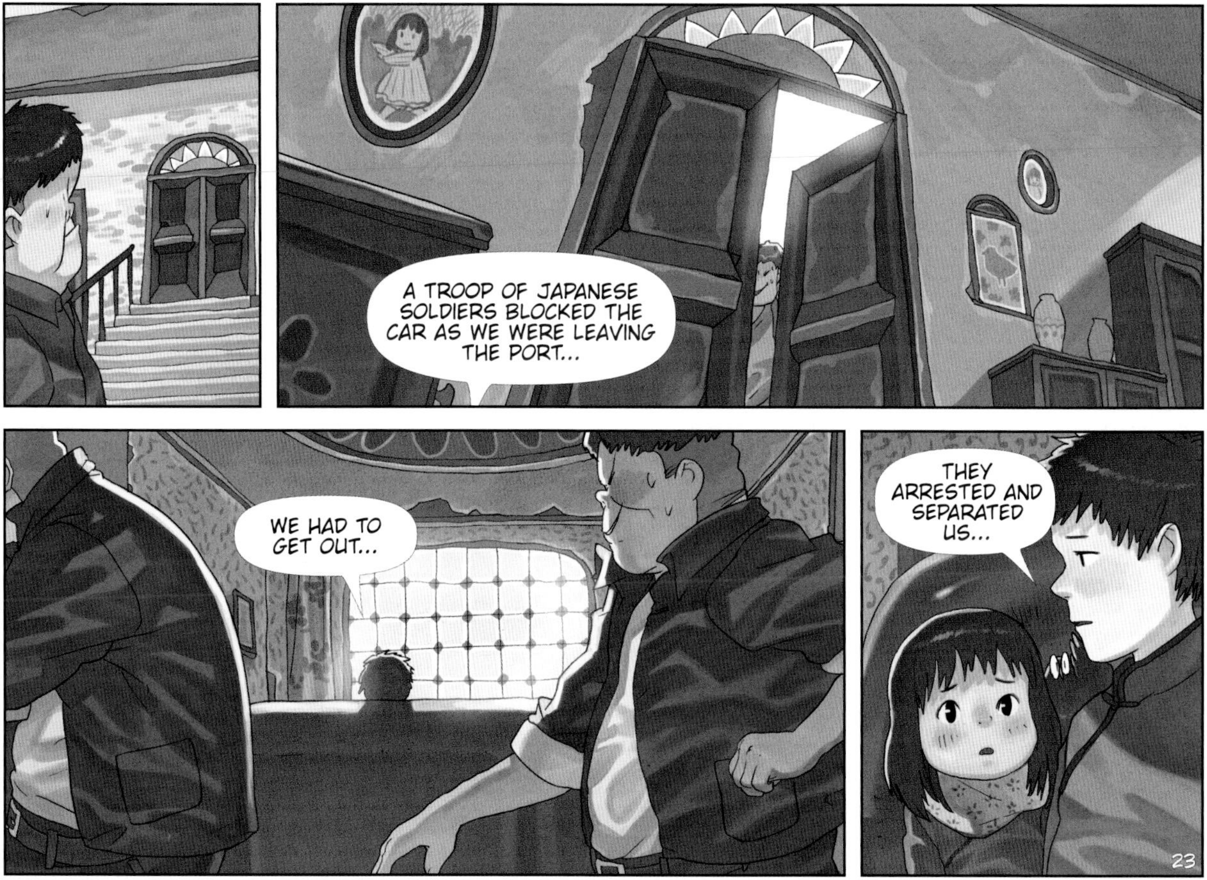
A TROOP OF JAPANESE SOLDIERS BLOCKED THE CAR AS WE WERE LEAVING THE PORT...
WE HAD TO GET OUT...
THEY ARRESTED AND SEPARATED US...

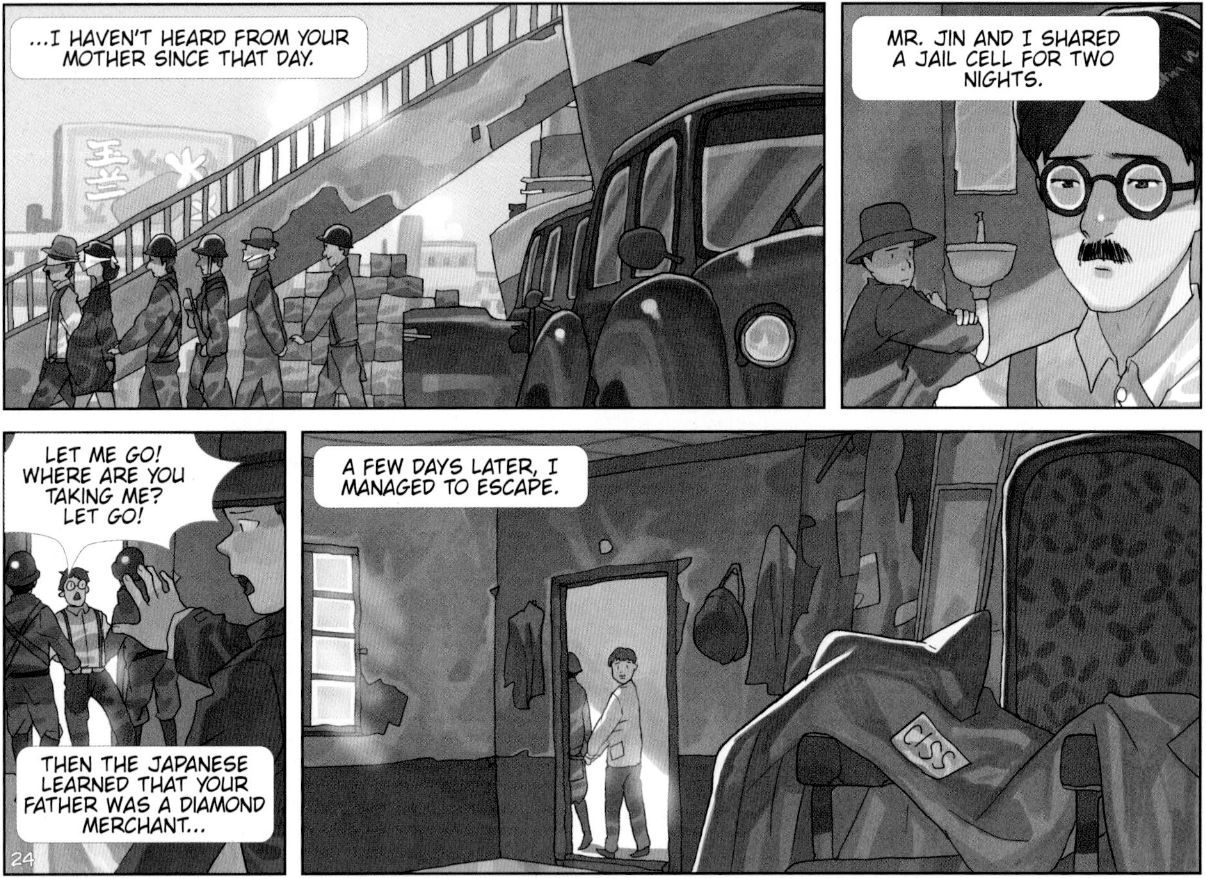
...I HAVEN'T HEARD FROM YOUR MOTHER SINCE THAT DAY.
MR. JIN AND I SHARED A JAIL CELL FOR TWO NIGHTS.
LET ME GO! WHERE ARE YOU TAKING ME? LET GO!
THEN THE JAPANESE LEARNED THAT YOUR FATHER WAS A DIAMOND MERCHANT...
A FEW DAYS LATER, I MANAGED TO ESCAPE.
CISS

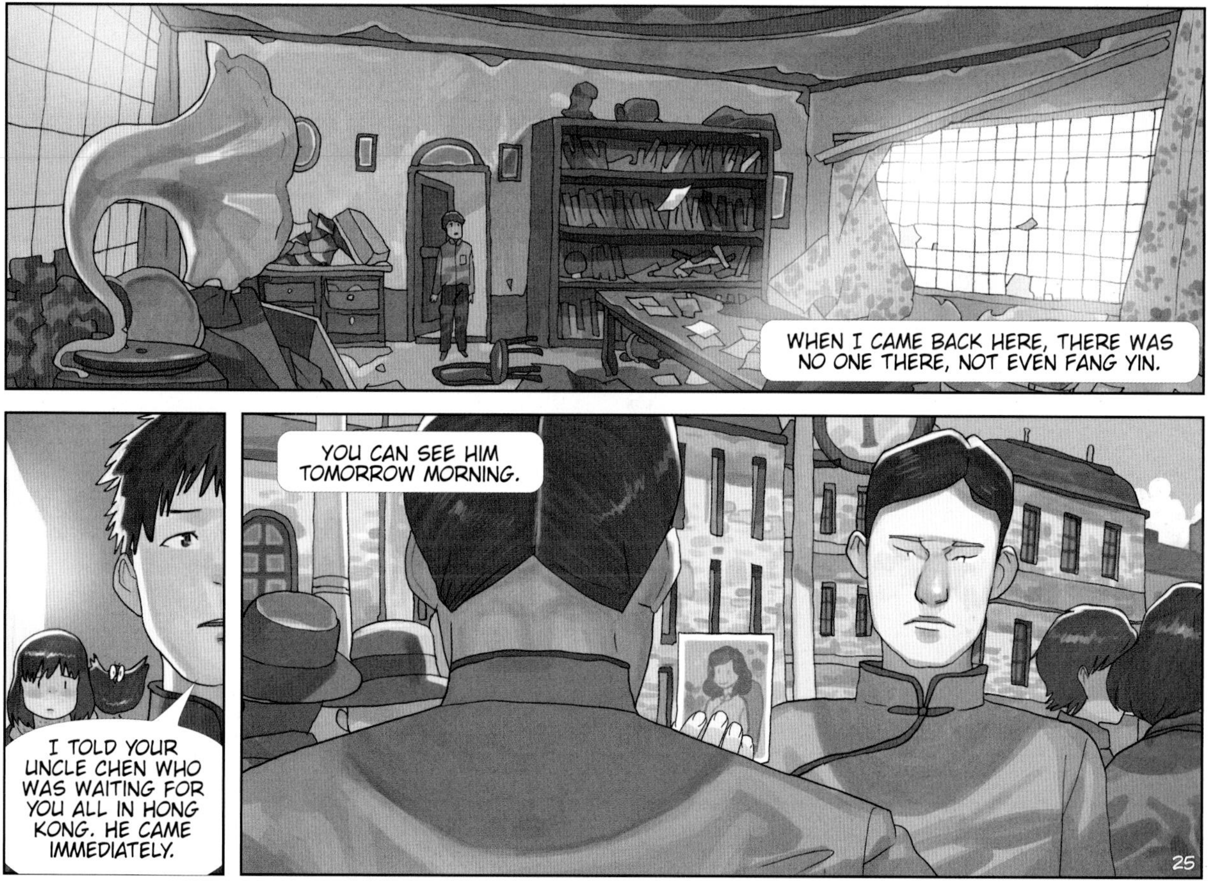
WHEN I CAME BACK HERE, THERE WAS NO ONE THERE, NOT EVEN FANG YIN.
I TOLD YOUR UNCLE CHEN WHO WAS WAITING FOR YOU ALL IN HONG KONG. HE CAME IMMEDIATELY.
YOU CAN SEE HIM TOMORROW MORNING.

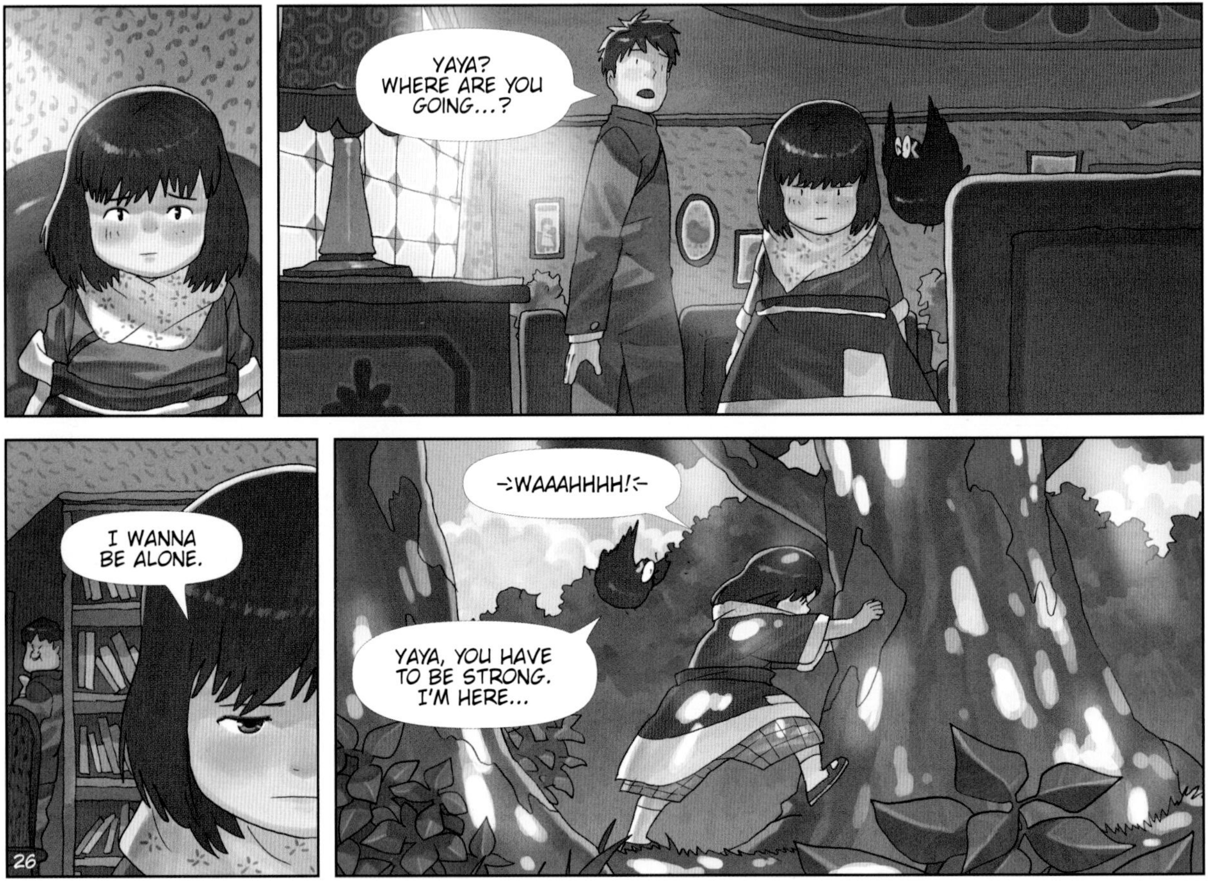
YAYA? WHERE ARE YOU GOING...?
I WANNA BE ALONE.
-WAAAHHHH!-
YAYA, YOU HAVE TO BE STRONG. I'M HERE...

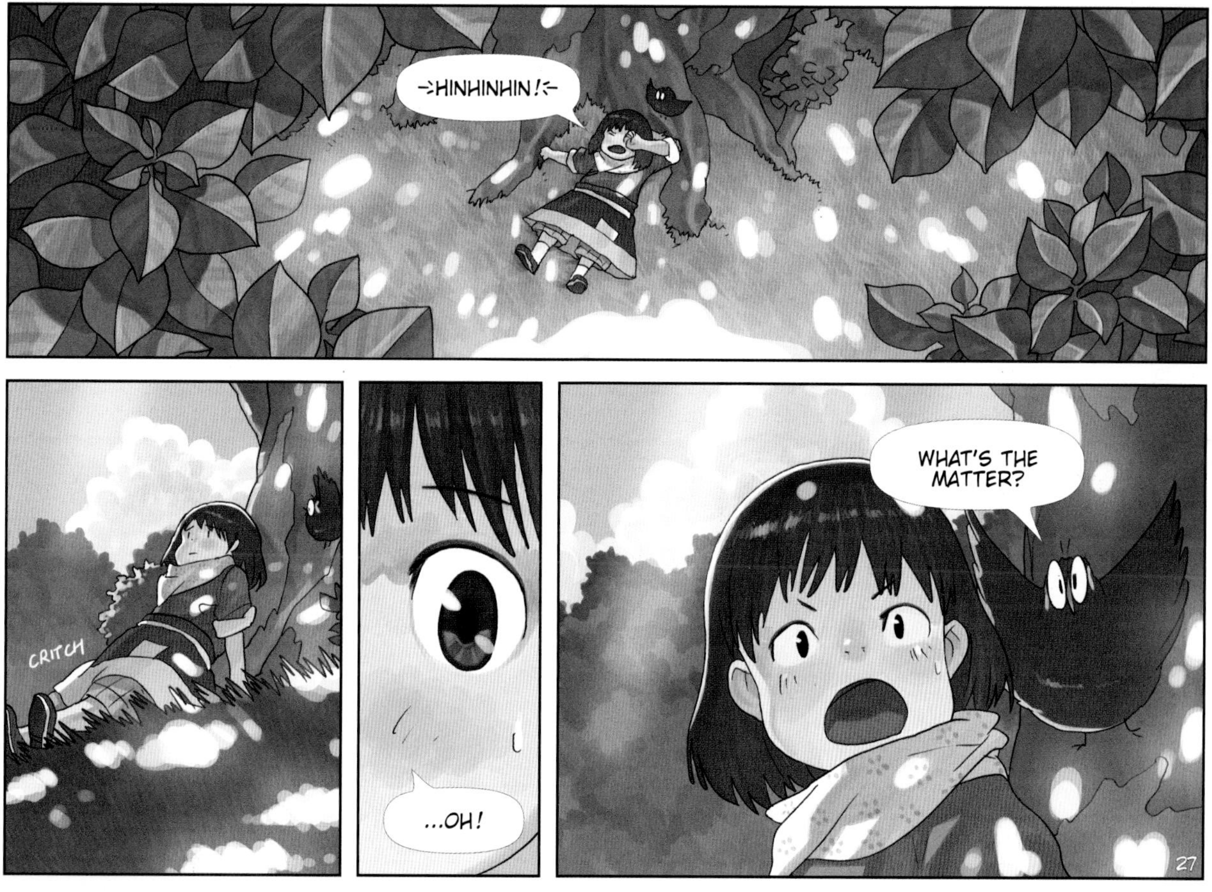
HINHINHIN!
CRITCH
...OH!
WHAT'S THE MATTER?

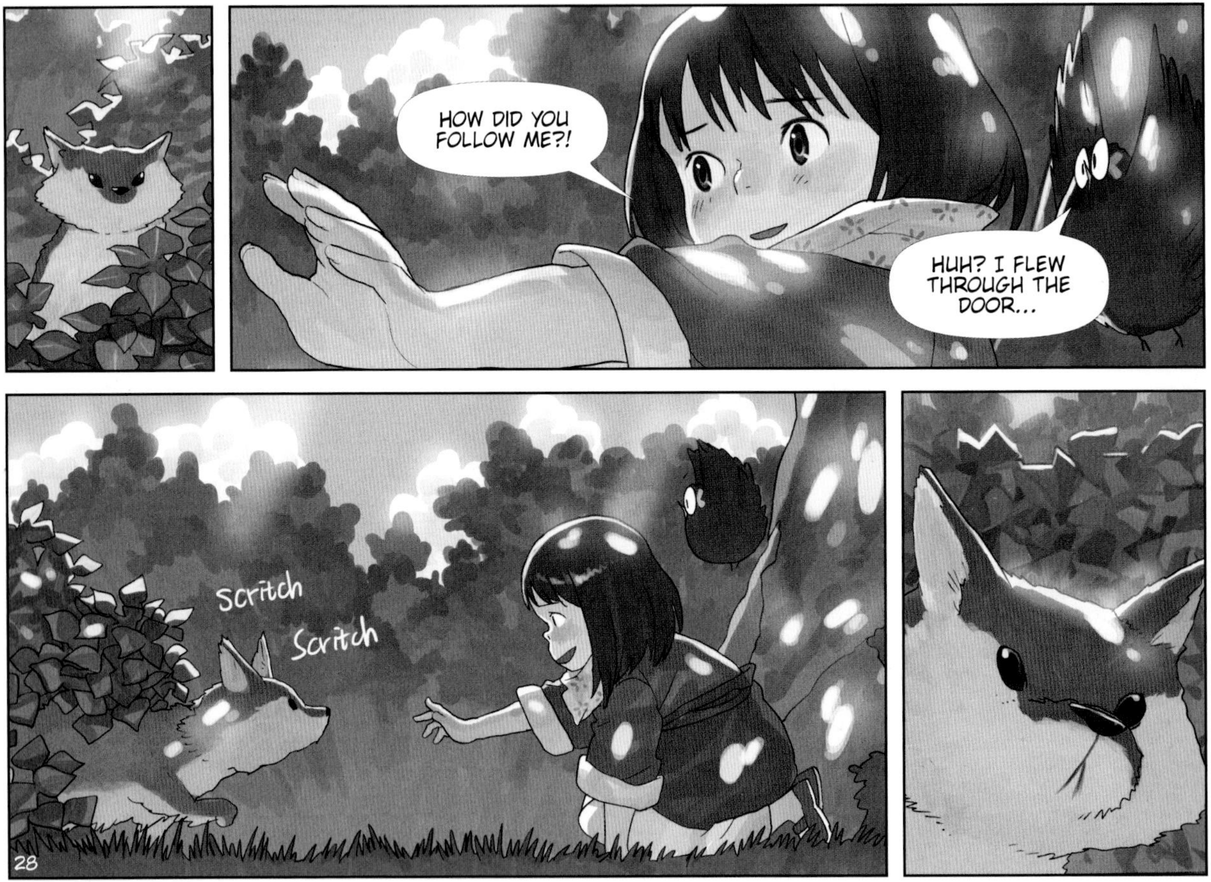
HOW DID YOU FOLLOW ME?!
HUH? I FLEW THROUGH THE DOOR...
scritch
scritch

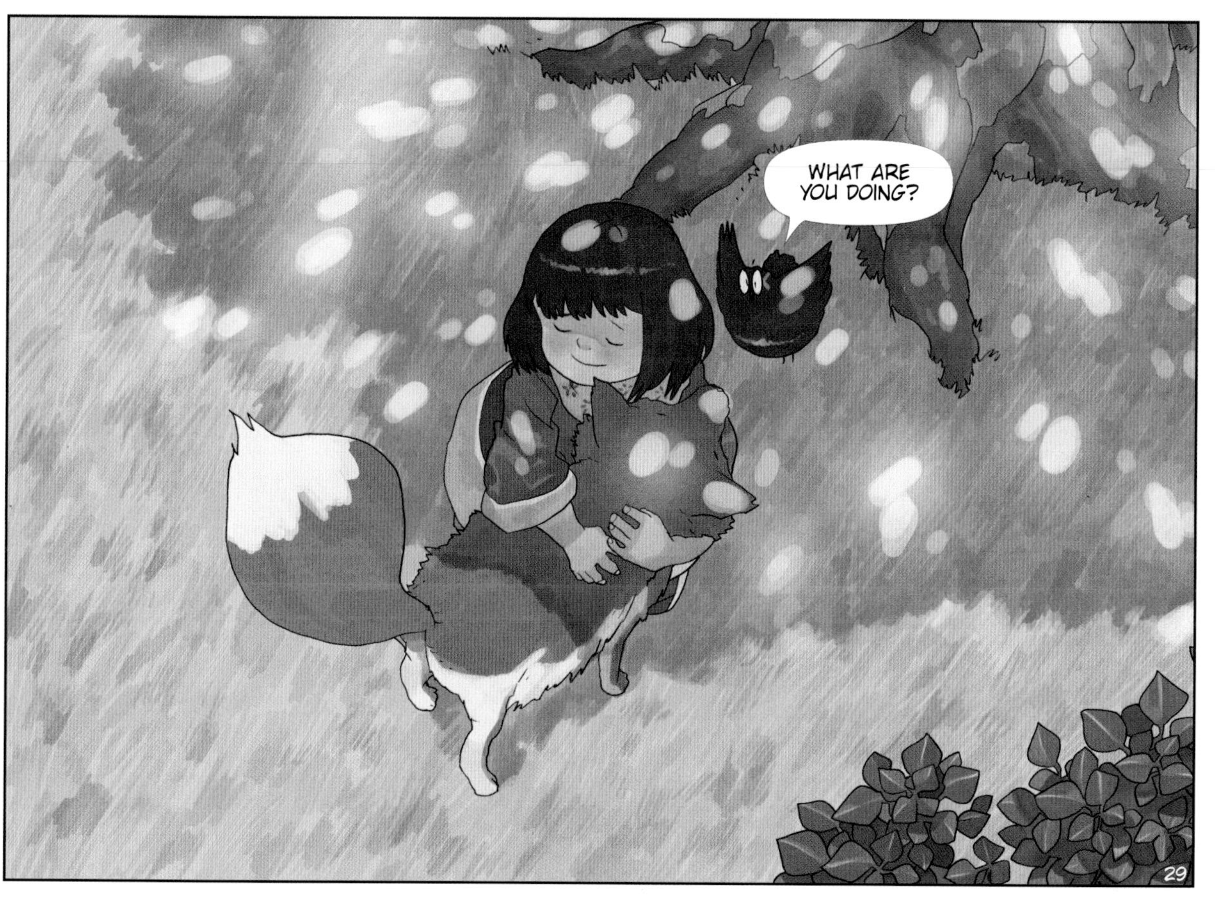
WHAT ARE YOU DOING?

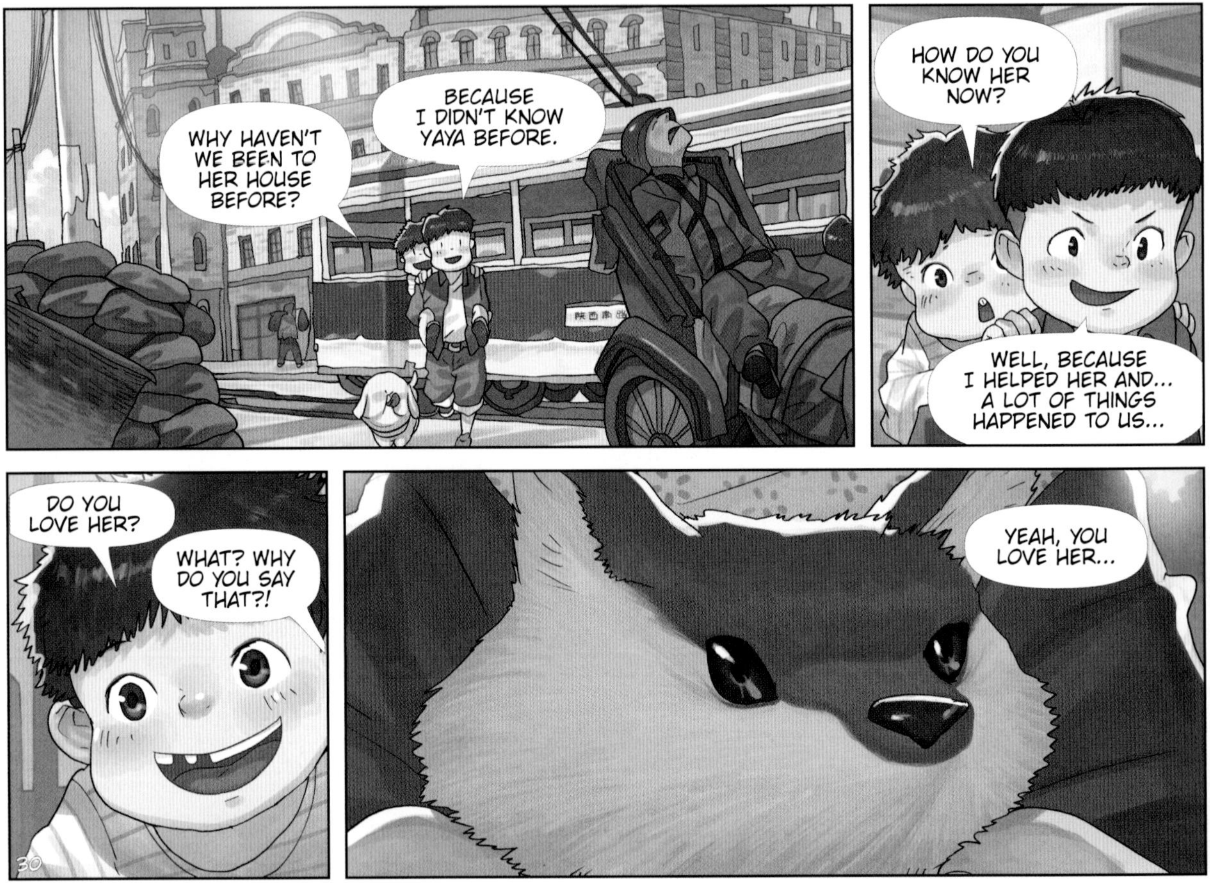
WHY HAVEN'T WE BEEN TO HER HOUSE BEFORE?
BECAUSE I DIDN'T KNOW YAYA BEFORE.
HOW DO YOU KNOW HER NOW?
WELL, BECAUSE I HELPED HER AND... A LOT OF THINGS HAPPENED TO US...
DO YOU LOVE HER?
WHAT? WHY DO YOU SAY THAT?!
YEAH, YOU LOVE HER...

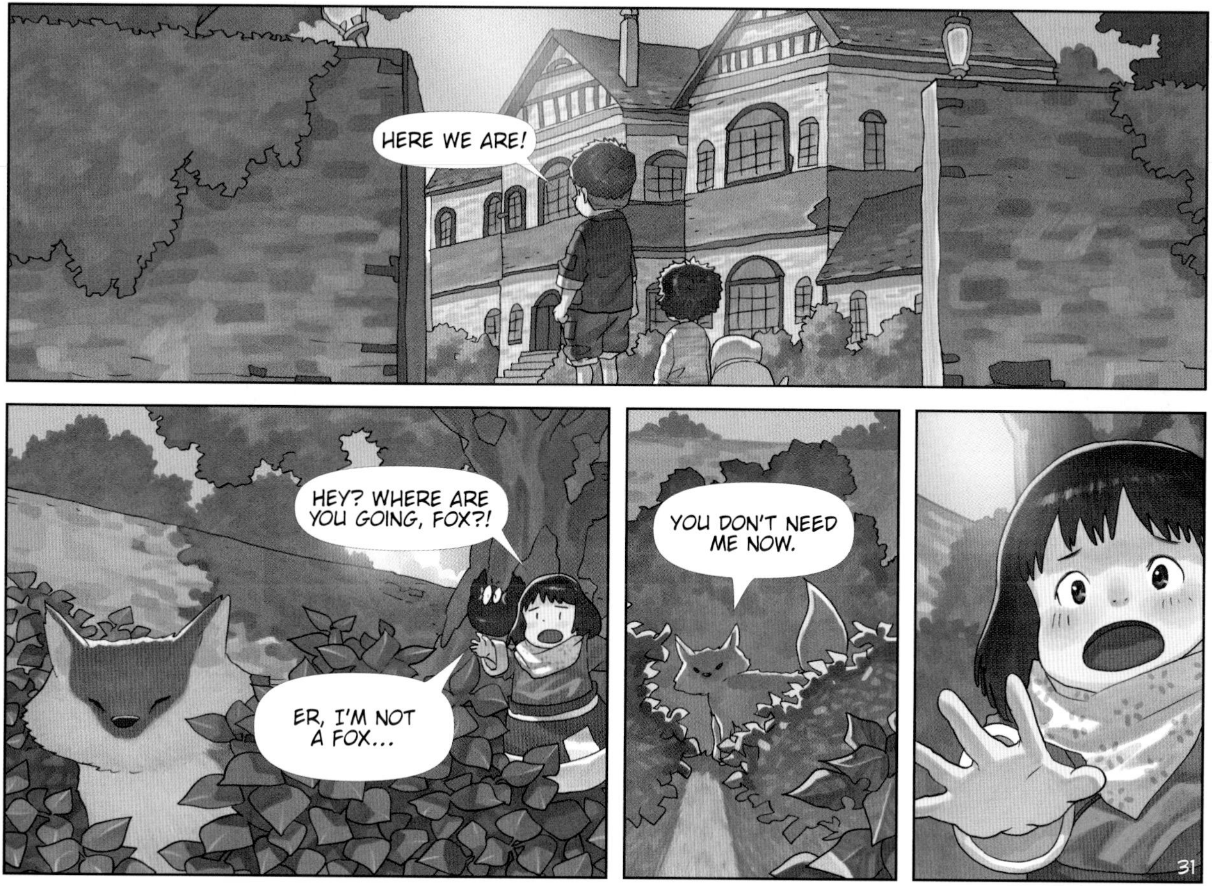
HERE WE ARE!
HEY? WHERE ARE YOU GOING, FOX?!
ER, I'M NOT A FOX...
YOU DON'T NEED ME NOW.

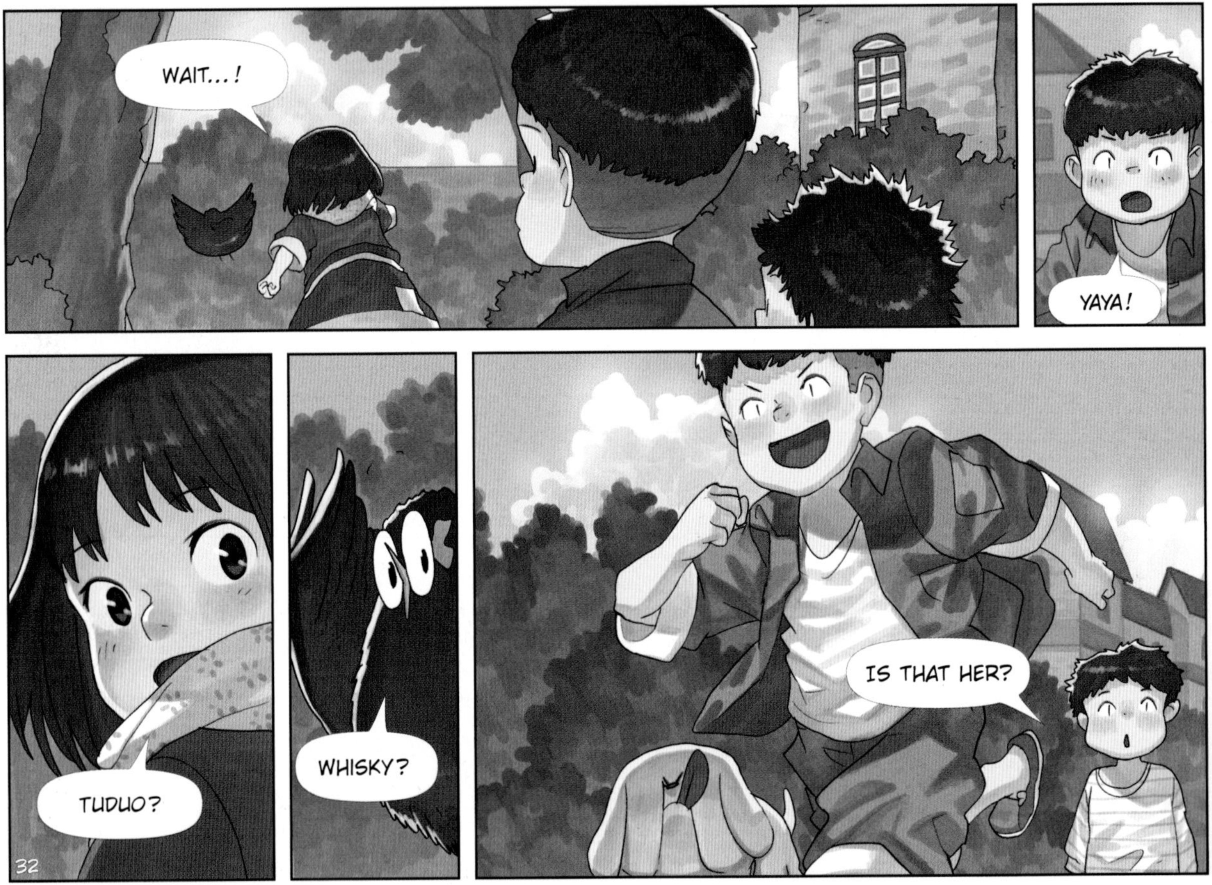
WAIT...!
YAYA!
TUDUO?
WHISKY?
IS THAT HER?

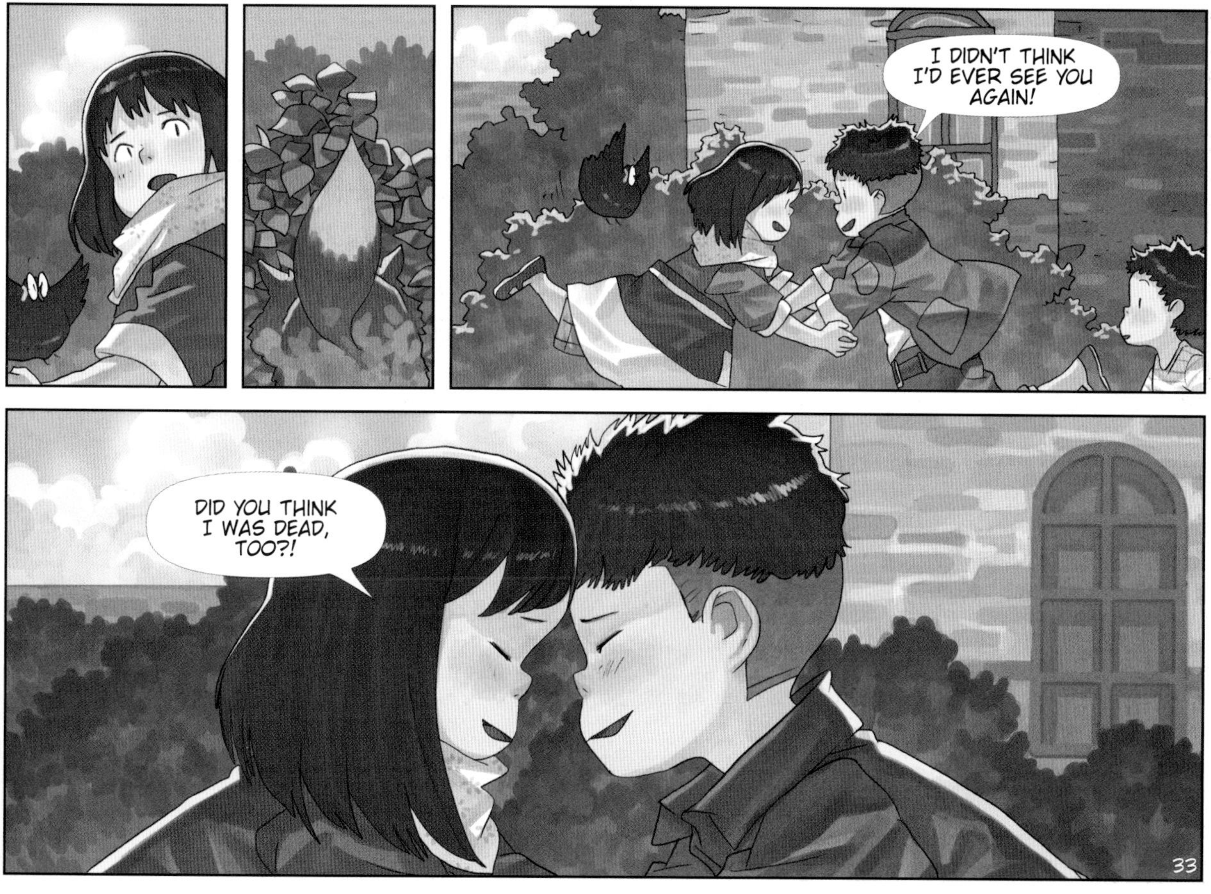
I DIDN'T THINK I'D EVER SEE YOU AGAIN!
DID YOU THINK I WAS DEAD, TOO?!

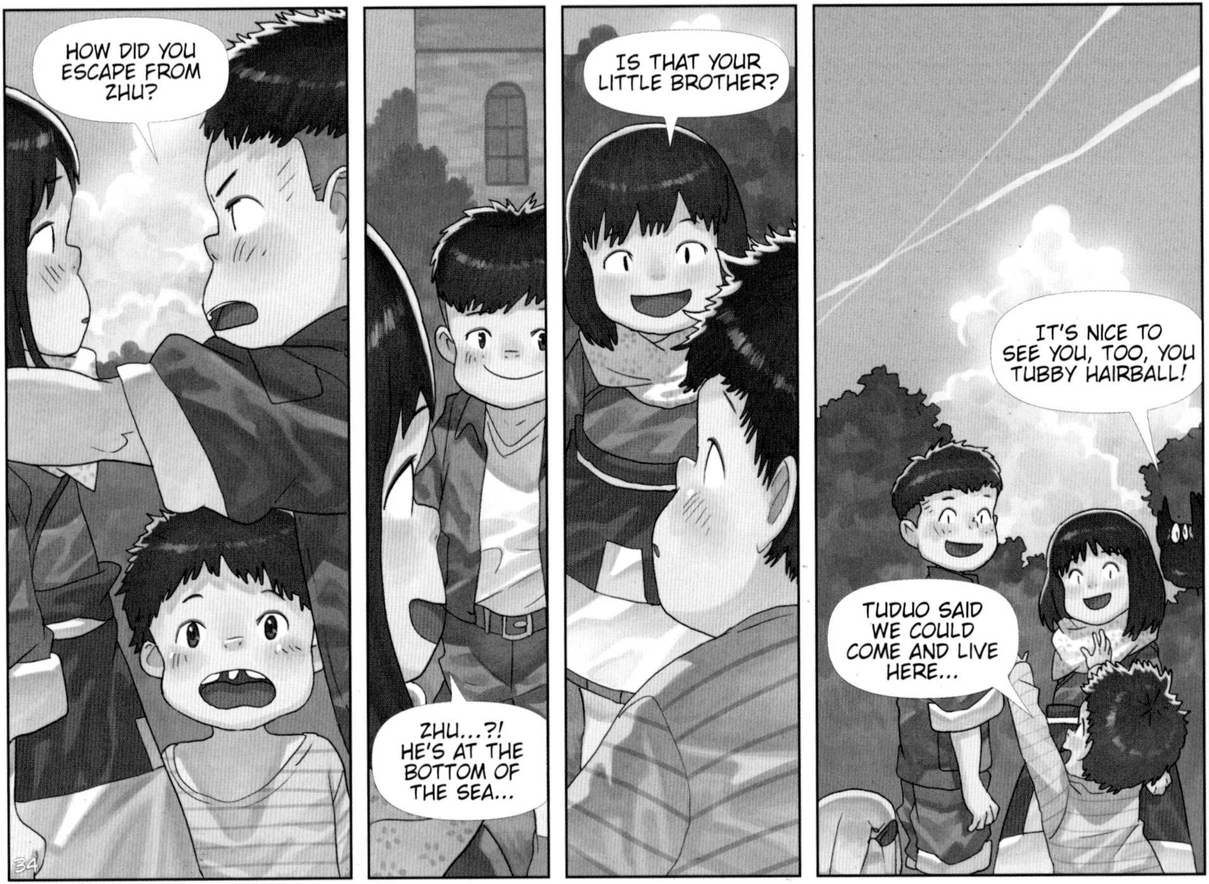
HOW DID YOU ESCAPE FROM ZHU?
ZHU...?! HE'S AT THE BOTTOM OF THE SEA...
IS THAT YOUR LITTLE BROTHER?
IT'S NICE TO SEE YOU, TOO, YOU TUBBY HAIRBALL!
TUDUO SAID WE COULD COME AND LIVE HERE...
34

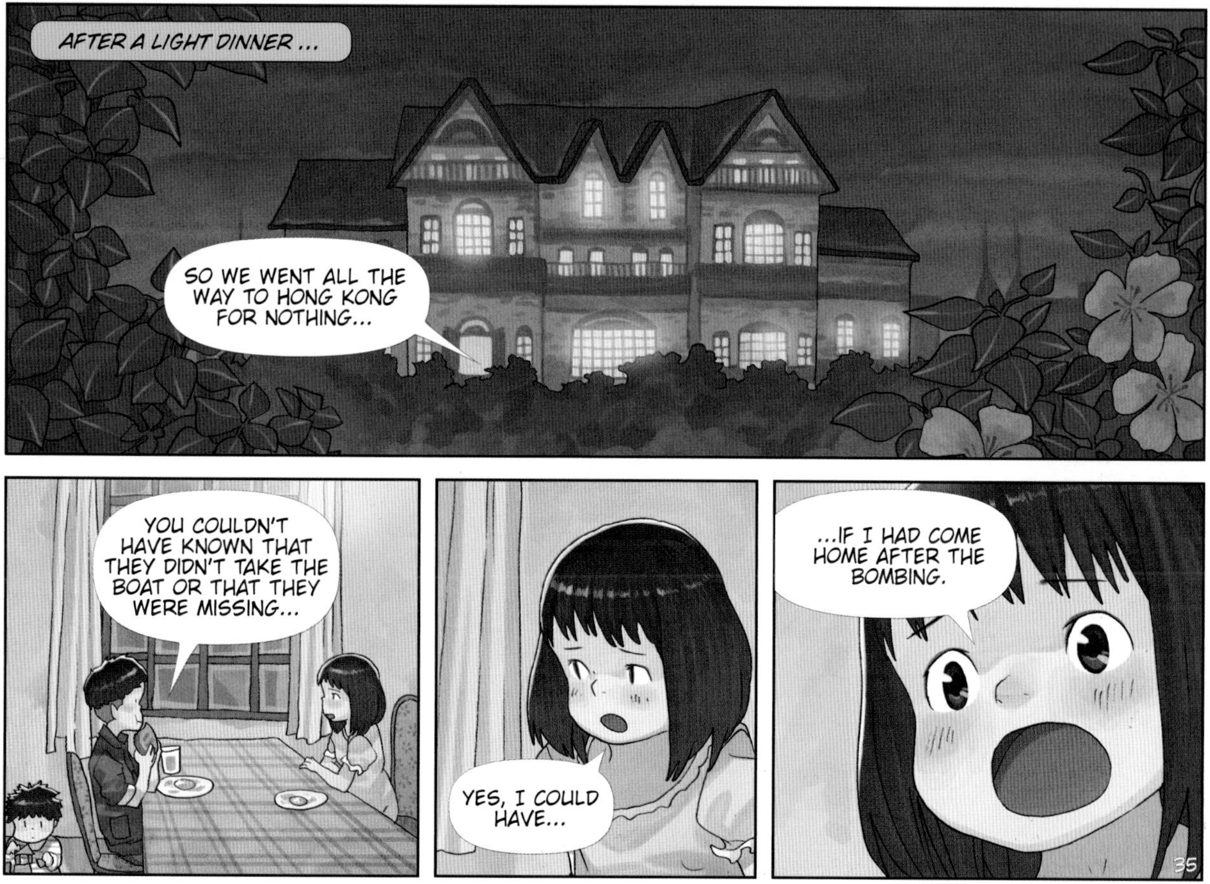
AFTER A LIGHT DINNER ...
SO WE WENT ALL THE WAY TO HONG KONG FOR NOTHING...
YOU COULDN'T HAVE KNOWN THAT THEY DIDN'T TAKE THE BOAT OR THAT THEY WERE MISSING...
YES, I COULD HAVE...
...IF I HAD COME HOME AFTER THE BOMBING.

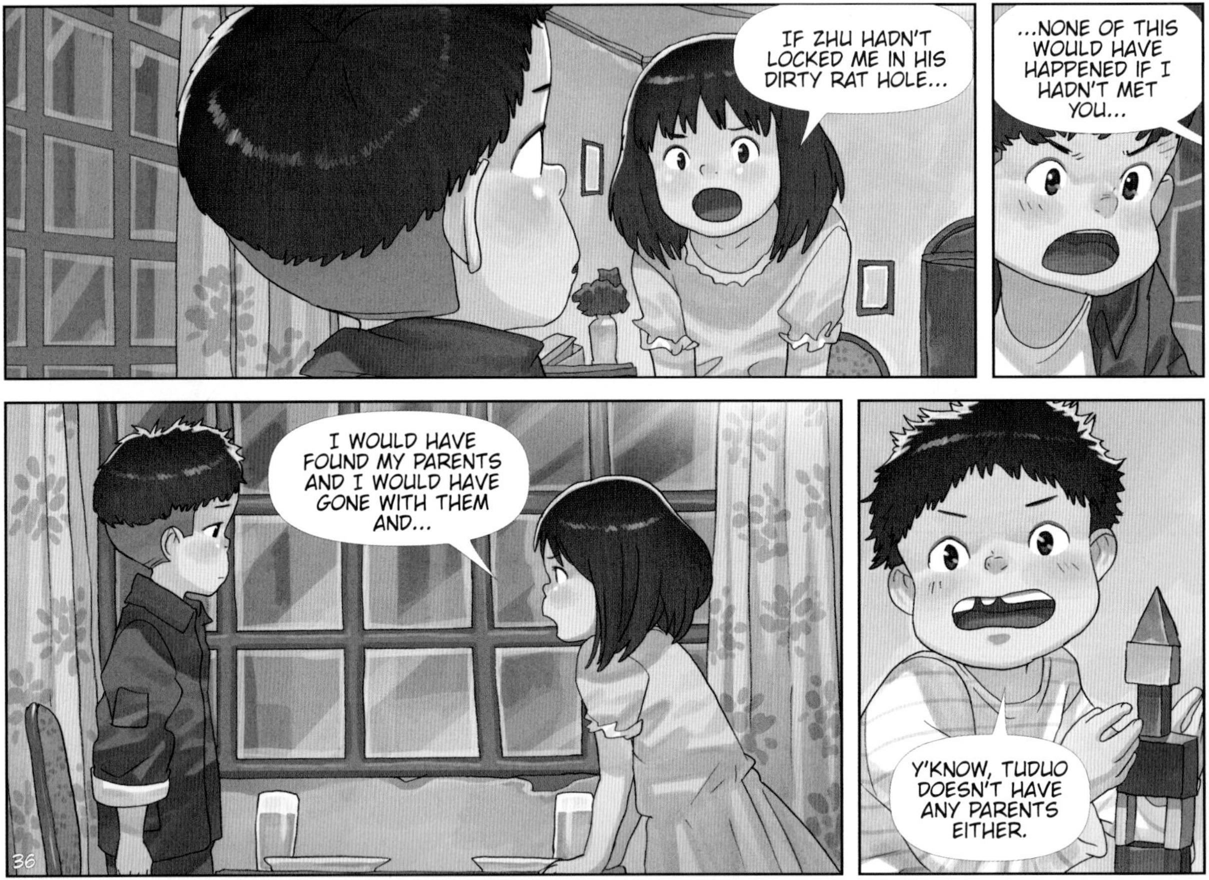

IF ZHU HADN'T LOCKED ME IN HIS DIRTY RAT HOLE...
...NONE OF THIS WOULD HAVE HAPPENED IF I HADN'T MET YOU...
I WOULD HAVE FOUND MY PARENTS AND I WOULD HAVE GONE WITH THEM AND...
Y'KNOW, TUDUO DOESN'T HAVE ANY PARENTS EITHER.

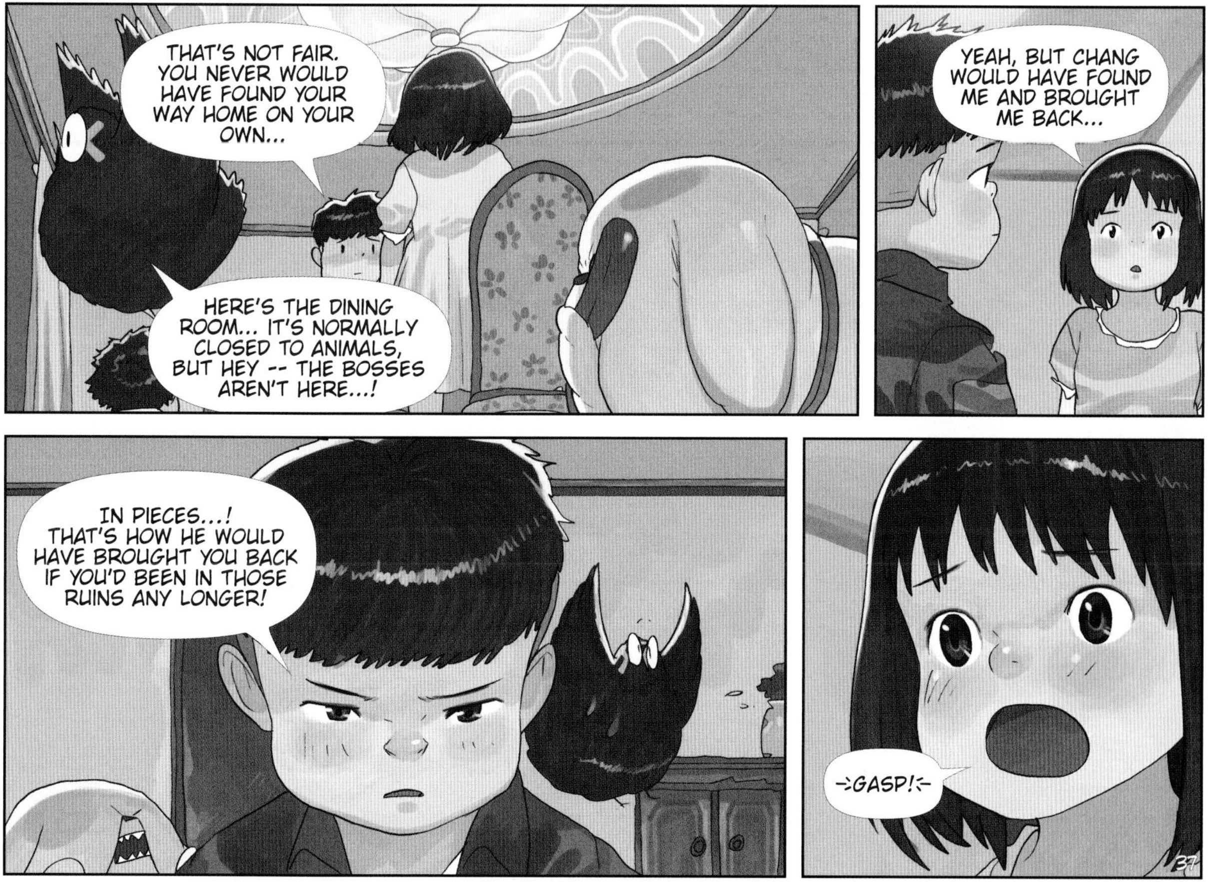
THAT'S NOT FAIR. YOU NEVER WOULD HAVE FOUND YOUR WAY HOME ON YOUR OWN...
HERE'S THE DINING ROOM... IT'S NORMALLY CLOSED TO ANIMALS, BUT HEY -- THE BOSSES AREN'T HERE...!
YEAH, BUT CHANG WOULD HAVE FOUND ME AND BROUGHT ME BACK...
IN PIECES...! THAT'S HOW HE WOULD HAVE BROUGHT YOU BACK IF YOU'D BEEN IN THOSE RUINS ANY LONGER!
GASP!

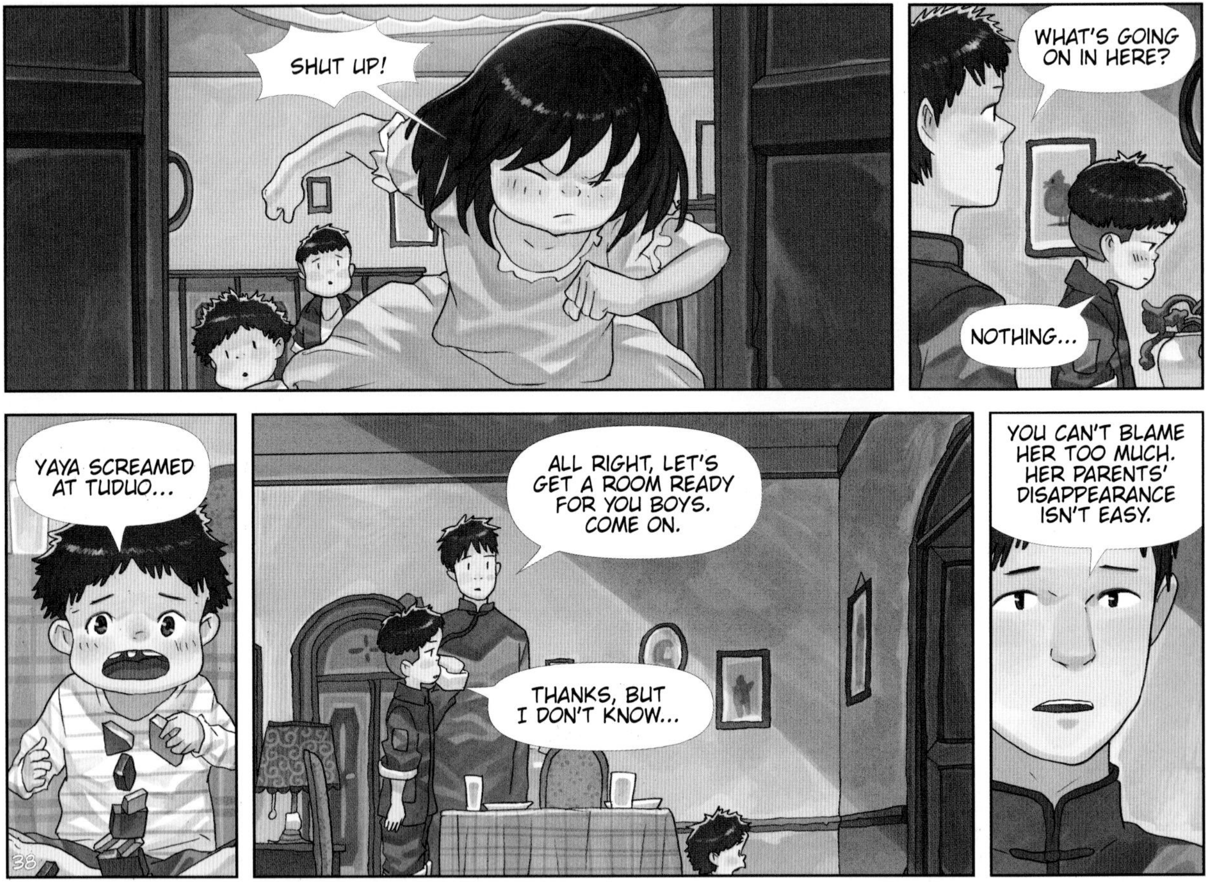

SHUT UP!
WHAT'S GOING ON IN HERE?
NOTHING...
YAYA SCREAMED AT TUDUO...
ALL RIGHT, LET'S GET A ROOM READY FOR YOU BOYS. COME ON.
THANKS, BUT I DON'T KNOW...
YOU CAN'T BLAME HER TOO MUCH. HER PARENTS' DISAPPEARANCE ISN'T EASY.

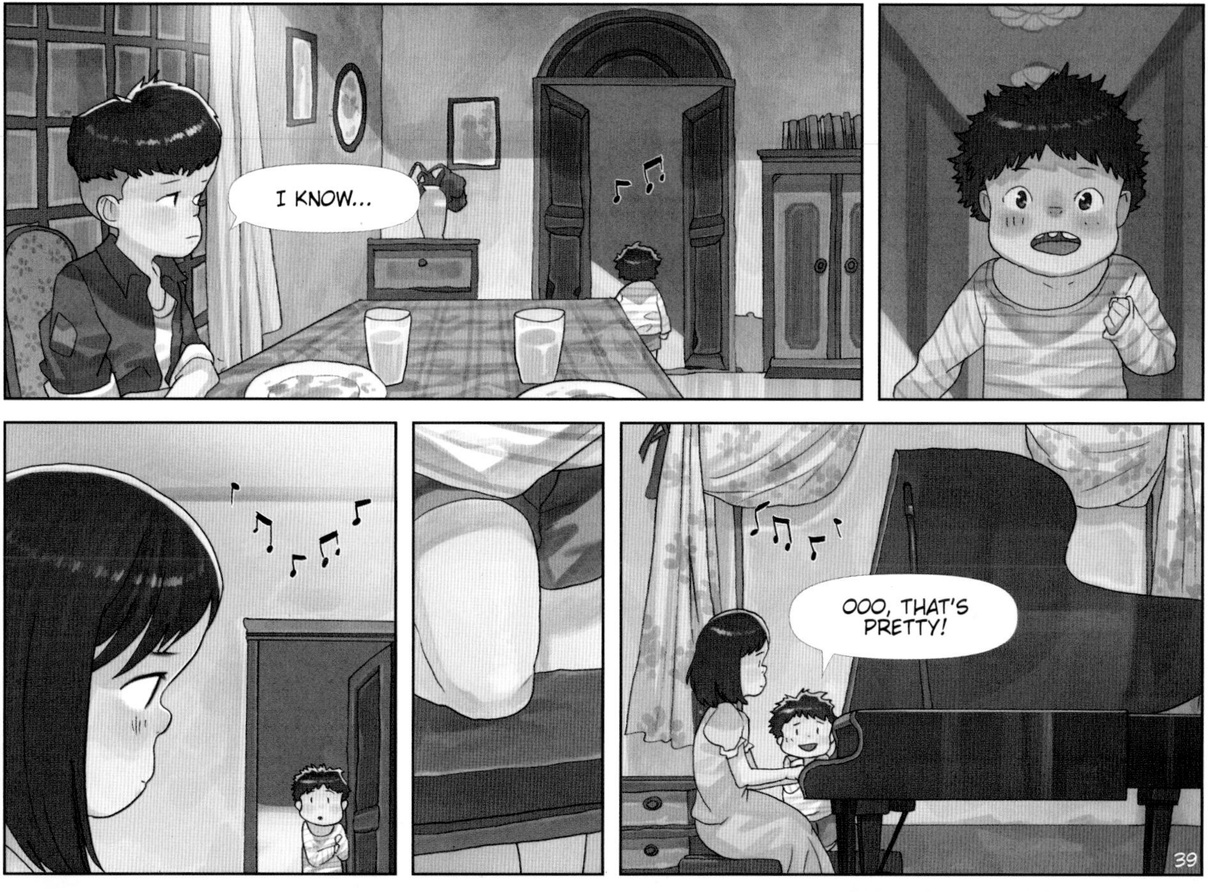
I KNOW...
OOO, THAT'S PRETTY!

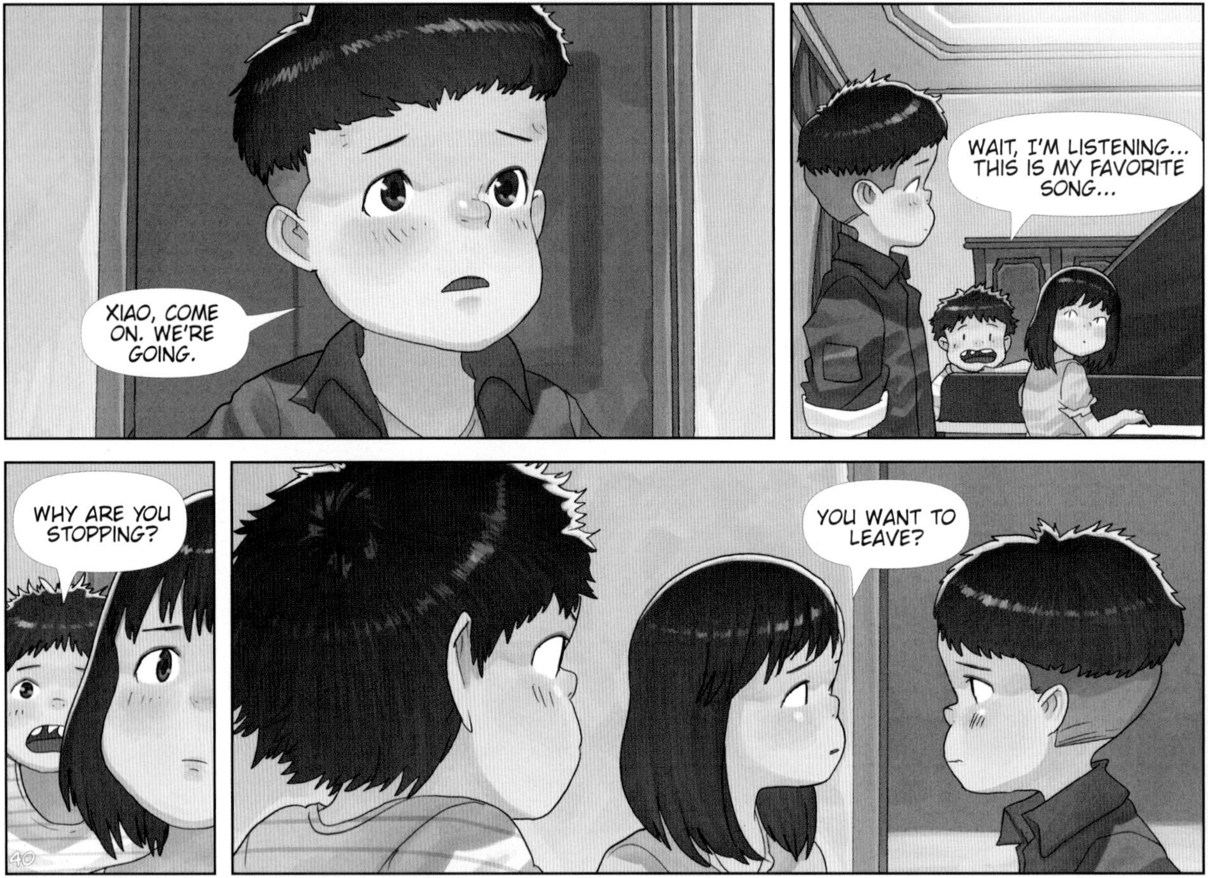
XIAO, COME ON. WE'RE GOING.
WAIT, I'M LISTENING... THIS IS MY FAVORITE SONG...
WHY ARE YOU STOPPING?
YOU WANT TO LEAVE?

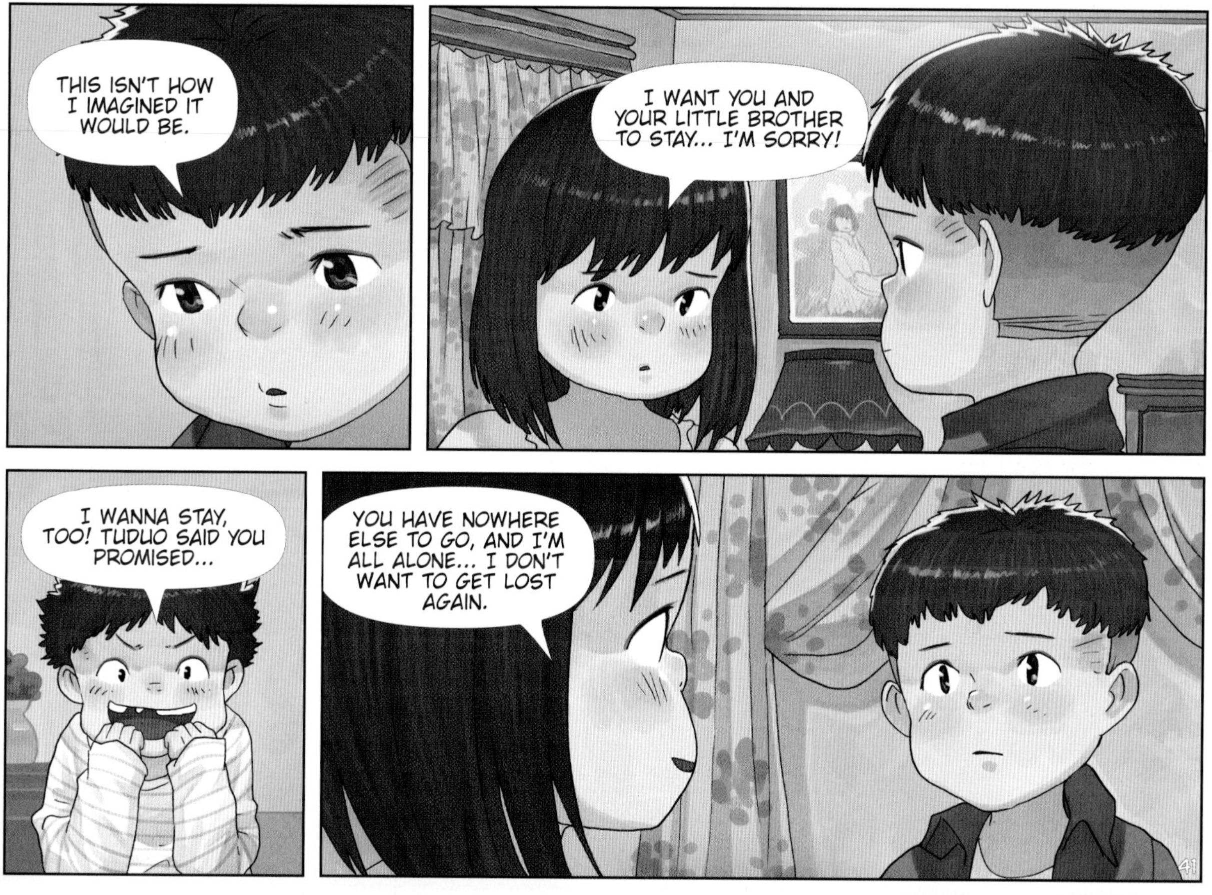
THIS ISN'T HOW I IMAGINED IT WOULD BE.
I WANT YOU AND YOUR LITTLE BROTHER TO STAY... I'M SORRY!
I WANNA STAY, TOO! TUDUO SAID YOU PROMISED...
YOU HAVE NOWHERE ELSE TO GO, AND I'M ALL ALONE... I DON'T WANT TO GET LOST AGAIN.

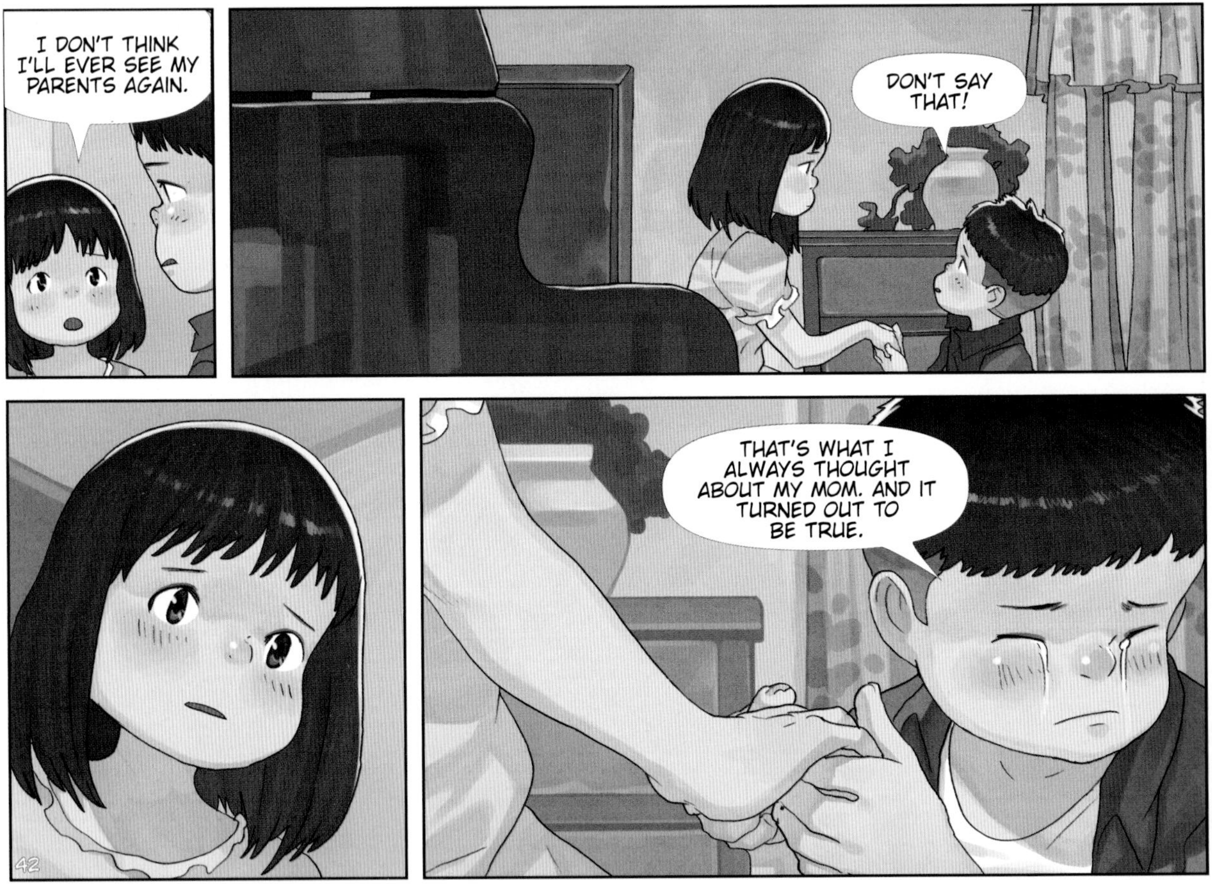
I DON'T THINK I'LL EVER SEE MY PARENTS AGAIN.
DON'T SAY THAT!
THAT'S WHAT I ALWAYS THOUGHT ABOUT MY MOM. AND IT TURNED OUT TO BE TRUE.

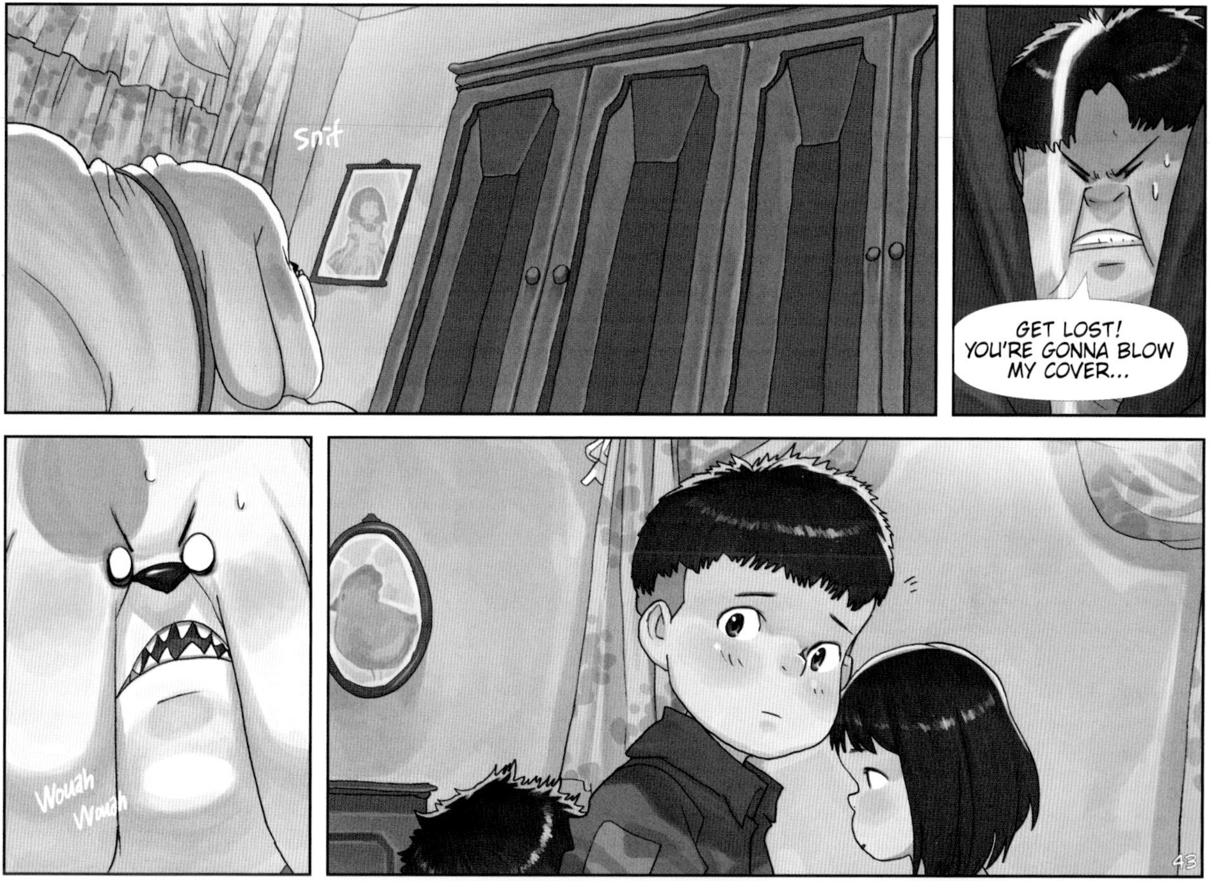
Snif
GET LOST! YOU'RE GONNA BLOW MY COVER...
Wouah Wouah

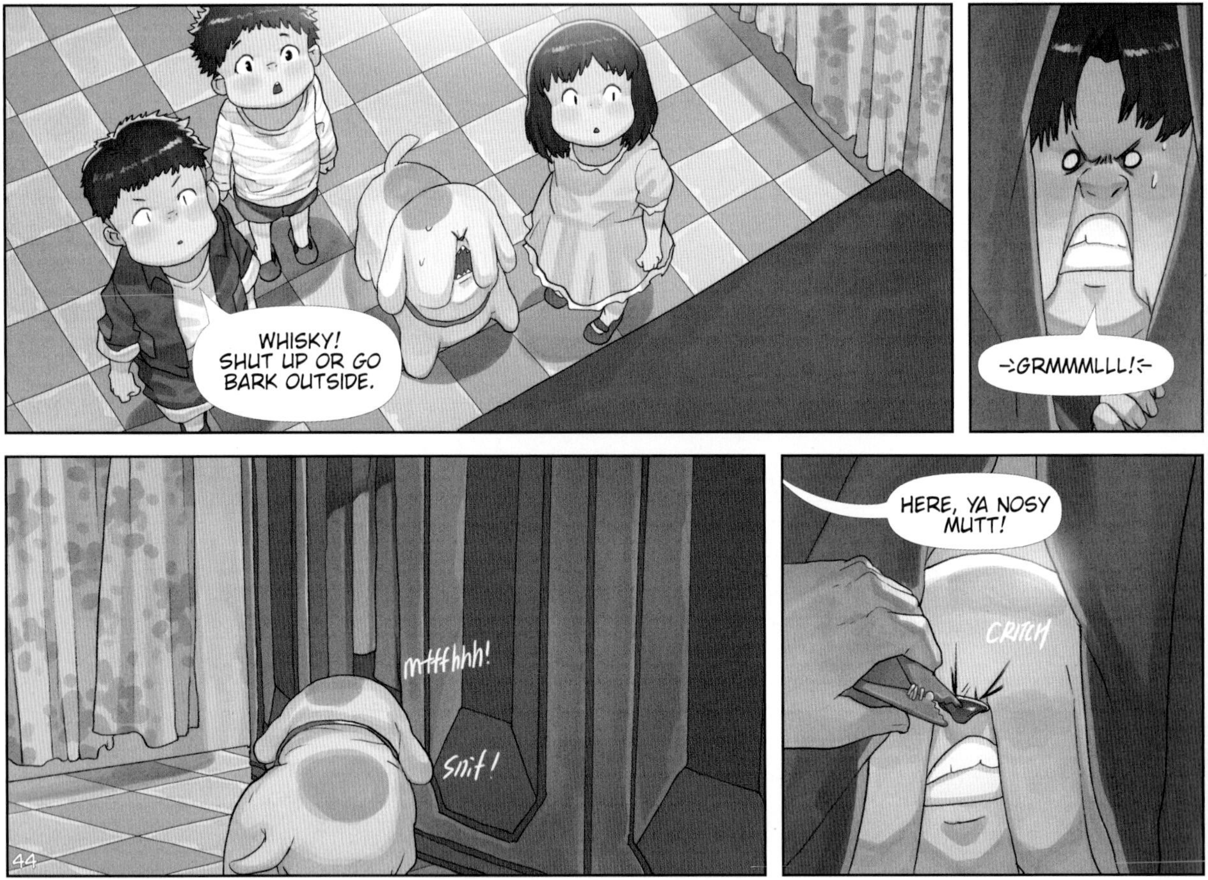
WHISKY! SHUT UP OR GO BARK OUTSIDE.
GRMMMLLL!
mtffhhh!
Snif!
HERE, YA NOSY MUTT!
CRITCH

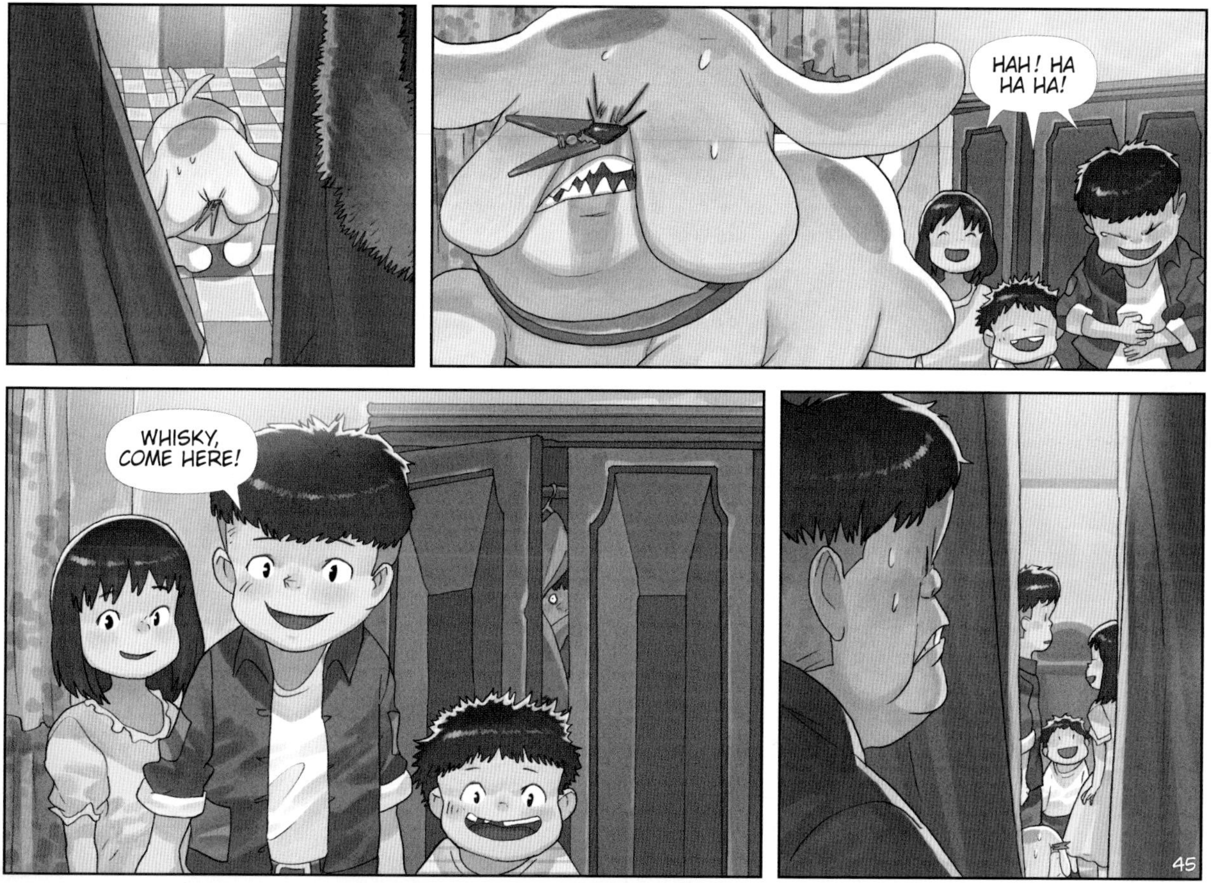
HAH! HA HA HA!
WHISKY, COME HERE!

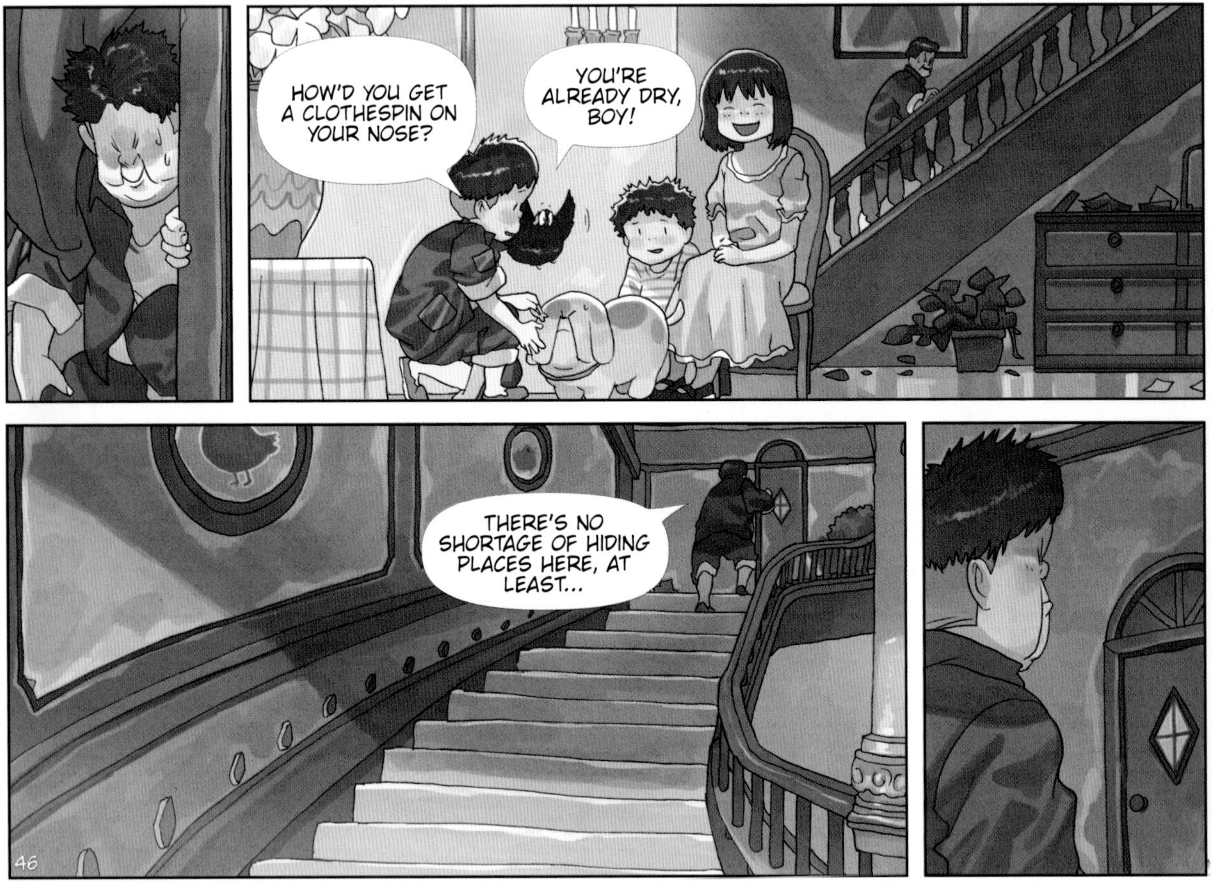
HOW'D YOU GET A CLOTHESPIN ON YOUR NOSE?
YOU'RE ALREADY DRY, BOY!
THERE'S NO SHORTAGE OF HIDING PLACES HERE, AT LEAST...

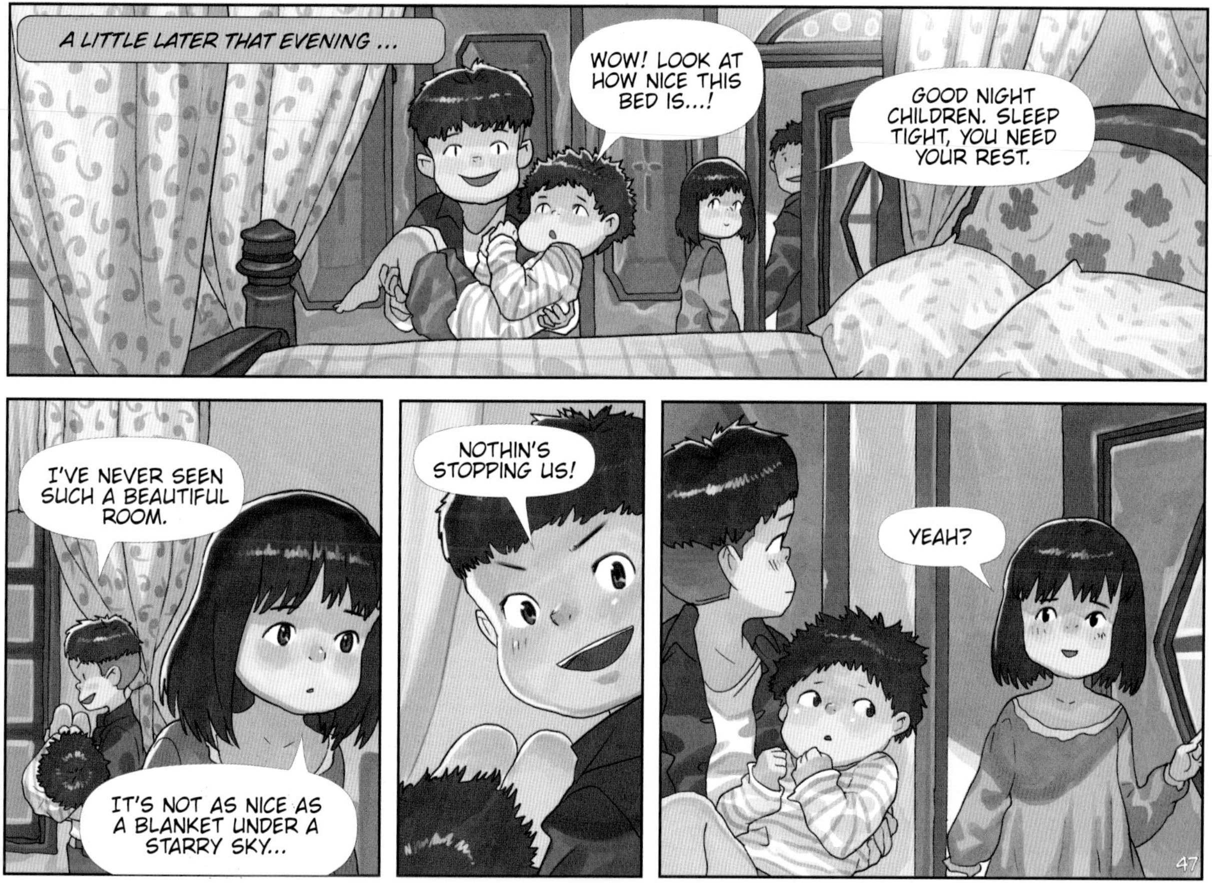
A LITTLE LATER THAT EVENING ...
WOW! LOOK AT HOW NICE THIS BED IS...!
GOOD NIGHT CHILDREN. SLEEP TIGHT, YOU NEED YOUR REST.
I'VE NEVER SEEN SUCH A BEAUTIFUL ROOM.
IT'S NOT AS NICE AS A BLANKET UNDER A STARRY SKY...
NOTHIN'S STOPPING US!
YEAH?

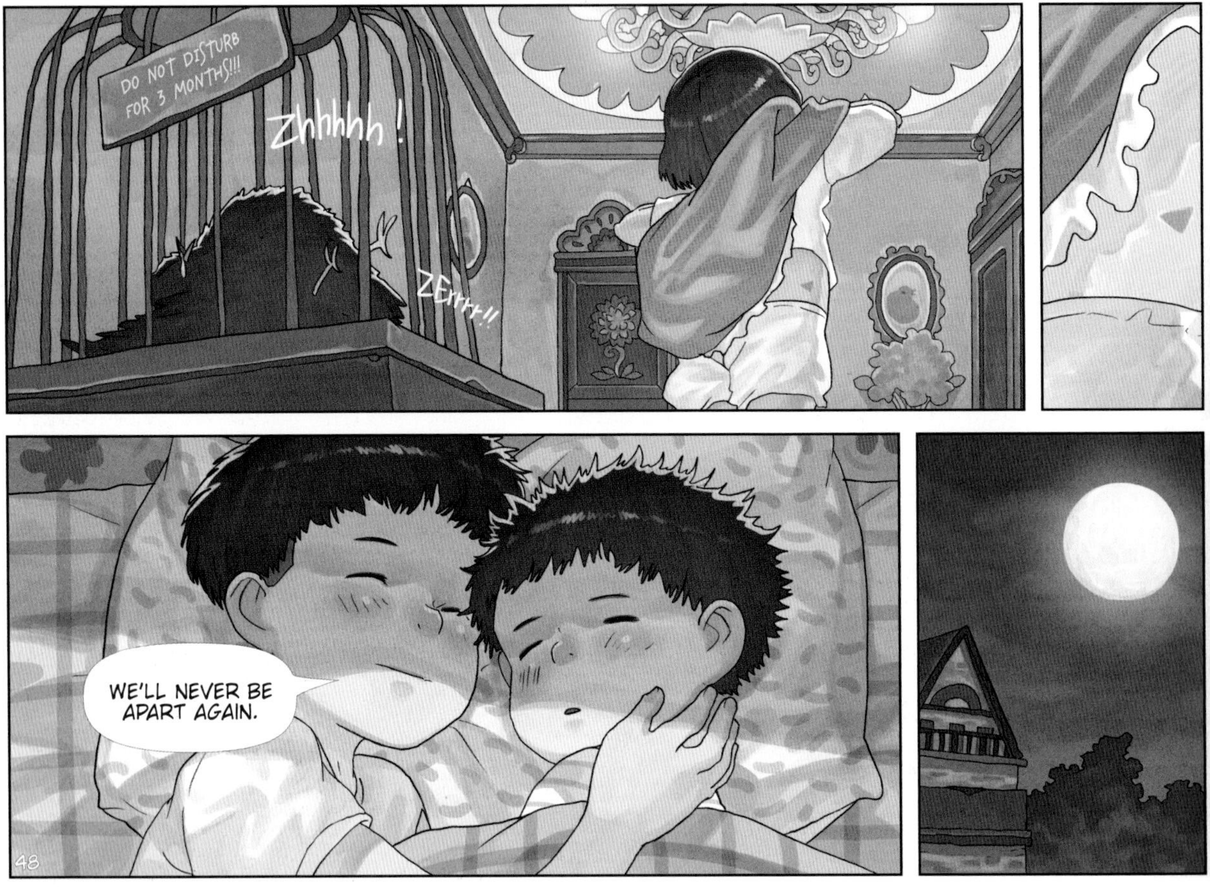
DO NOT DISTURB FOR 3 MONTHS!!!
Zhhhhh !
ZErrrr!!
WE'LL NEVER BE APART AGAIN.

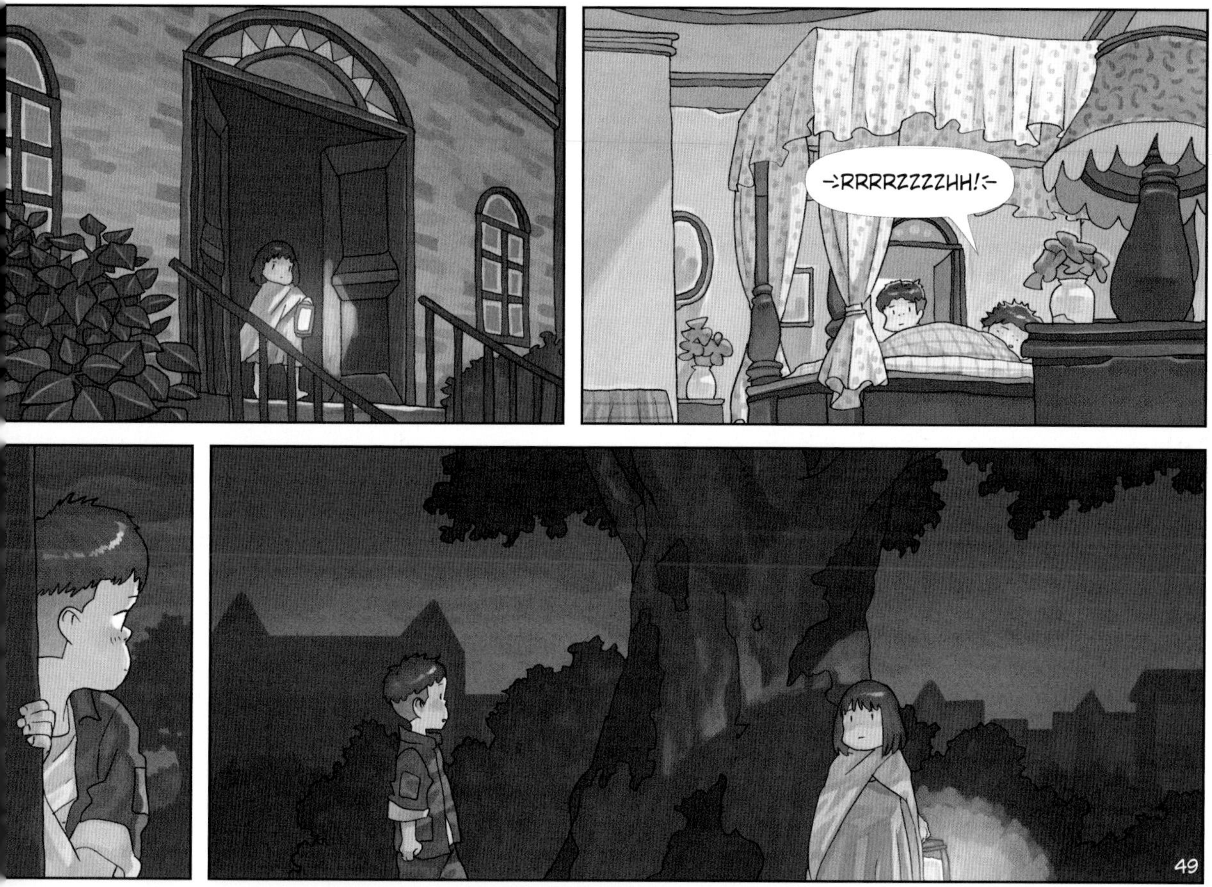
RRRRZZZZHH!

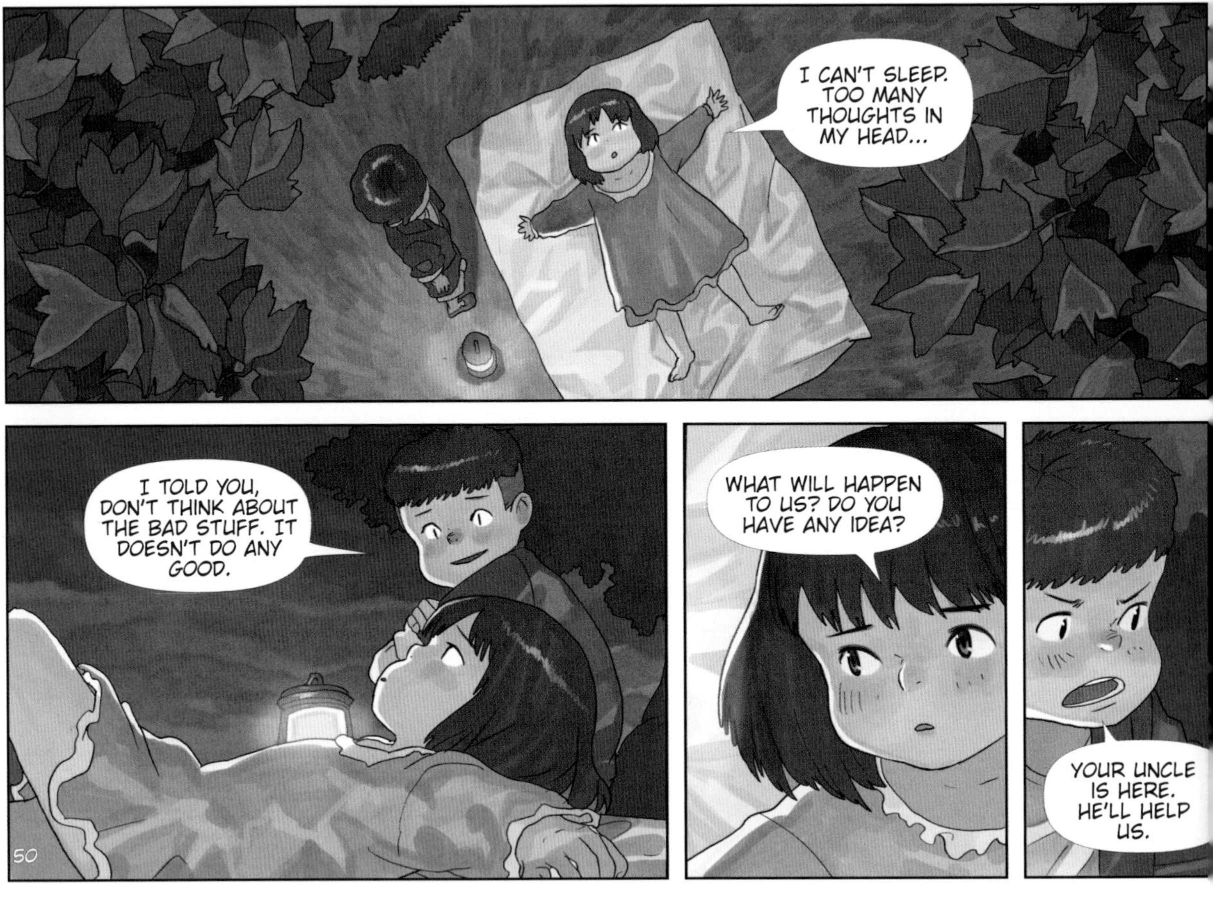
I CAN'T SLEEP. TOO MANY THOUGHTS IN MY HEAD...
I TOLD YOU, DON'T THINK ABOUT THE BAD STUFF. IT DOESN'T DO ANY GOOD.
WHAT WILL HAPPEN TO US? DO YOU HAVE ANY IDEA?
YOUR UNCLE IS HERE. HE'LL HELP US.

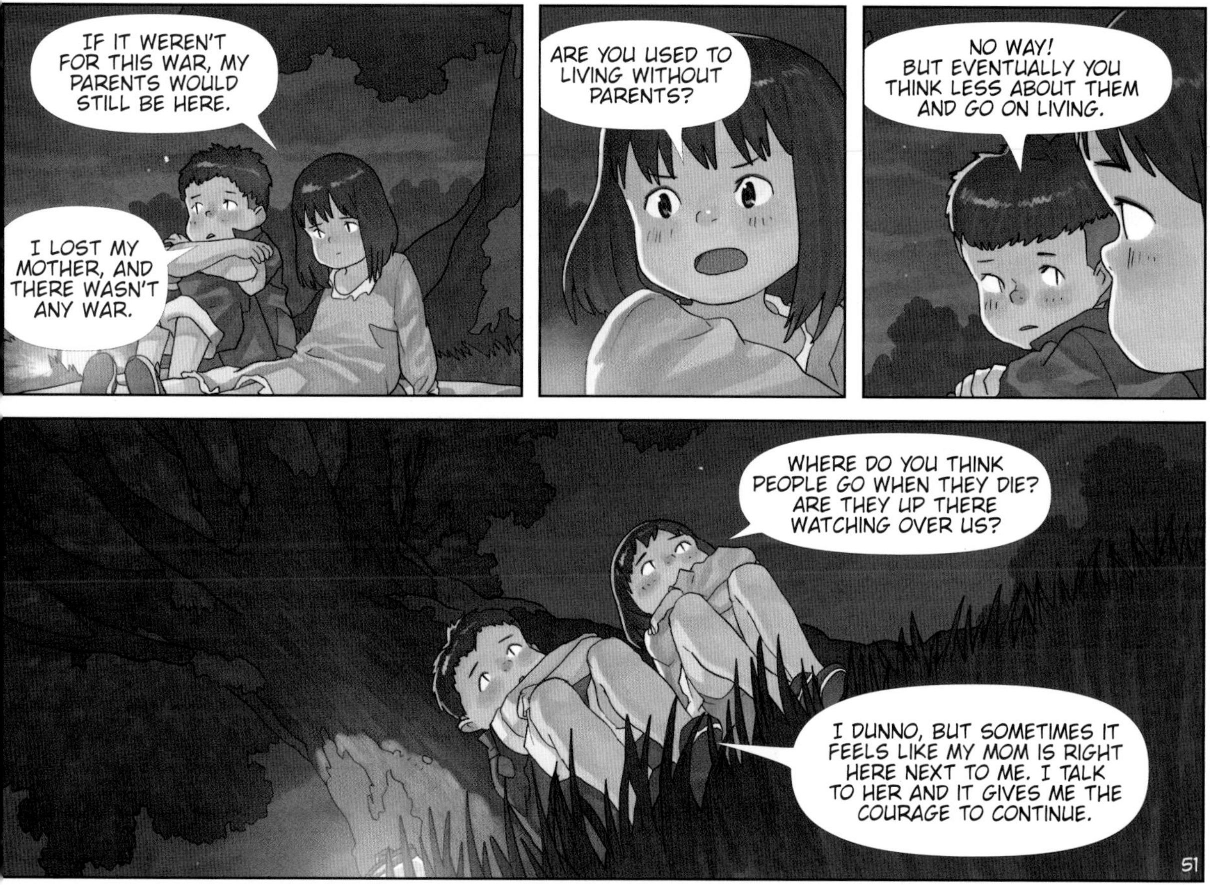
IF IT WEREN'T FOR THIS WAR, MY PARENTS WOULD STILL BE HERE.
I LOST MY MOTHER, AND THERE WASN'T ANY WAR.
ARE YOU USED TO LIVING WITHOUT PARENTS?
NO WAY! BUT EVENTUALLY YOU THINK LESS ABOUT THEM AND GO ON LIVING.
WHERE DO YOU THINK PEOPLE GO WHEN THEY DIE? ARE THEY UP THERE WATCHING OVER US?
I DUNNO, BUT SOMETIMES IT FEELS LIKE MY MOM IS RIGHT HERE NEXT TO ME. I TALK TO HER AND IT GIVES ME THE COURAGE TO CONTINUE.

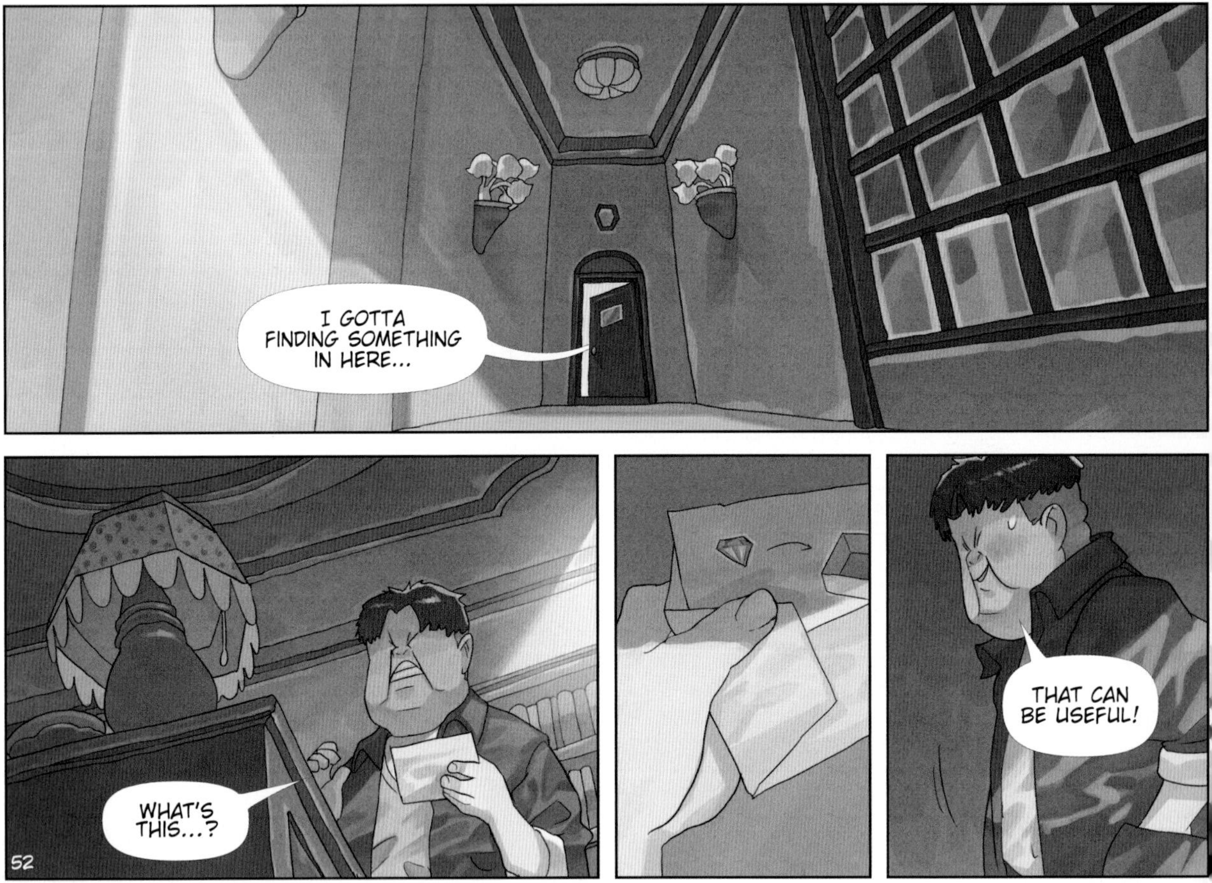
I GOTTA FINDING SOMETHING IN HERE...
WHAT'S THIS...?
THAT CAN BE USEFUL!

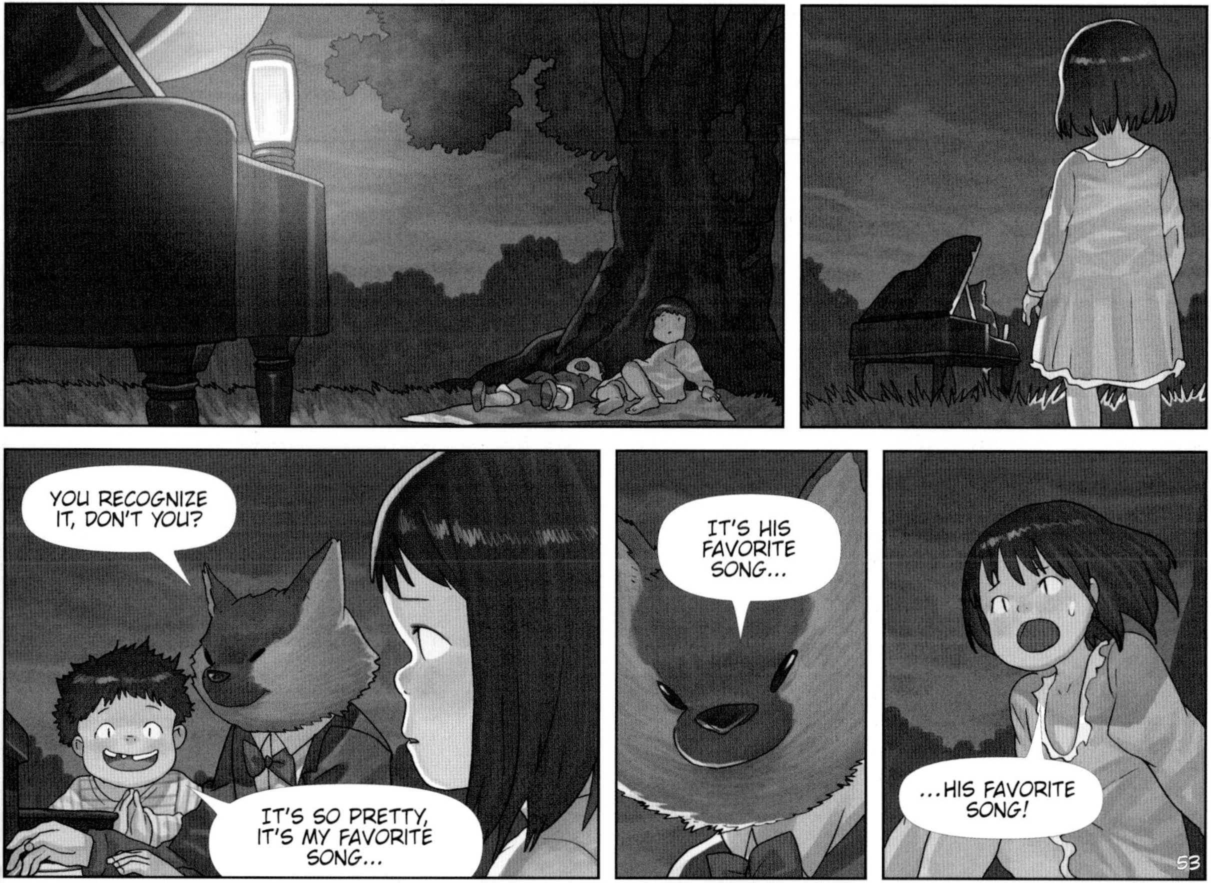
YOU RECOGNIZE IT, DON'T YOU?
IT'S SO PRETTY, IT'S MY FAVORITE SONG...
IT'S HIS FAVORITE SONG...
...HIS FAVORITE SONG!

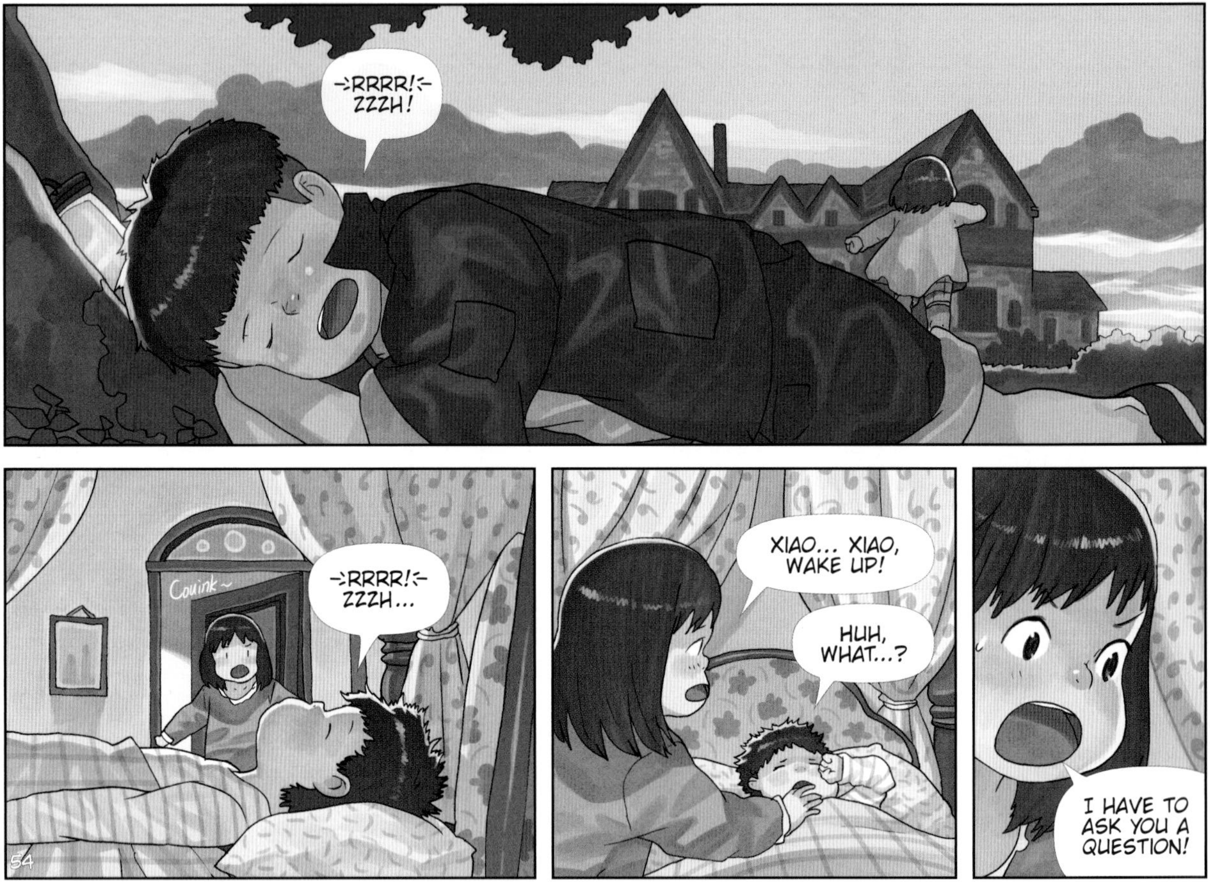
RRRR!
ZZZH!
Couink ~
RRRR!
ZZZH...
XIAO... XIAO, WAKE UP!
HUH, WHAT...?
I HAVE TO ASK YOU A QUESTION!

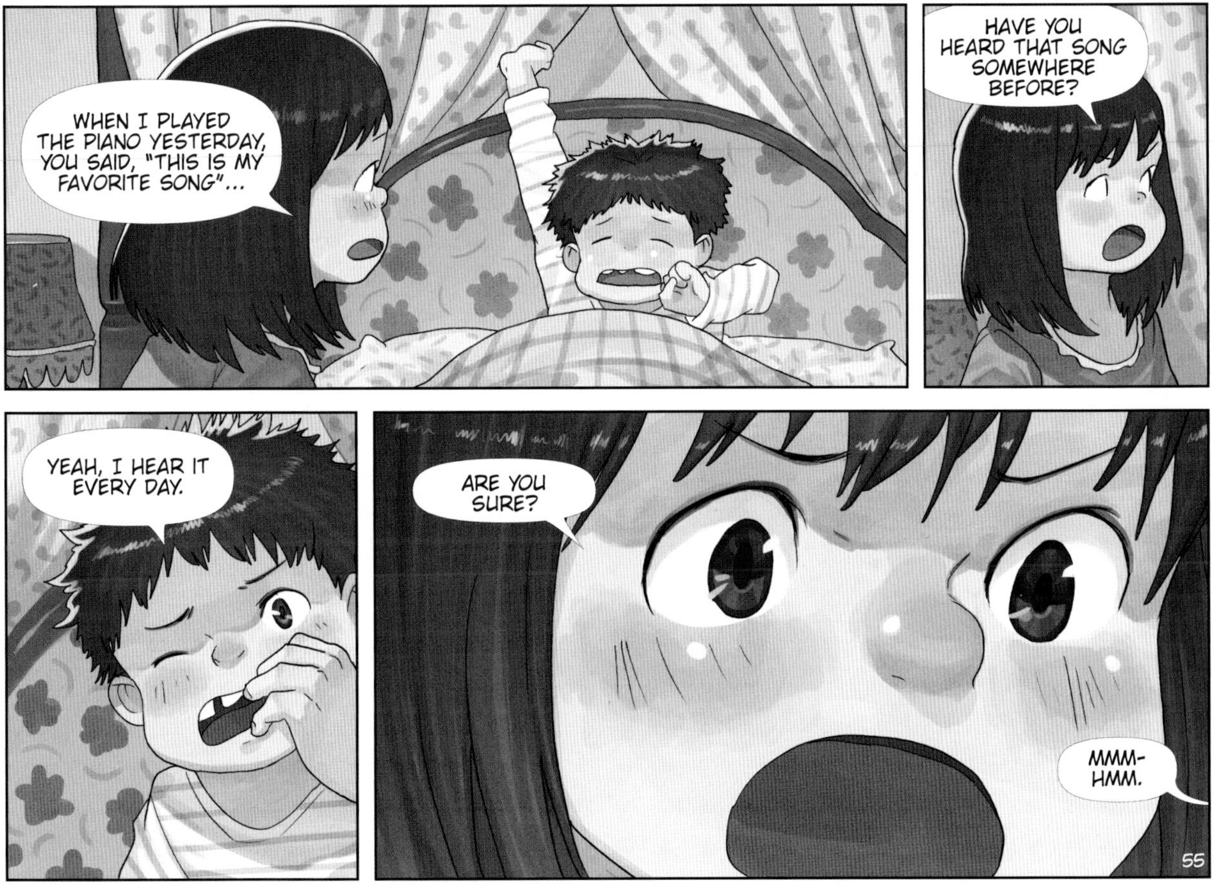
WHEN I PLAYED THE PIANO YESTERDAY, YOU SAID, "THIS IS MY FAVORITE SONG"...
HAVE YOU HEARD THAT SONG SOMEWHERE BEFORE?
YEAH, I HEAR IT EVERY DAY.
ARE YOU SURE?
MMM-HMM.

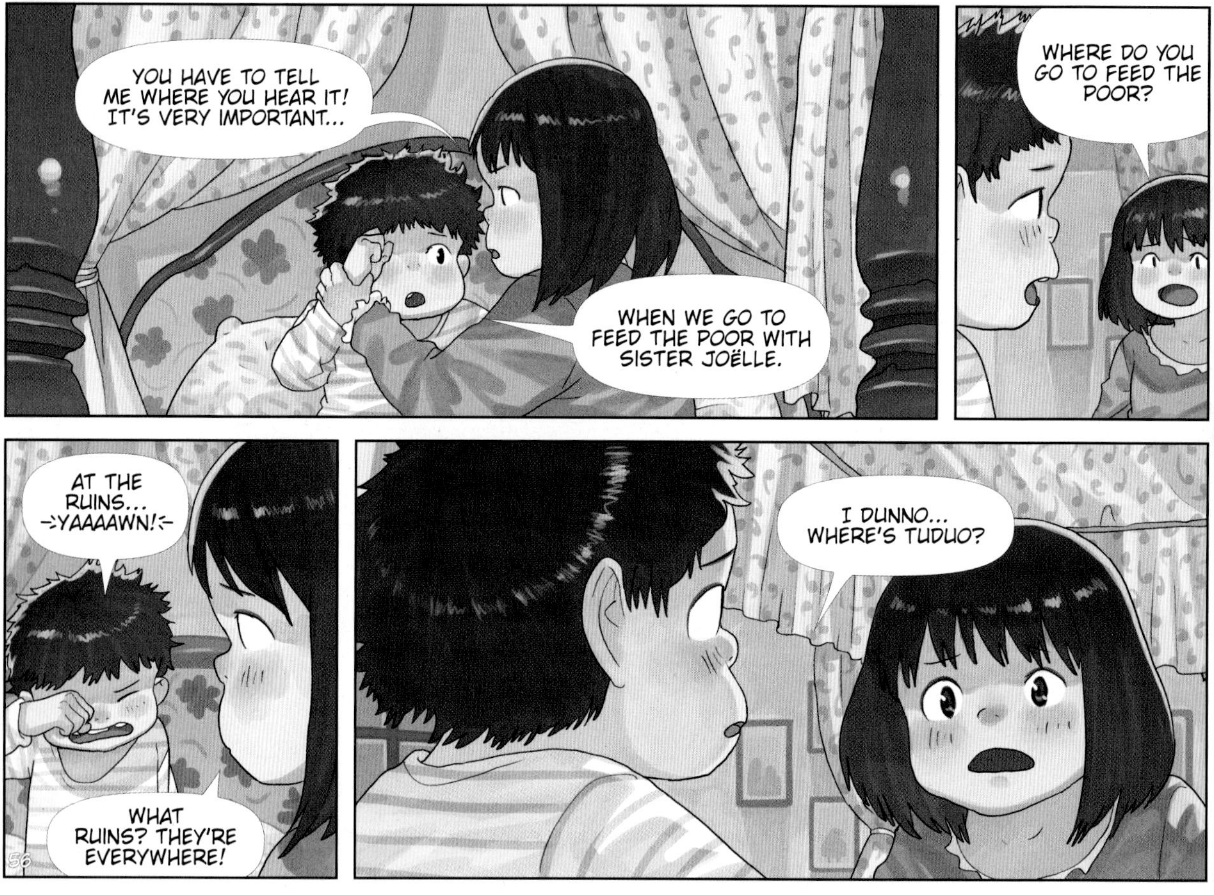
YOU HAVE TO TELL ME WHERE YOU HEAR IT! IT'S VERY IMPORTANT...
WHEN WE GO TO FEED THE POOR WITH SISTER JOËLLE.
WHERE DO YOU GO TO FEED THE POOR?
AT THE RUINS... -YAAAAWN!-
WHAT RUINS? THEY'RE EVERYWHERE!
I DUNNO... WHERE'S TUDUO?

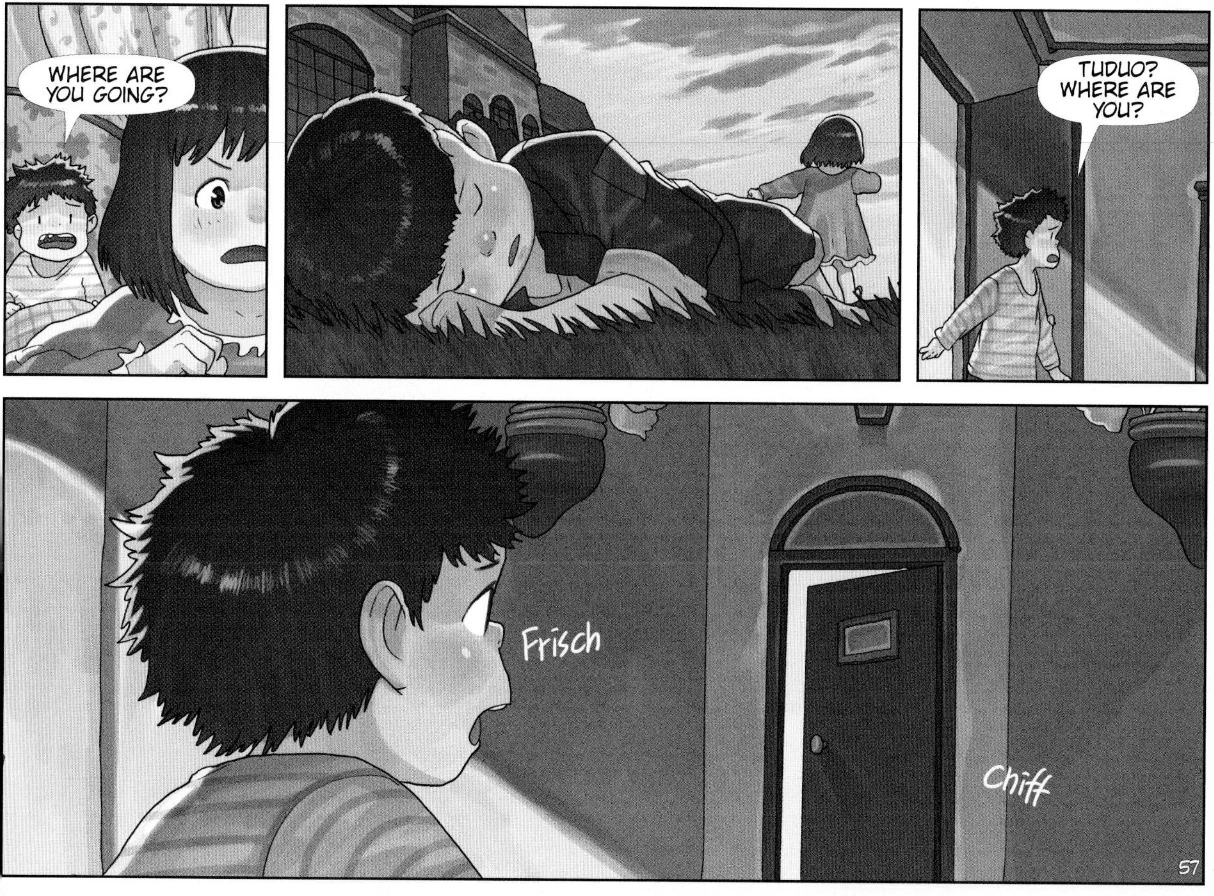
WHERE ARE YOU GOING?
TUDUO? WHERE ARE YOU?
Frisch
Chiff

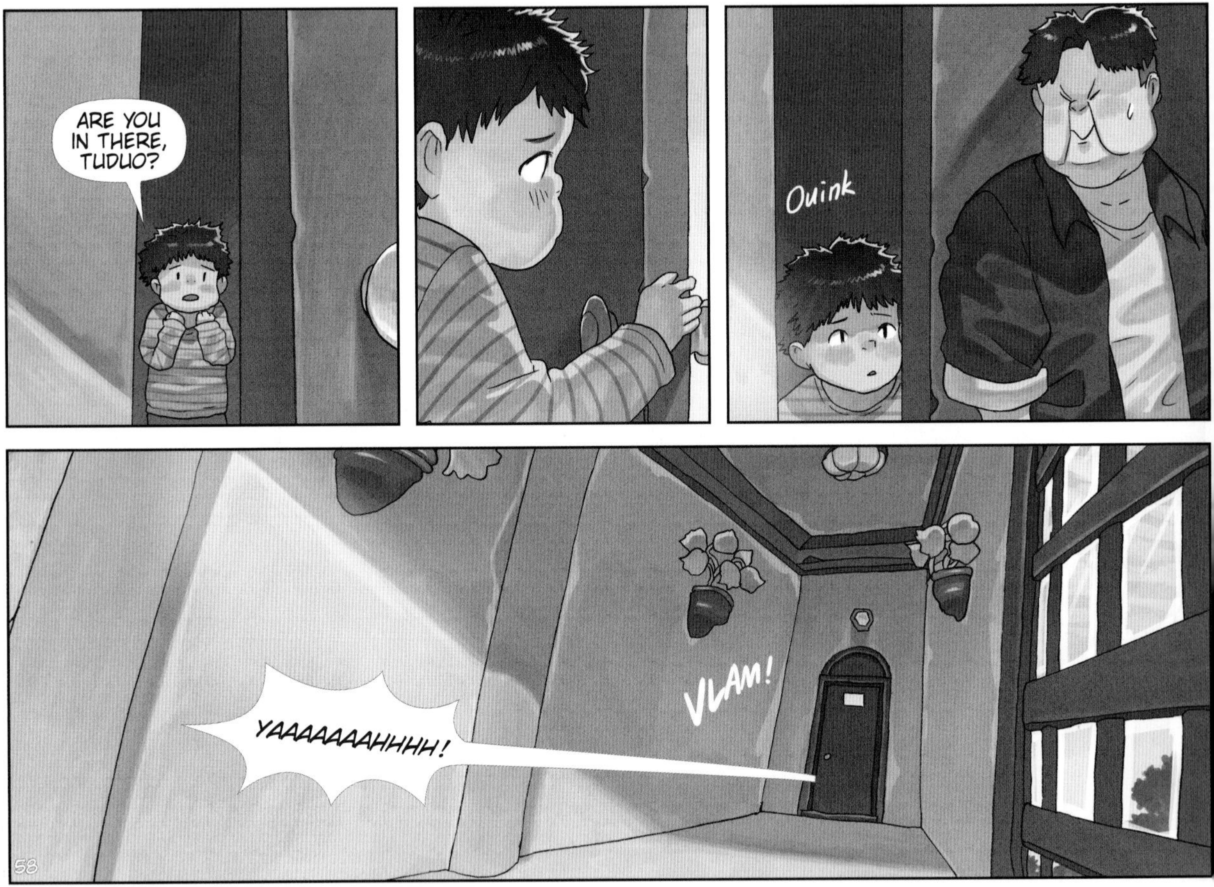
ARE YOU IN THERE, TUDUO?
Ouink
VLAM!
YAAAAAAAHHHH!

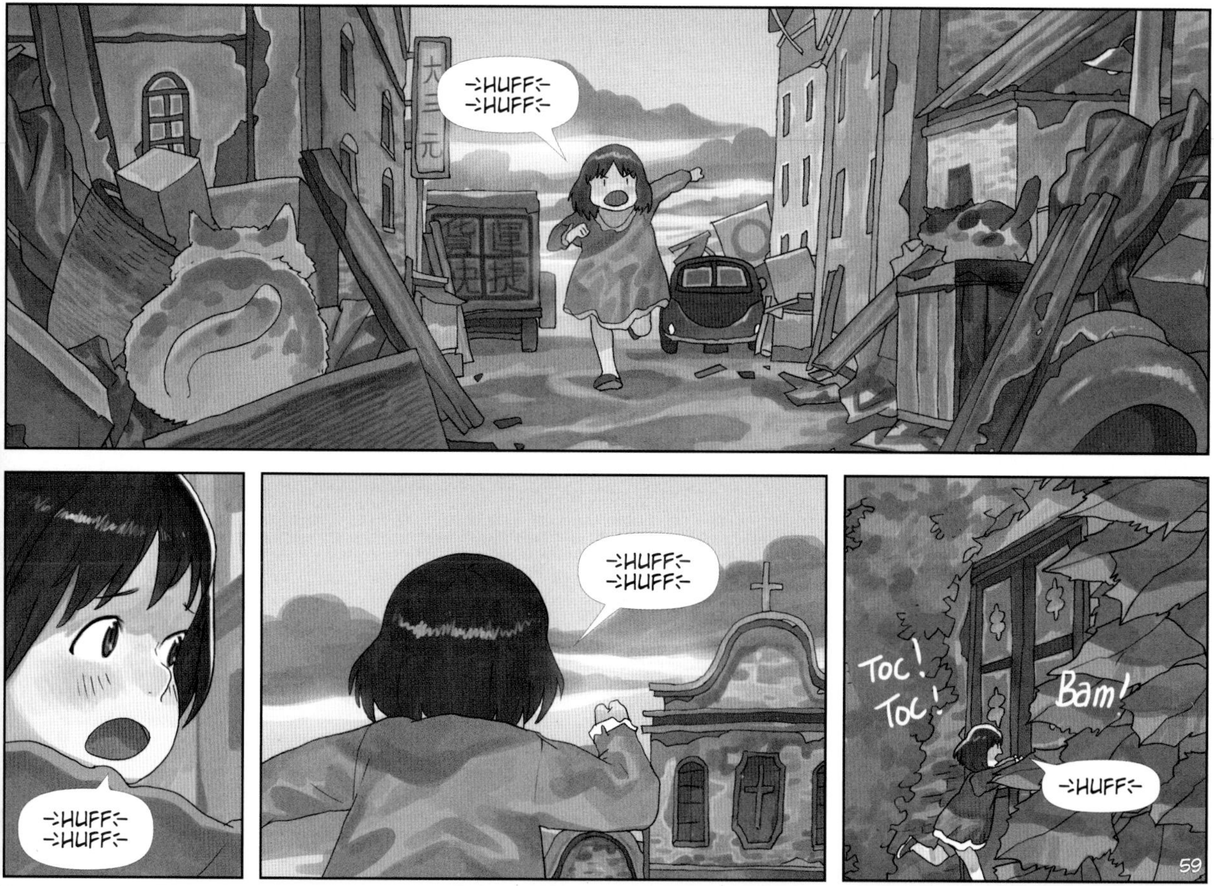
HUFF
HUFF
HUFF
HUFF
HUFF
HUFF
Toc!
Toc!
Bam!
HUFF

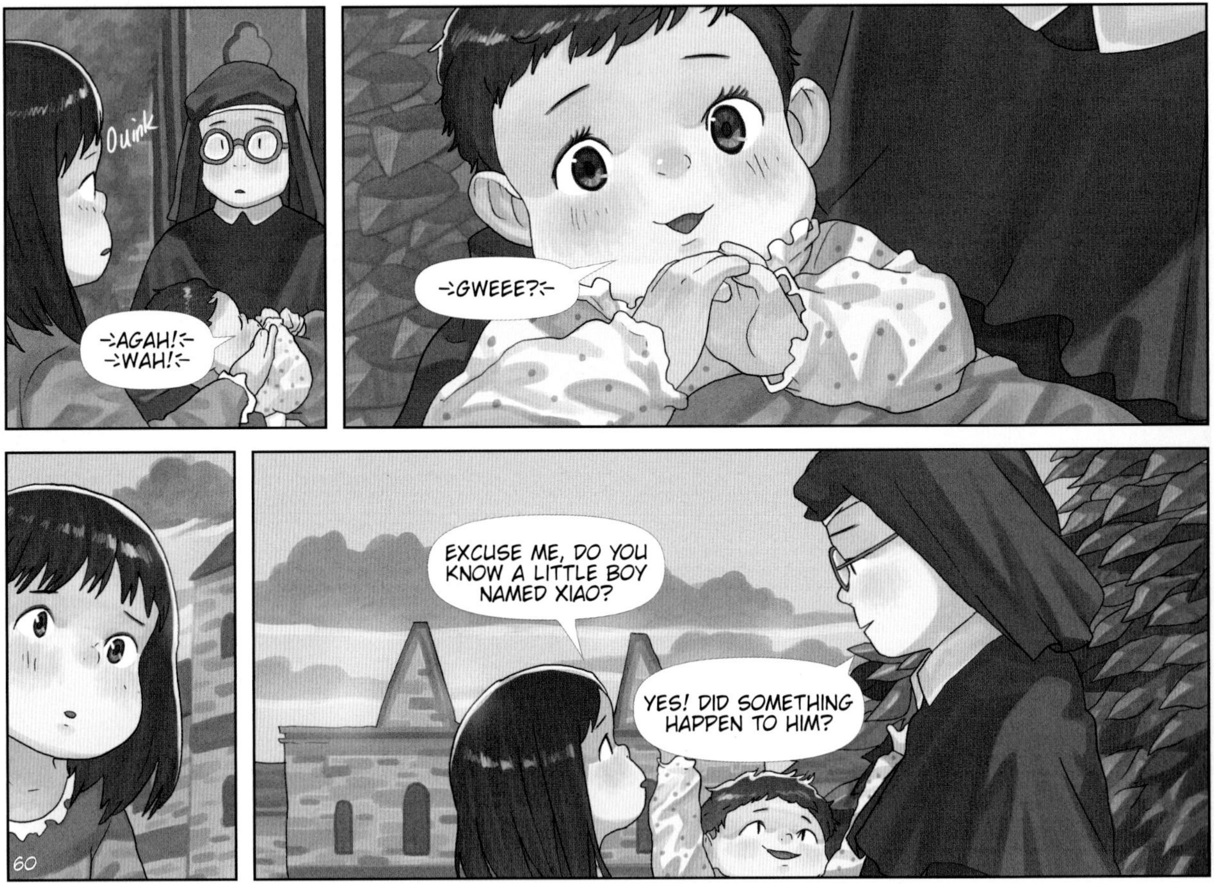
Ouink
AGAH! WAH!
GWEEE?
EXCUSE ME, DO YOU KNOW A LITTLE BOY NAMED XIAO?
YES! DID SOMETHING HAPPEN TO HIM?

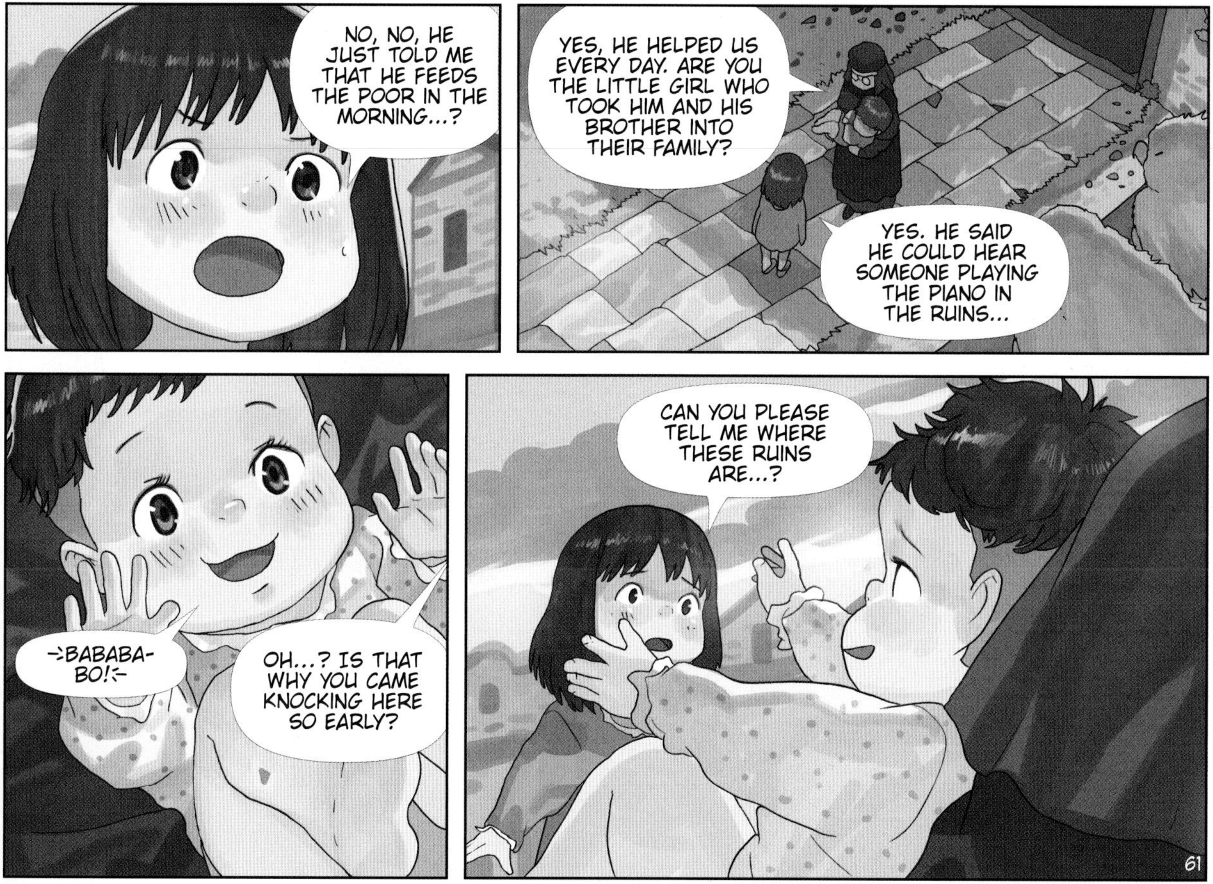
NO, NO, HE JUST TOLD ME THAT HE FEEDS THE POOR IN THE MORNING...?
YES, HE HELPED US EVERY DAY. ARE YOU THE LITTLE GIRL WHO TOOK HIM AND HIS BROTHER INTO THEIR FAMILY?
YES. HE SAID HE COULD HEAR SOMEONE PLAYING THE PIANO IN THE RUINS...
BABABA-BO!
OH...? IS THAT WHY YOU CAME KNOCKING HERE SO EARLY?
CAN YOU PLEASE TELL ME WHERE THESE RUINS ARE...?

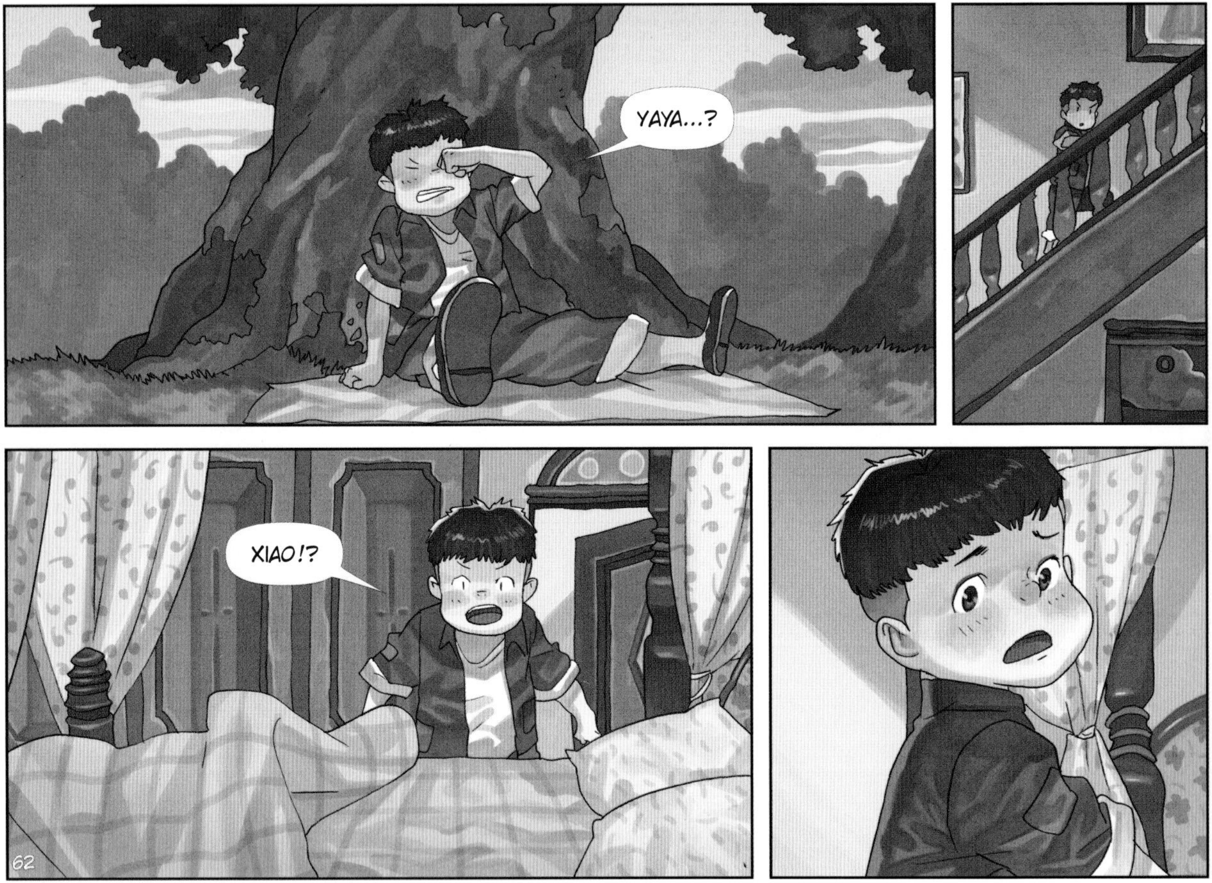
YAYA...?
XIAO!?

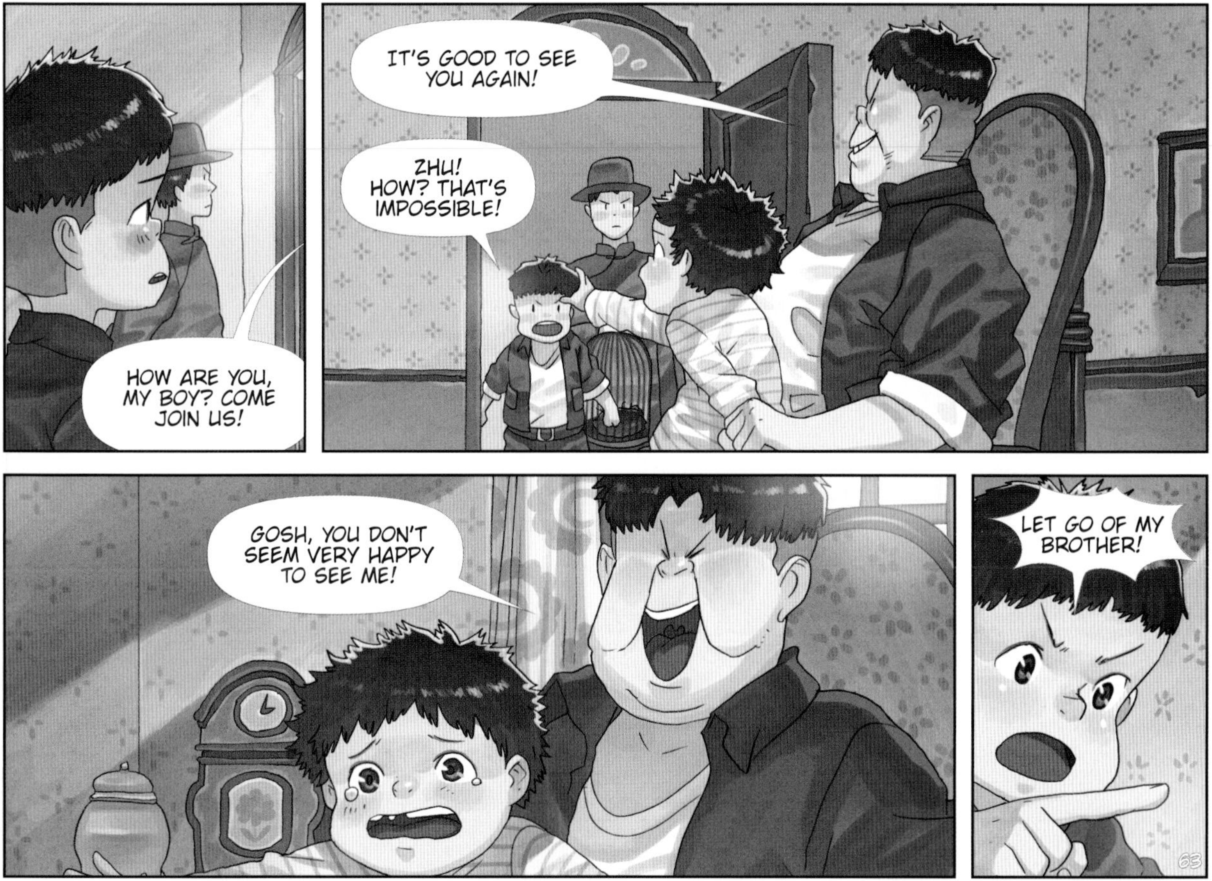

IT'S GOOD TO SEE YOU AGAIN!
ZHU! HOW? THAT'S IMPOSSIBLE!
HOW ARE YOU, MY BOY? COME JOIN US!
GOSH, YOU DON'T SEEM VERY HAPPY TO SEE ME!
LET GO OF MY BROTHER!

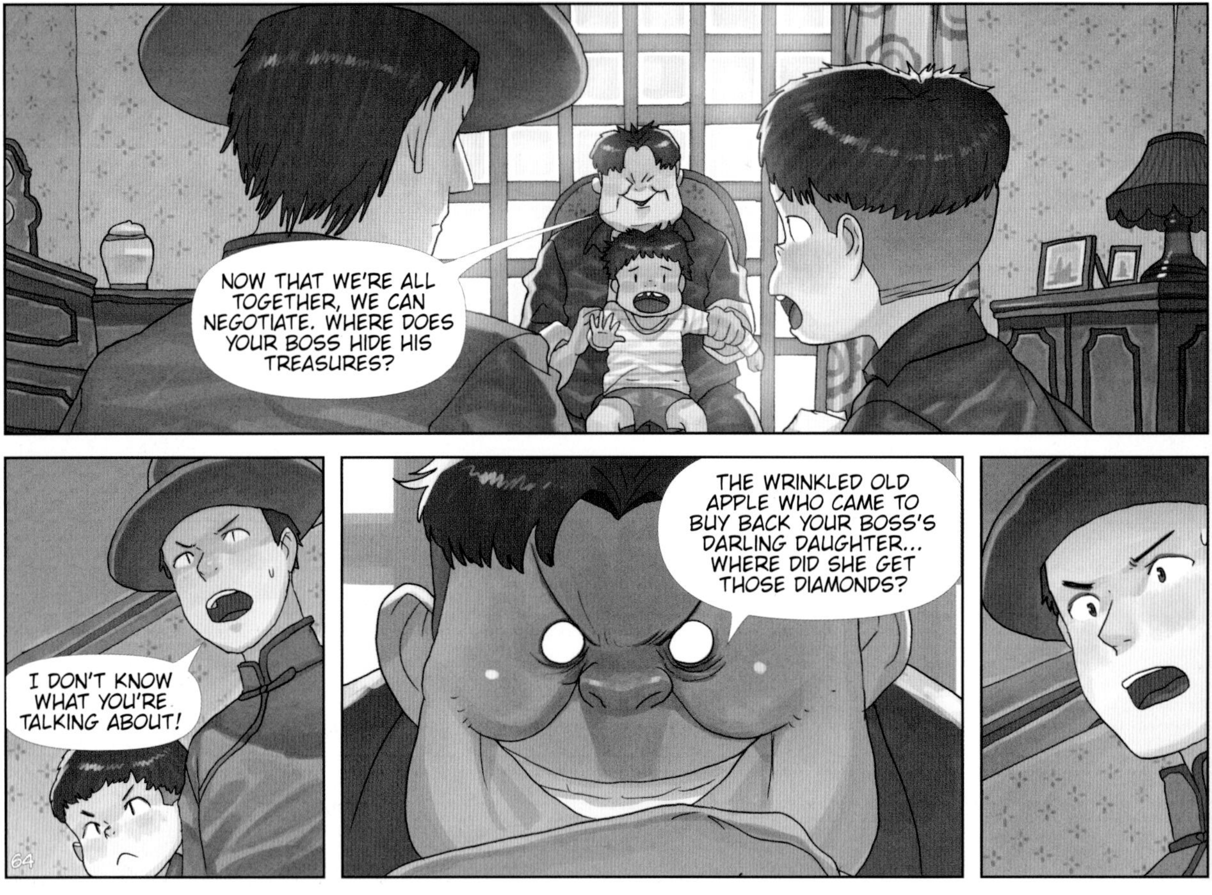
NOW THAT WE'RE ALL TOGETHER, WE CAN NEGOTIATE. WHERE DOES YOUR BOSS HIDE HIS TREASURES?
I DON'T KNOW WHAT YOU'RE TALKING ABOUT!
THE WRINKLED OLD APPLE WHO CAME TO BUY BACK YOUR BOSS'S DARLING DAUGHTER... WHERE DID SHE GET THOSE DIAMONDS?

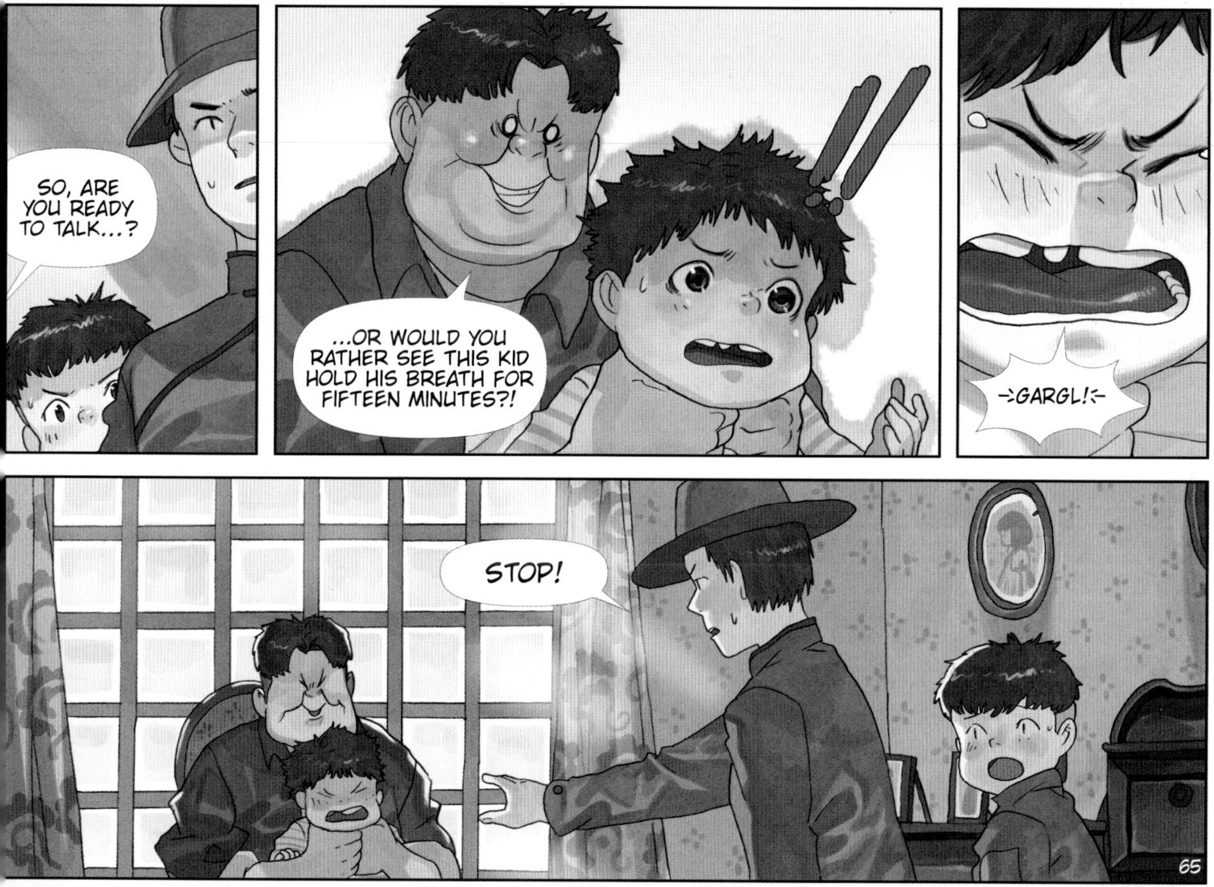
SO, ARE YOU READY TO TALK...?
...OR WOULD YOU RATHER SEE THIS KID HOLD HIS BREATH FOR FIFTEEN MINUTES?!
GARGL!
STOP!

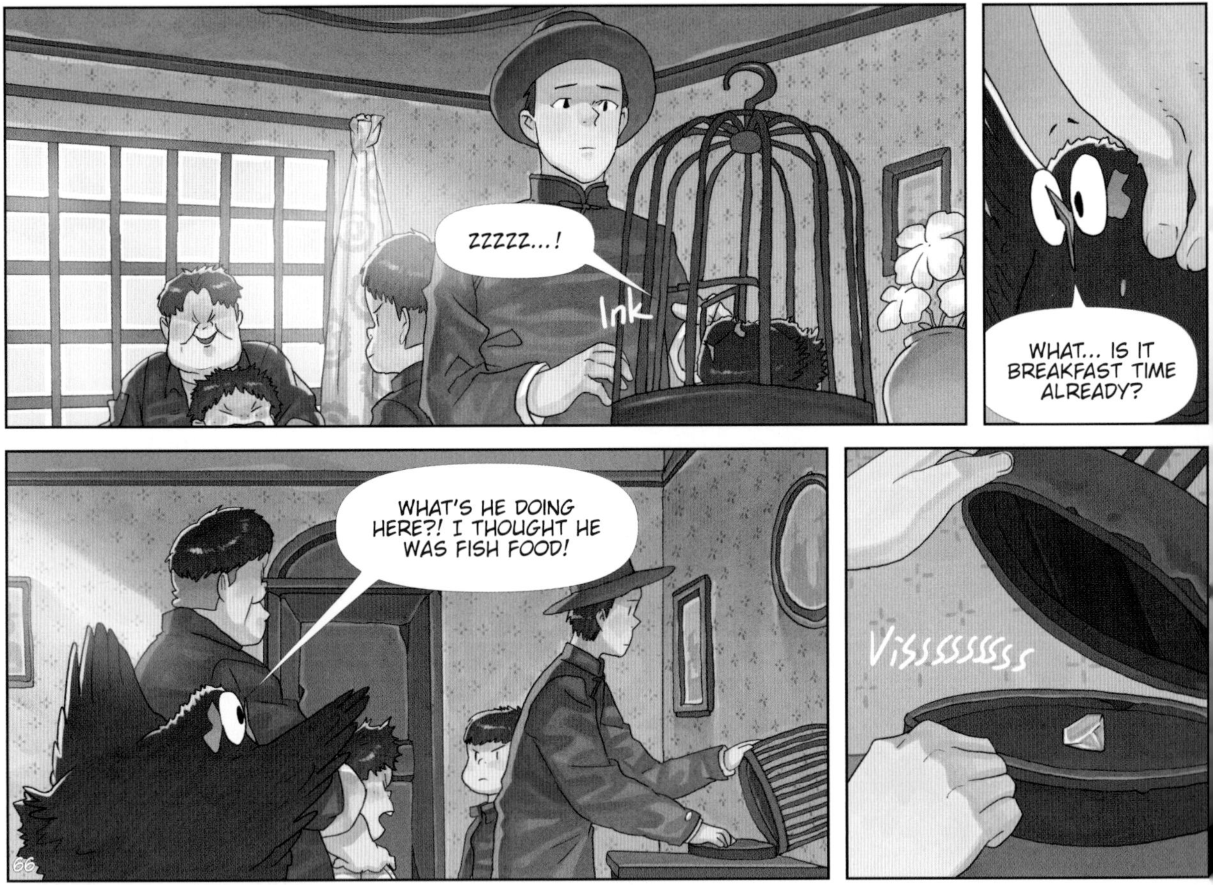
ZZZZZ...!
Ink
WHAT... IS IT BREAKFAST TIME ALREADY?
WHAT'S HE DOING HERE?! I THOUGHT HE WAS FISH FOOD!
Vissssssss

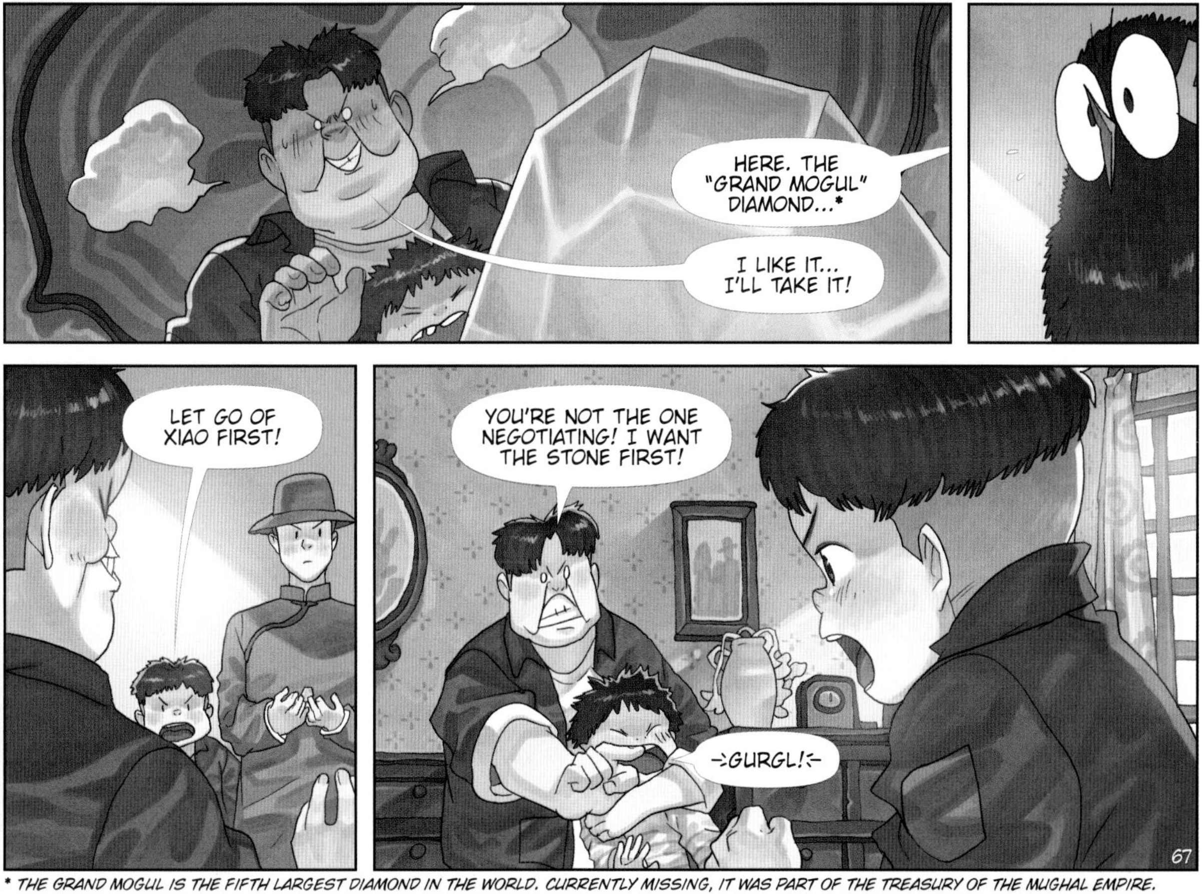
HERE. THE "GRAND MOGUL" DIAMOND...*
I LIKE IT... I'LL TAKE IT!
LET GO OF XIAO FIRST!
YOU'RE NOT THE ONE NEGOTIATING! I WANT THE STONE FIRST!
-GURGL!-

* THE GRAND MOGUL IS THE FIFTH LARGEST DIAMOND IN THE WORLD. CURRENTLY MISSING, IT WAS PART OF THE TREASURY OF THE MUGHAL EMPIRE.

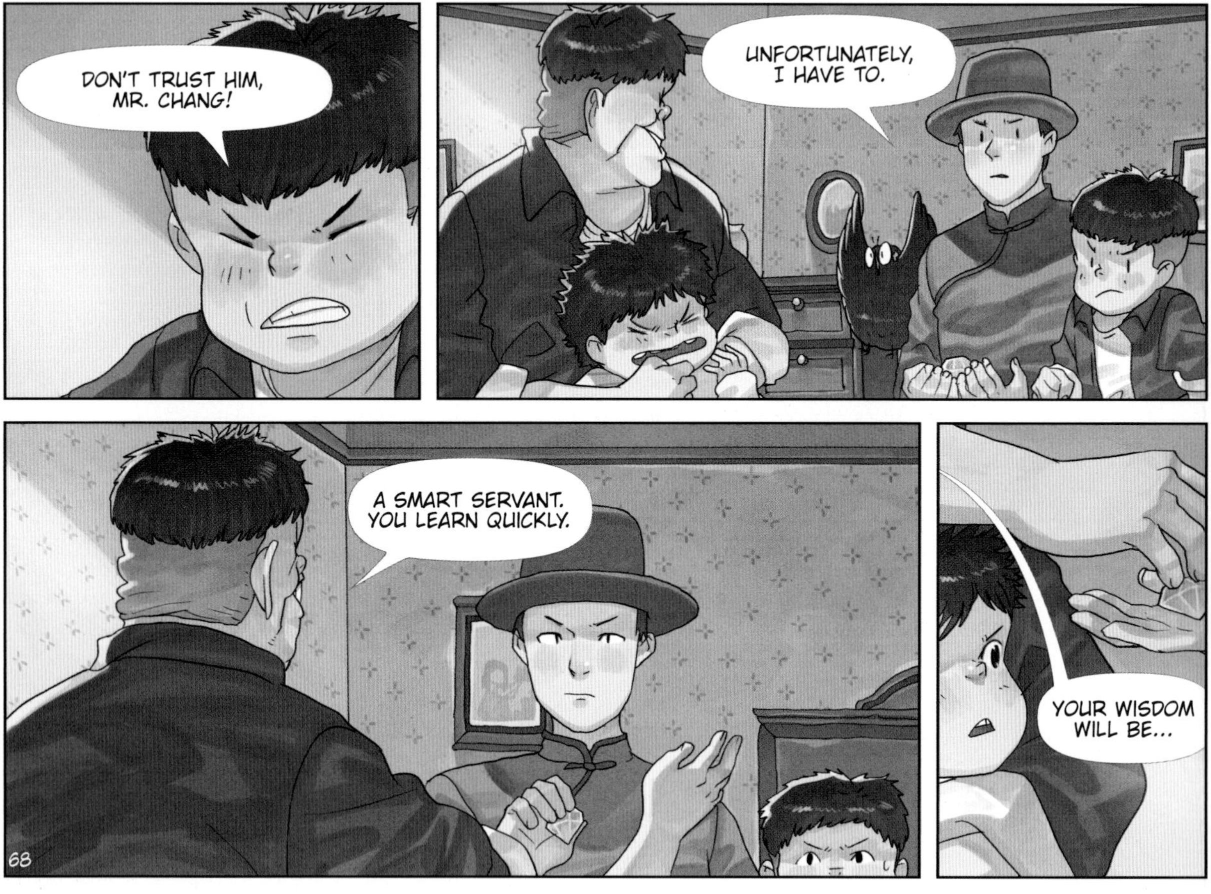
DON'T TRUST HIM, MR. CHANG!
UNFORTUNATELY, I HAVE TO.
A SMART SERVANT. YOU LEARN QUICKLY.
YOUR WISDOM WILL BE...

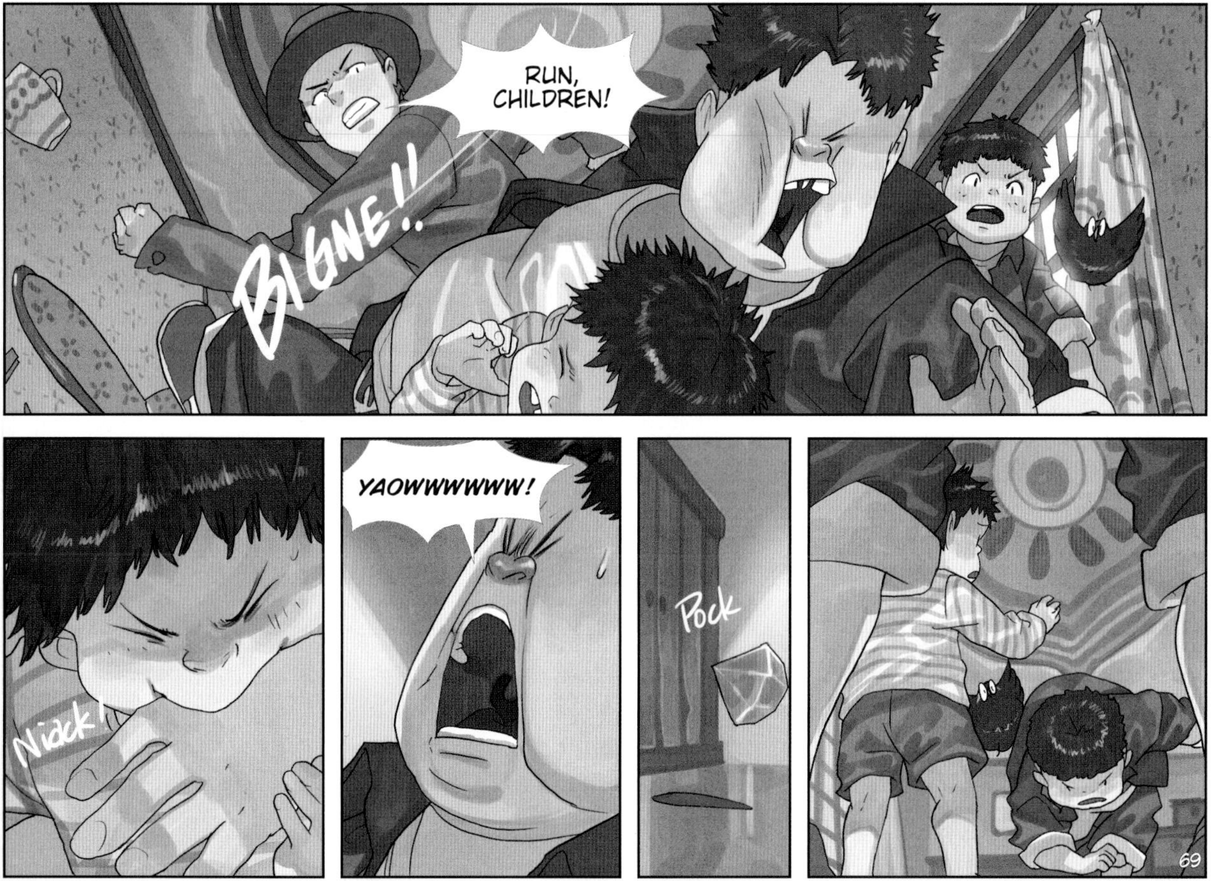
RUN, CHILDREN!
BIGNE!!
Niack!
YAOWWWWWW!
Pock

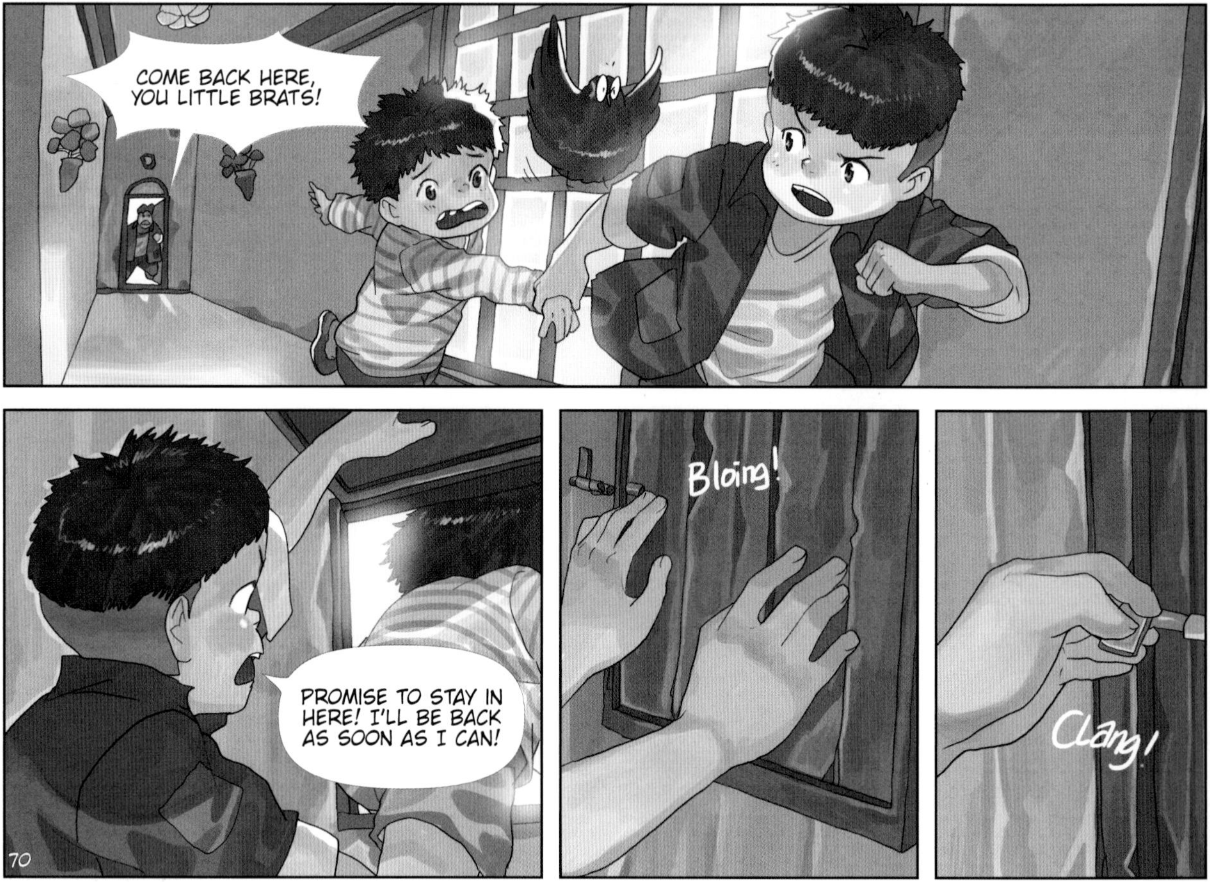
COME BACK HERE, YOU LITTLE BRATS!
PROMISE TO STAY IN HERE! I'LL BE BACK AS SOON AS I CAN!
Bloing!
Clang!

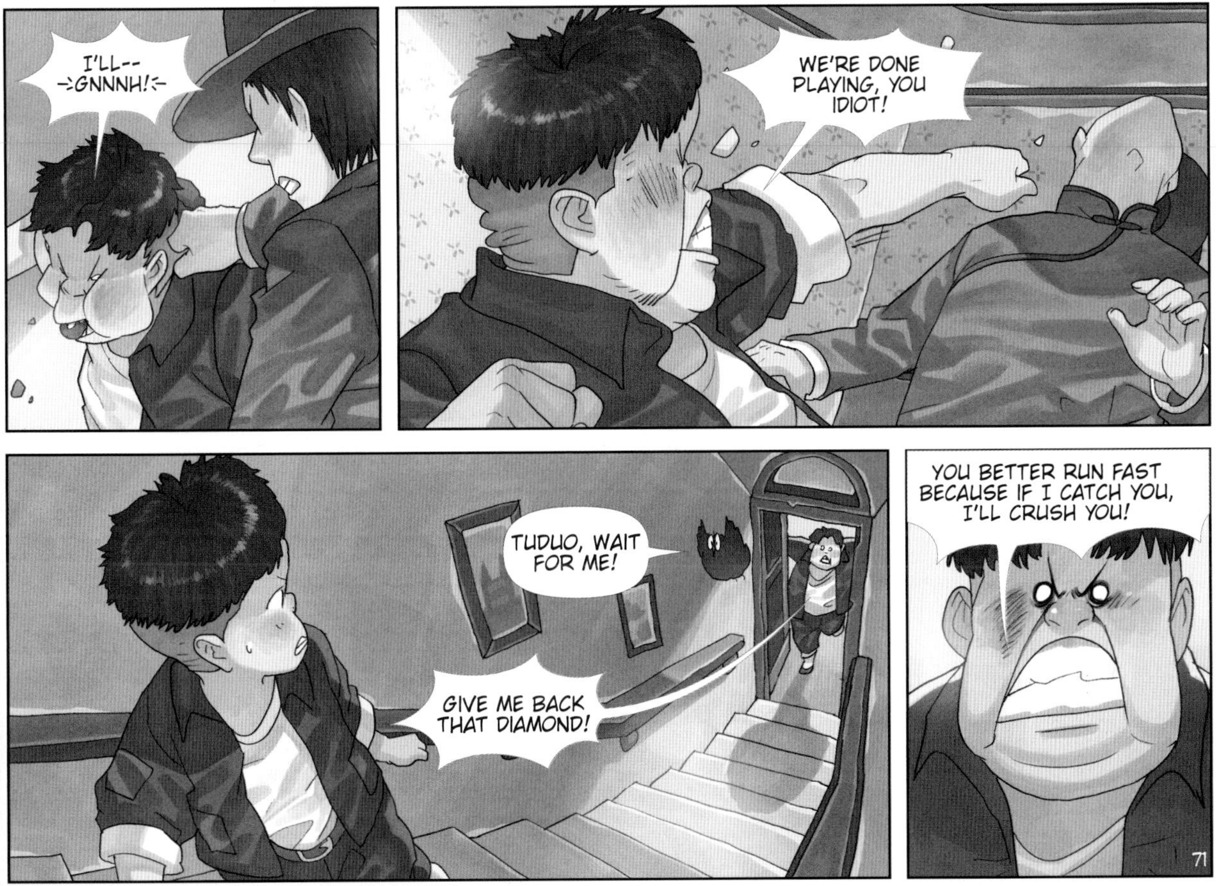
I'LL--
-GNNNH!-
WE'RE DONE PLAYING, YOU IDIOT!
TUDUO, WAIT FOR ME!
GIVE ME BACK THAT DIAMOND!
YOU BETTER RUN FAST BECAUSE IF I CATCH YOU, I'LL CRUSH YOU!

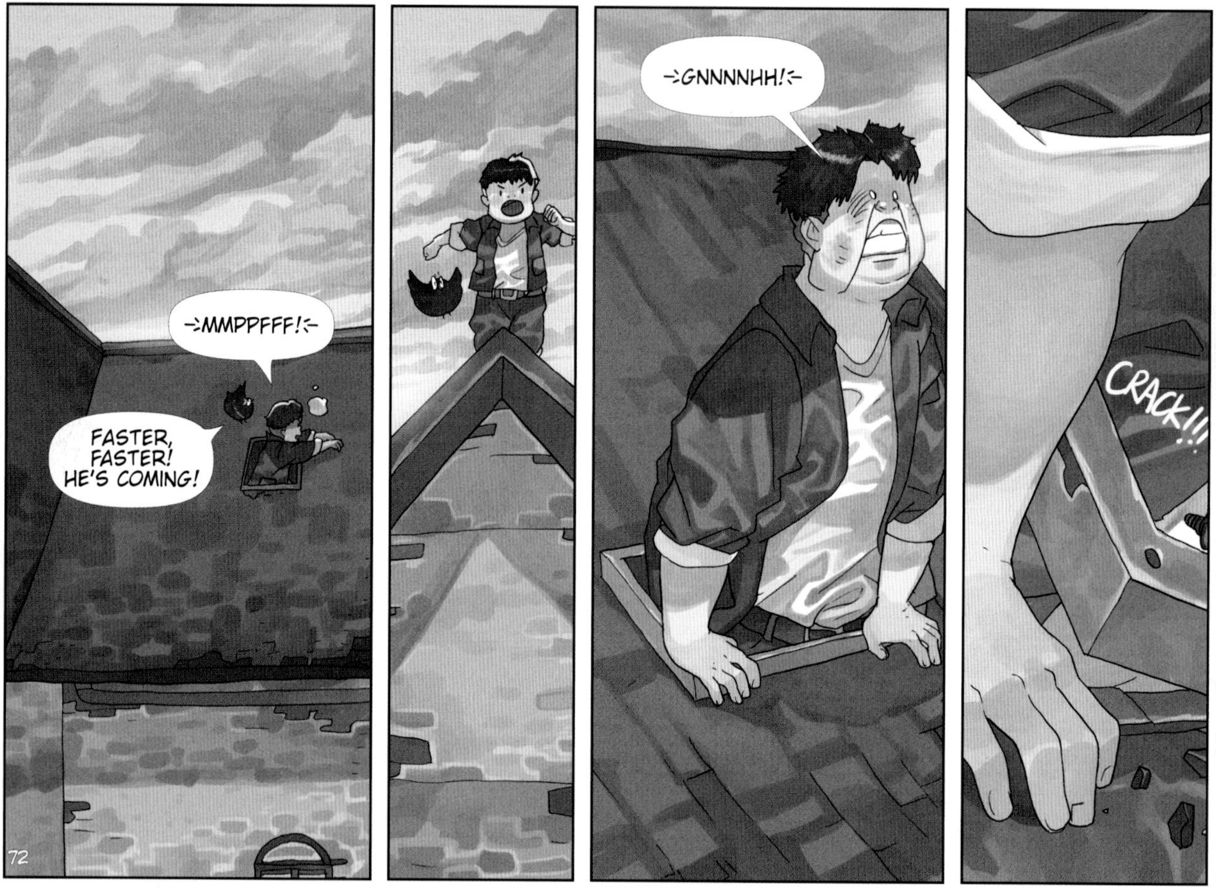
-MMPPFFF!-
FASTER, FASTER! HE'S COMING!
-GNNNNHH!-
CRACK!!!

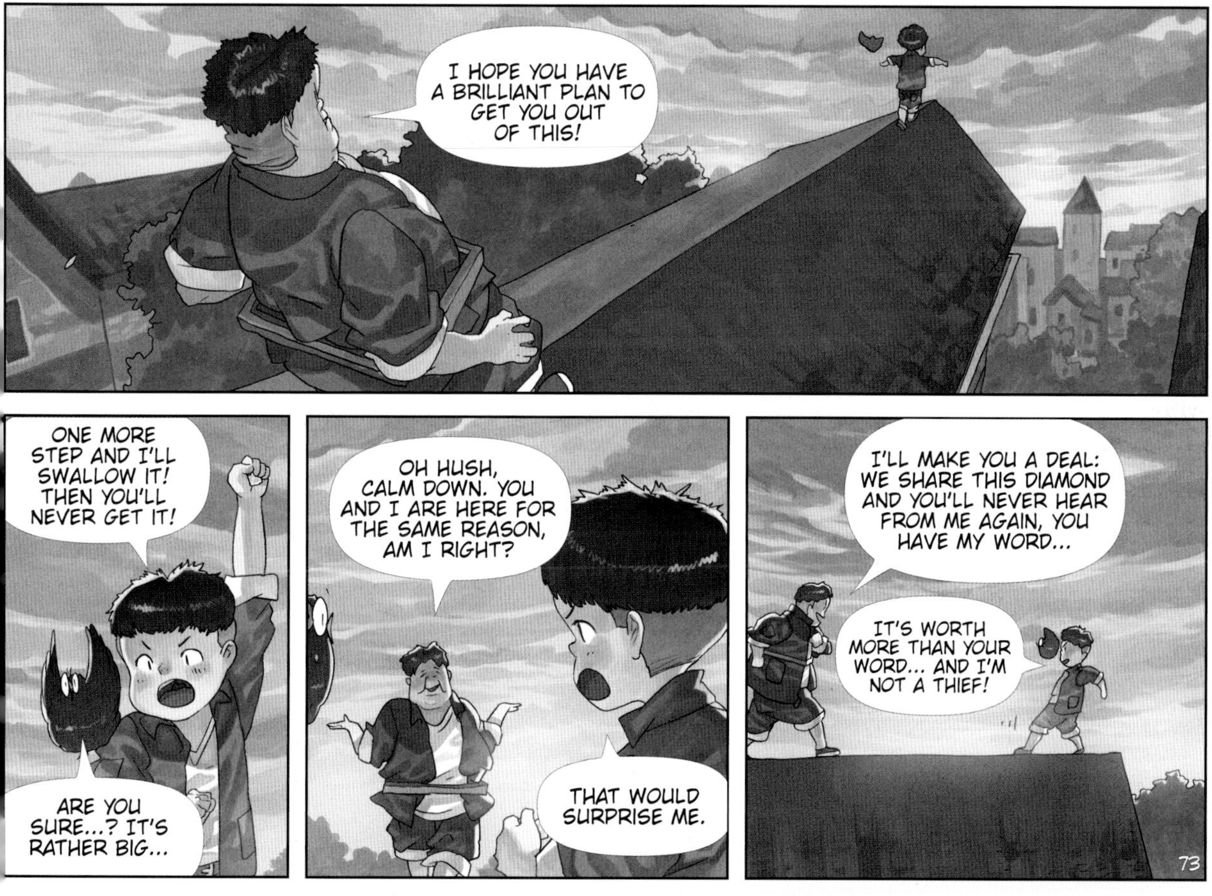
I HOPE YOU HAVE A BRILLIANT PLAN TO GET YOU OUT OF THIS!
ONE MORE STEP AND I'LL SWALLOW IT! THEN YOU'LL NEVER GET IT!
ARE YOU SURE...? IT'S RATHER BIG...
OH HUSH, CALM DOWN. YOU AND I ARE HERE FOR THE SAME REASON, AM I RIGHT?
THAT WOULD SURPRISE ME.
I'LL MAKE YOU A DEAL: WE SHARE THIS DIAMOND AND YOU'LL NEVER HEAR FROM ME AGAIN, YOU HAVE MY WORD...
IT'S WORTH MORE THAN YOUR WORD... AND I'M NOT A THIEF!

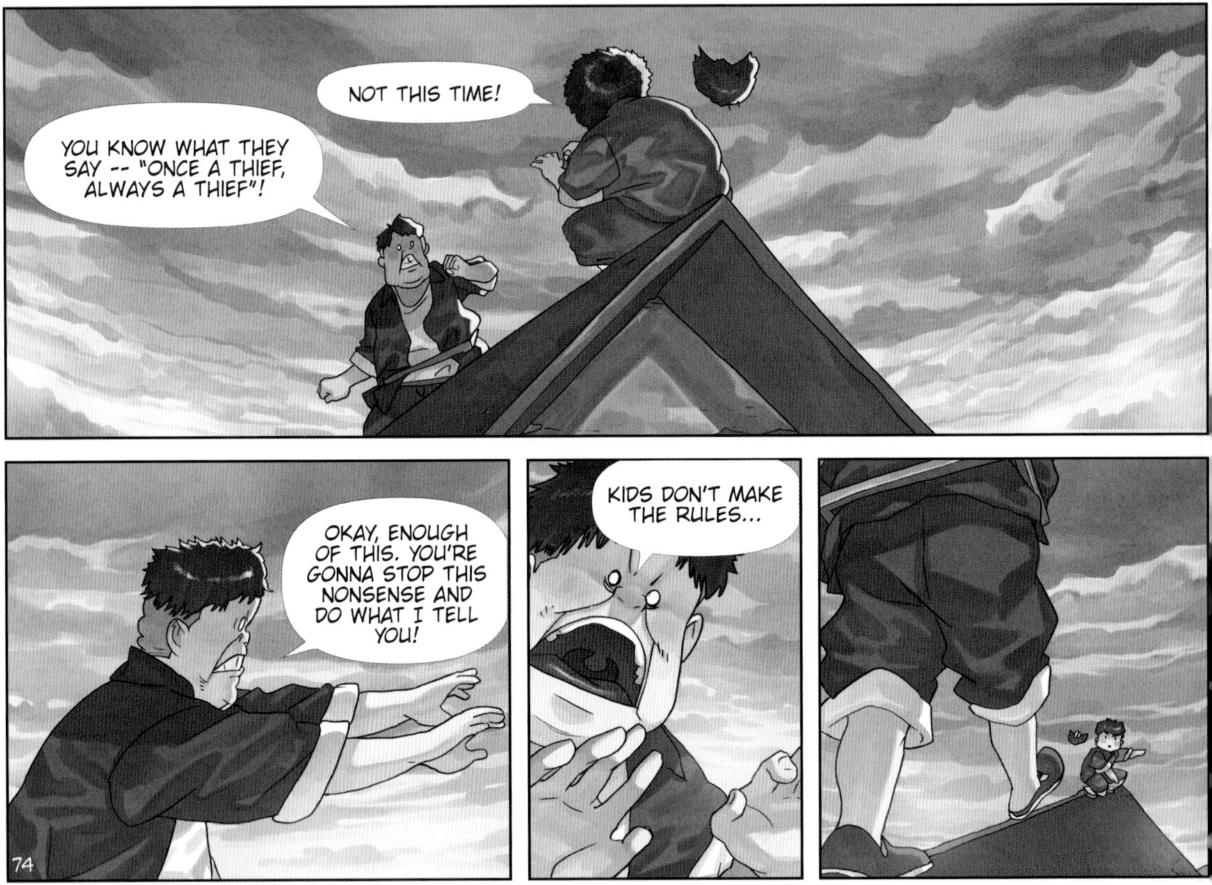
YOU KNOW WHAT THEY SAY -- "ONCE A THIEF, ALWAYS A THIEF"!
NOT THIS TIME!
OKAY, ENOUGH OF THIS. YOU'RE GONNA STOP THIS NONSENSE AND DO WHAT I TELL YOU!
KIDS DON'T MAKE THE RULES...

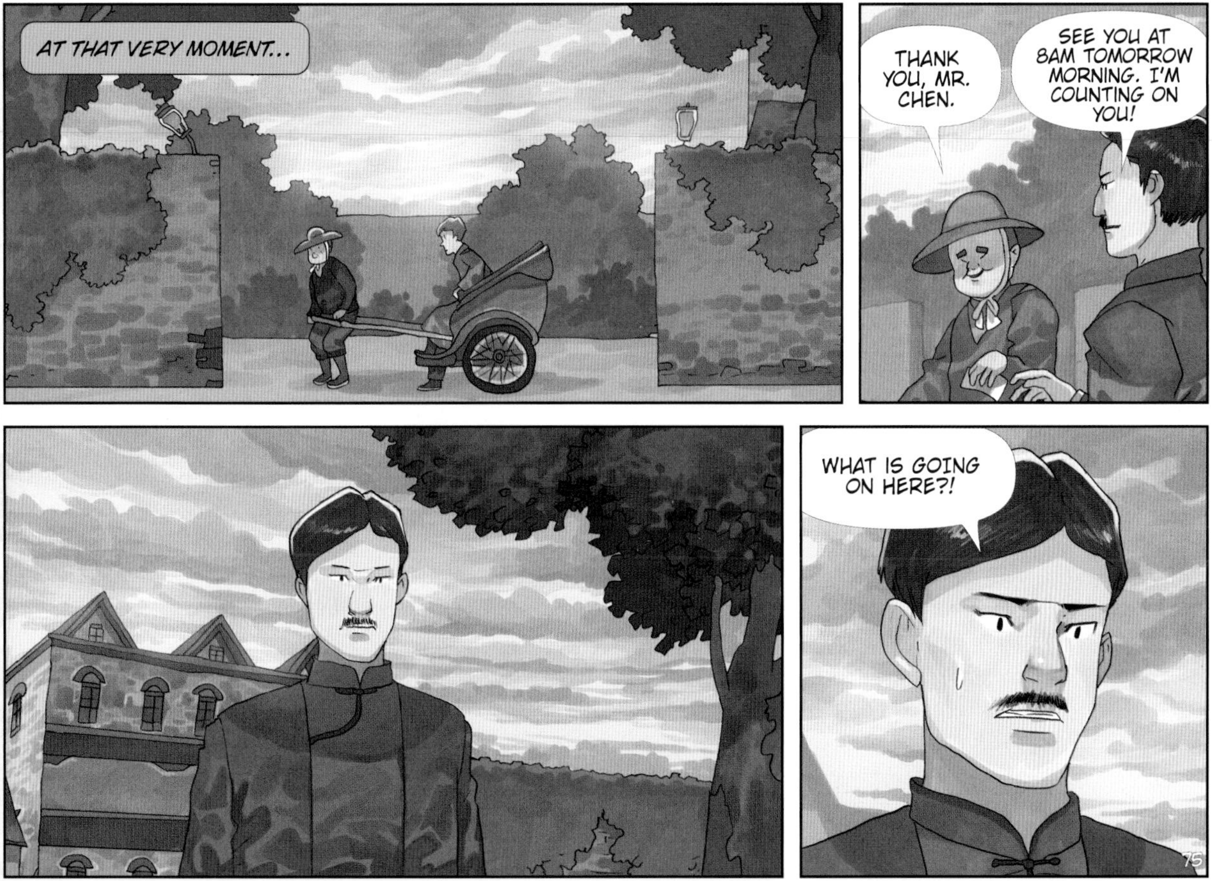
AT THAT VERY MOMENT...
THANK YOU, MR. CHEN.
SEE YOU AT 8AM TOMORROW MORNING. I'M COUNTING ON YOU!
WHAT IS GOING ON HERE?!

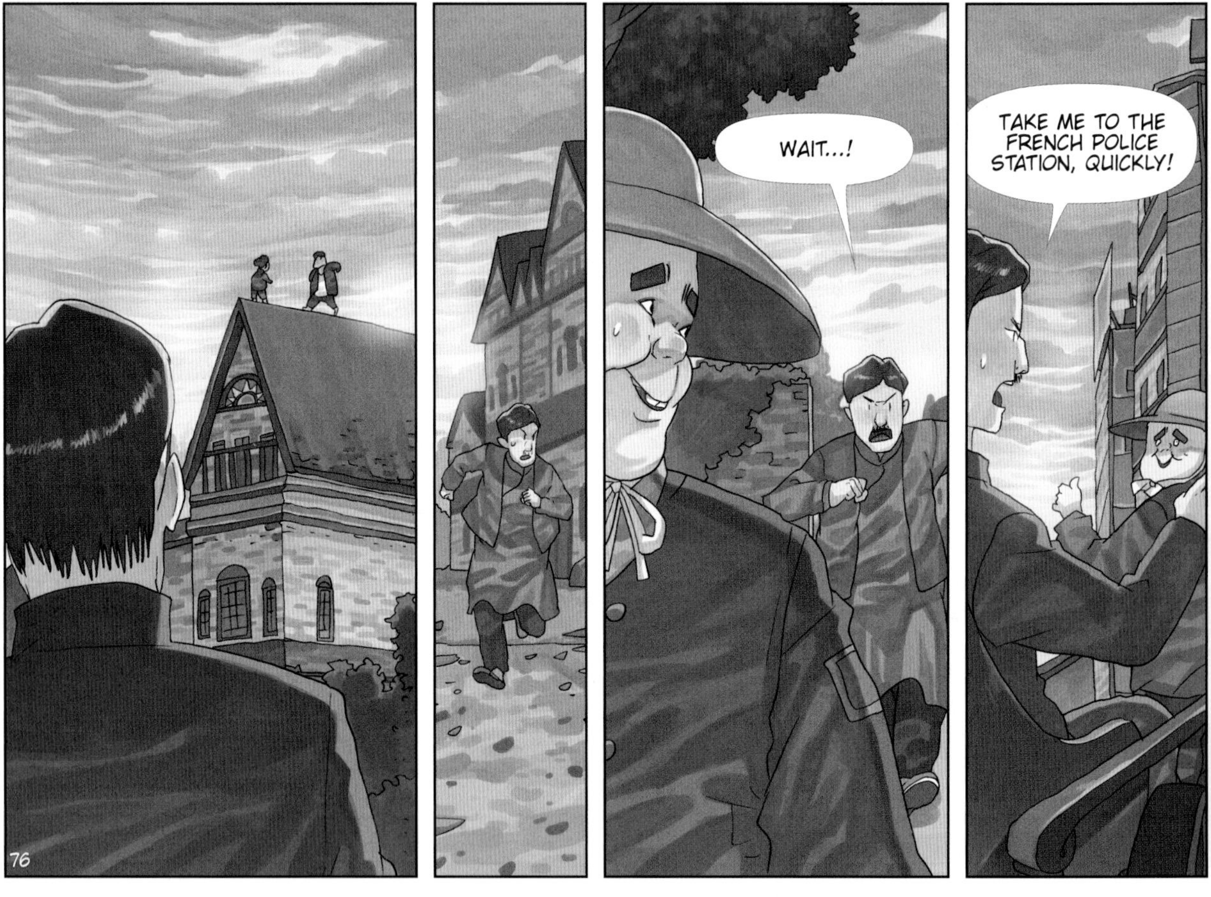
WAIT...!
TAKE ME TO THE FRENCH POLICE STATION, QUICKLY!

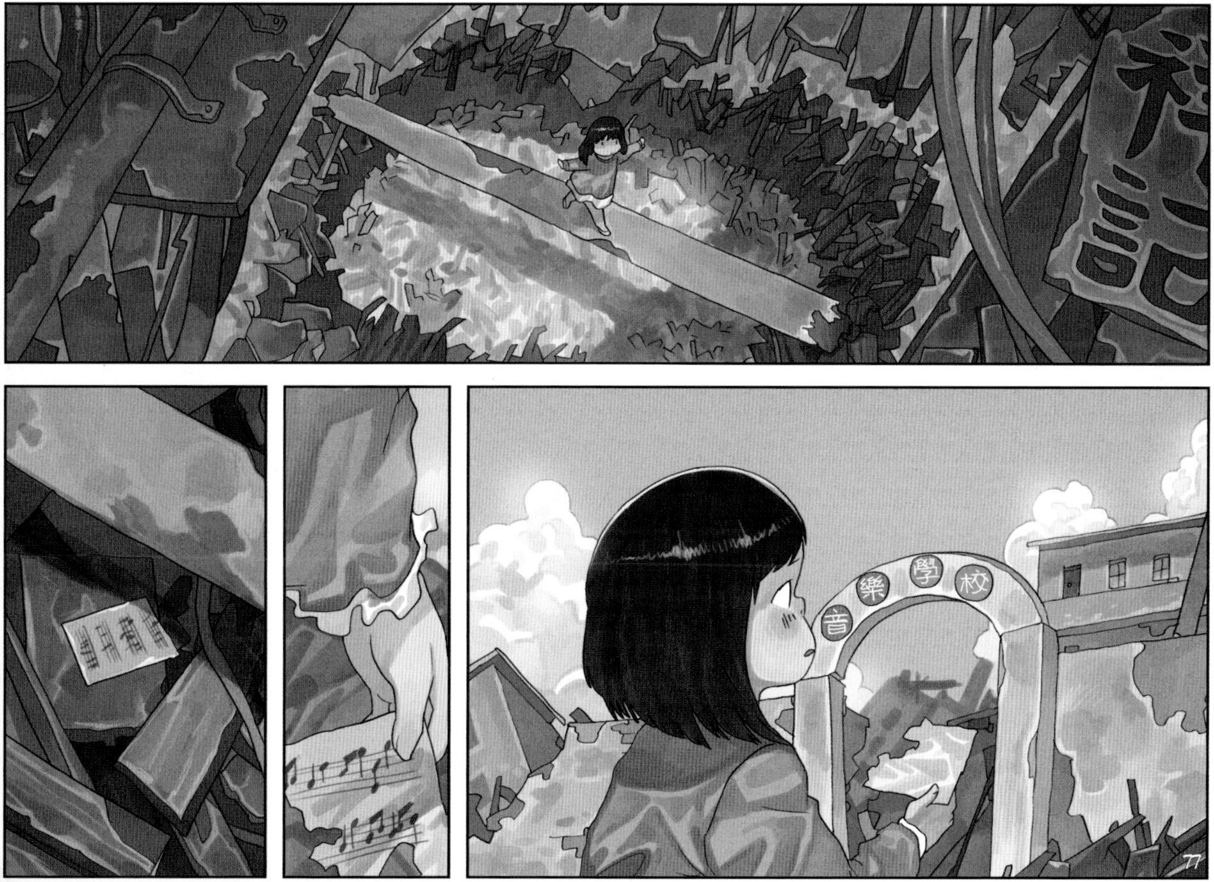
記
音樂學校

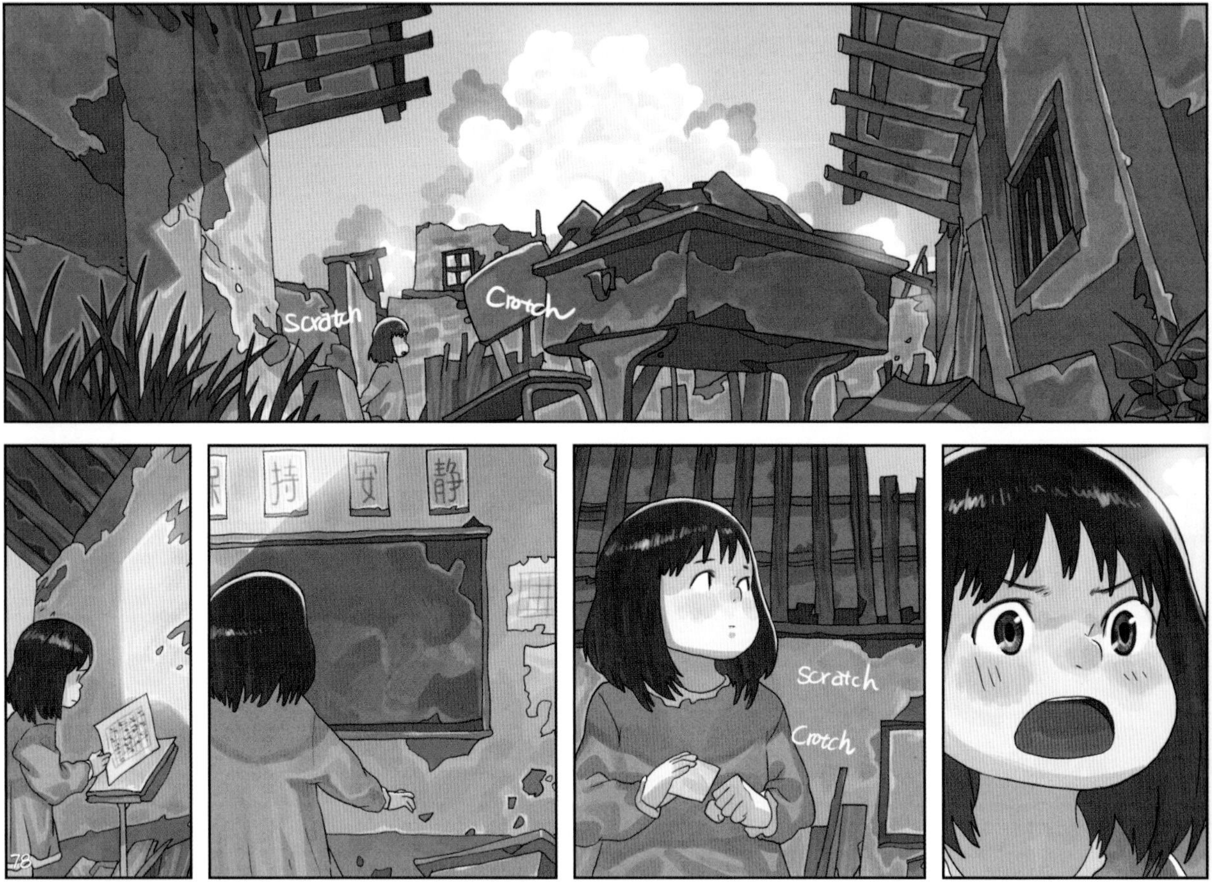
scratch
Crotch
持
安
静
scratch
Crotch

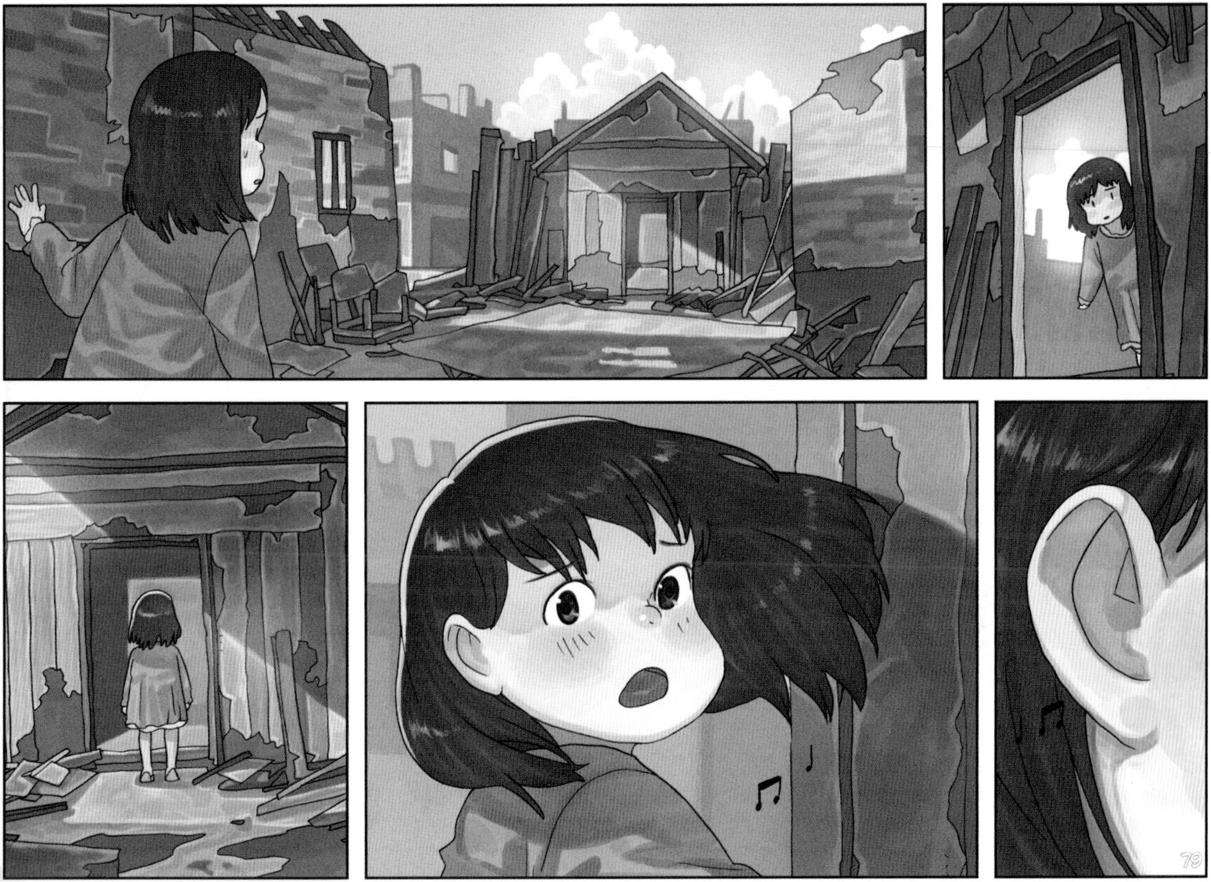

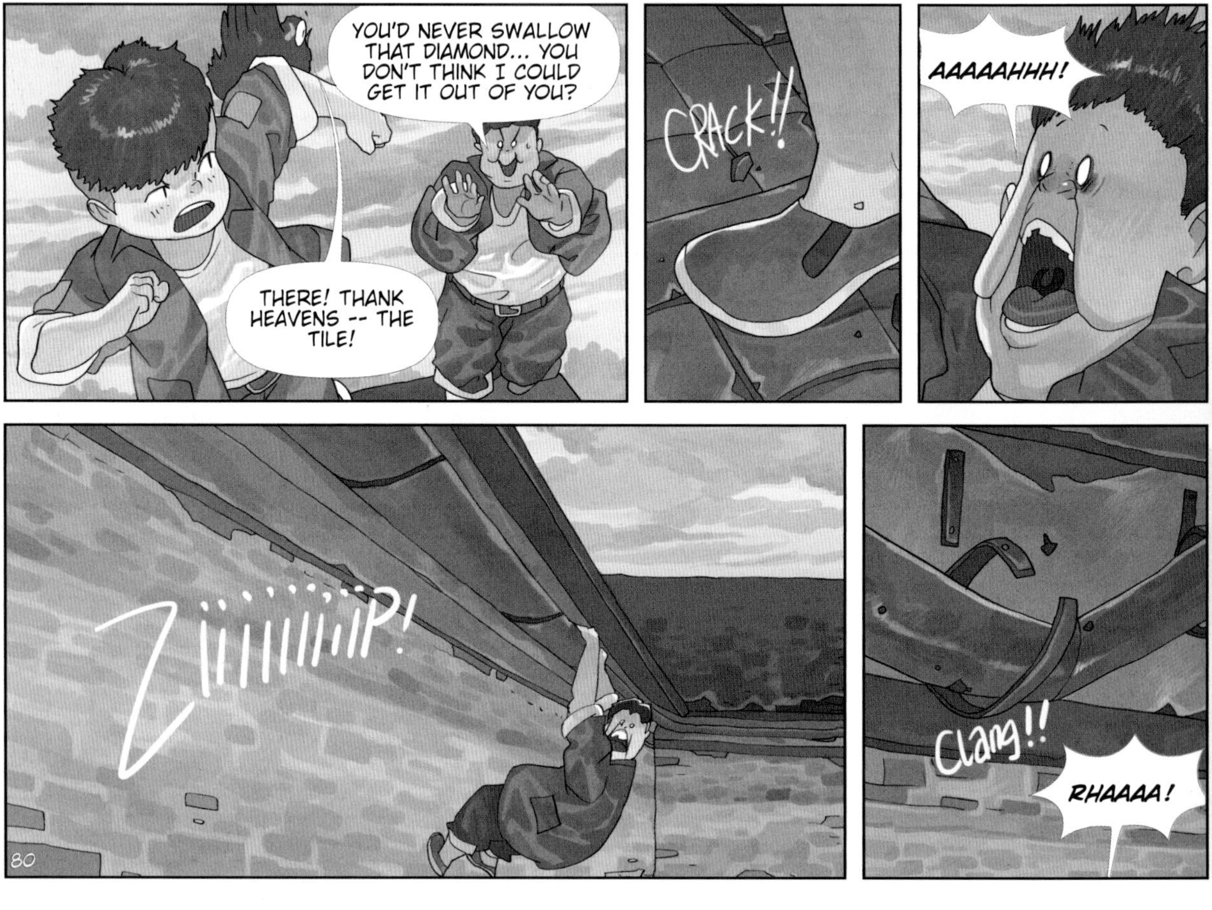
YOU'D NEVER SWALLOW THAT DIAMOND... YOU DON'T THINK I COULD GET IT OUT OF YOU?
THERE! THANK HEAVENS -- THE TILE!
CRACK!!
AAAAAHHH!
ZIIIIIIIIP!
CLANG!!
RHAAAA!

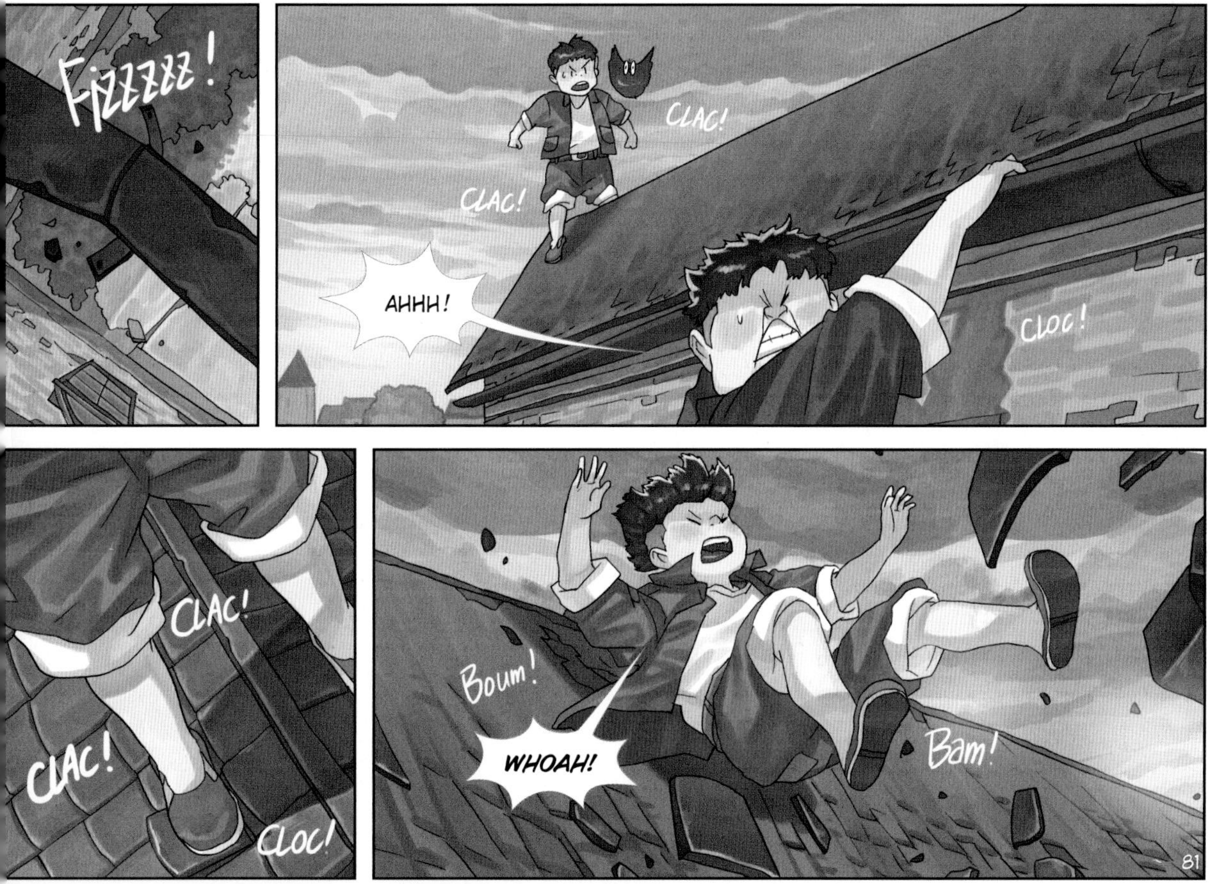
Fizzzzz!
CLAC!
CLAC!
AHHH!
CLOC!
CLAC!
CLAC!
CLOC!
Boum!
WHOAH!
Bam!

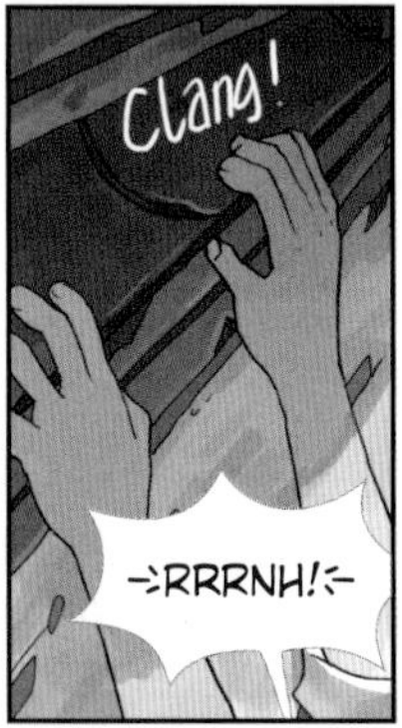
Clang!
RRRNH!

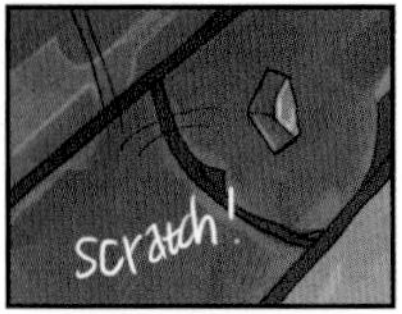
scratch!

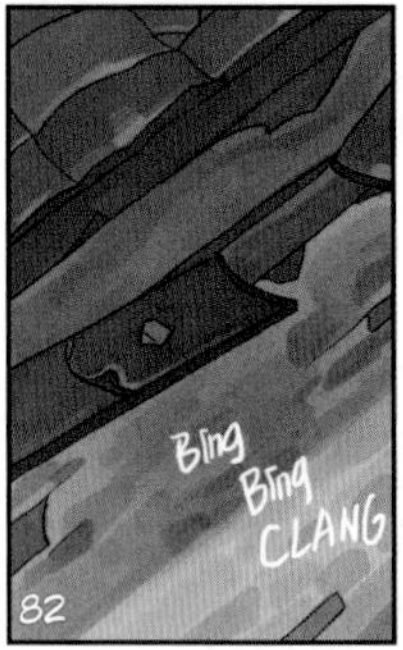
Bing
Bing
CLANG

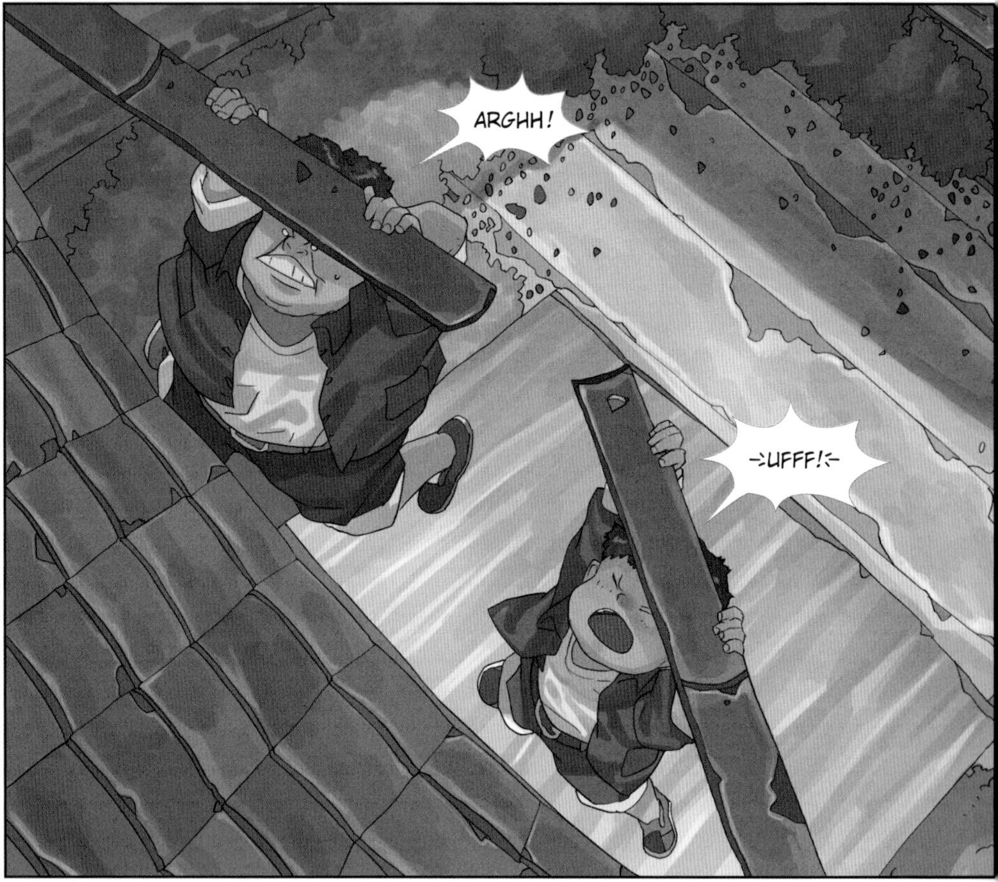
ARGHH!
UFFF!

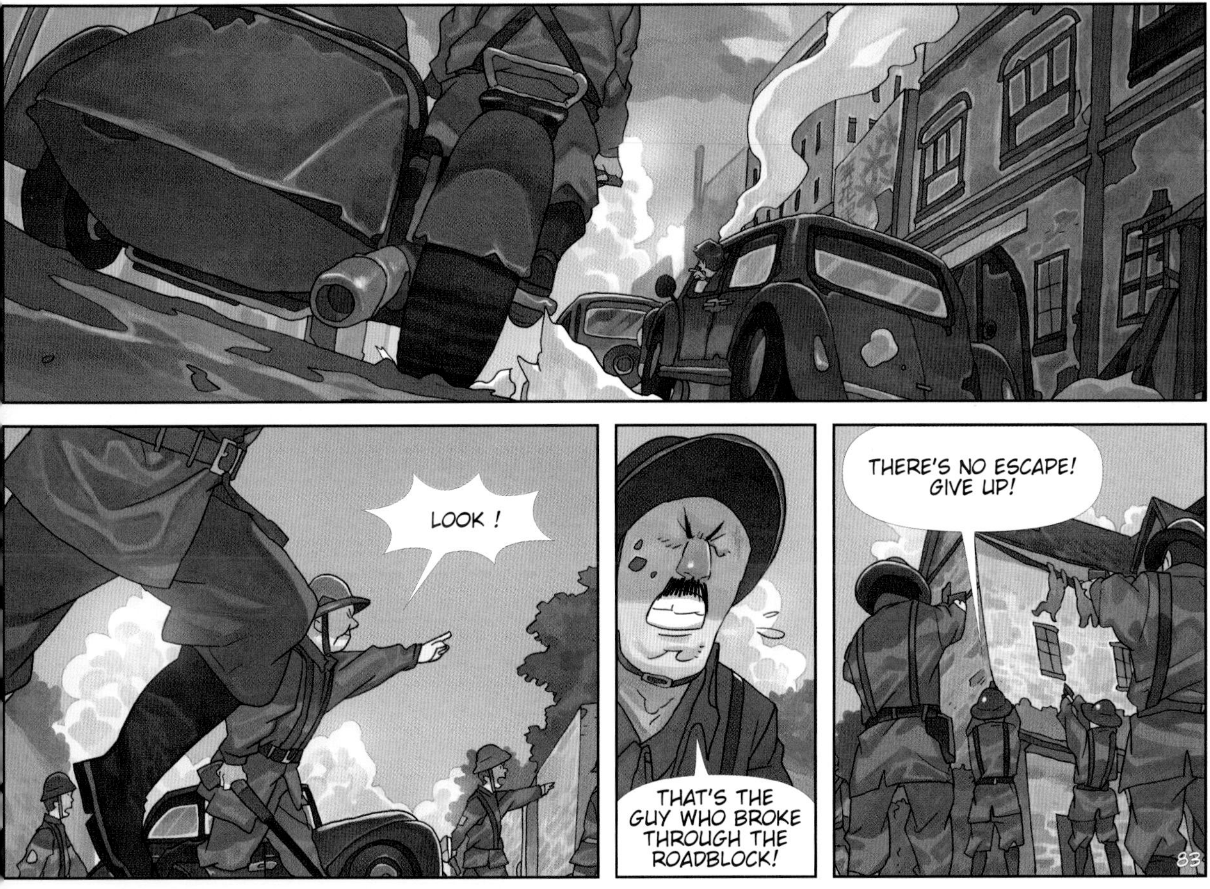
LOOK !
THAT'S THE GUY WHO BROKE THROUGH THE ROADBLOCK!
THERE'S NO ESCAPE! GIVE UP!

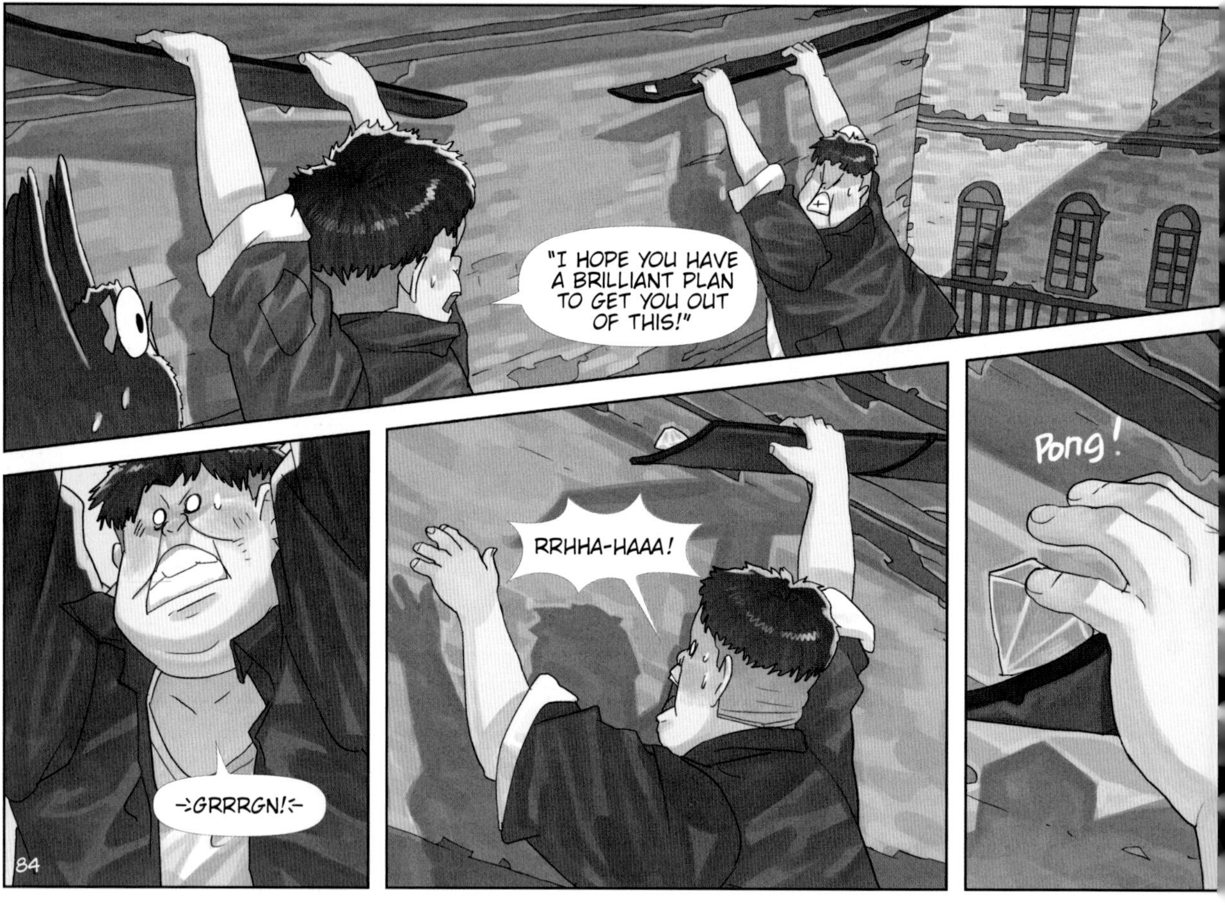
"I HOPE YOU HAVE A BRILLIANT PLAN TO GET YOU OUT OF THIS!"
-GRRRGN!-
RRHHA-HAAA!
Pong!

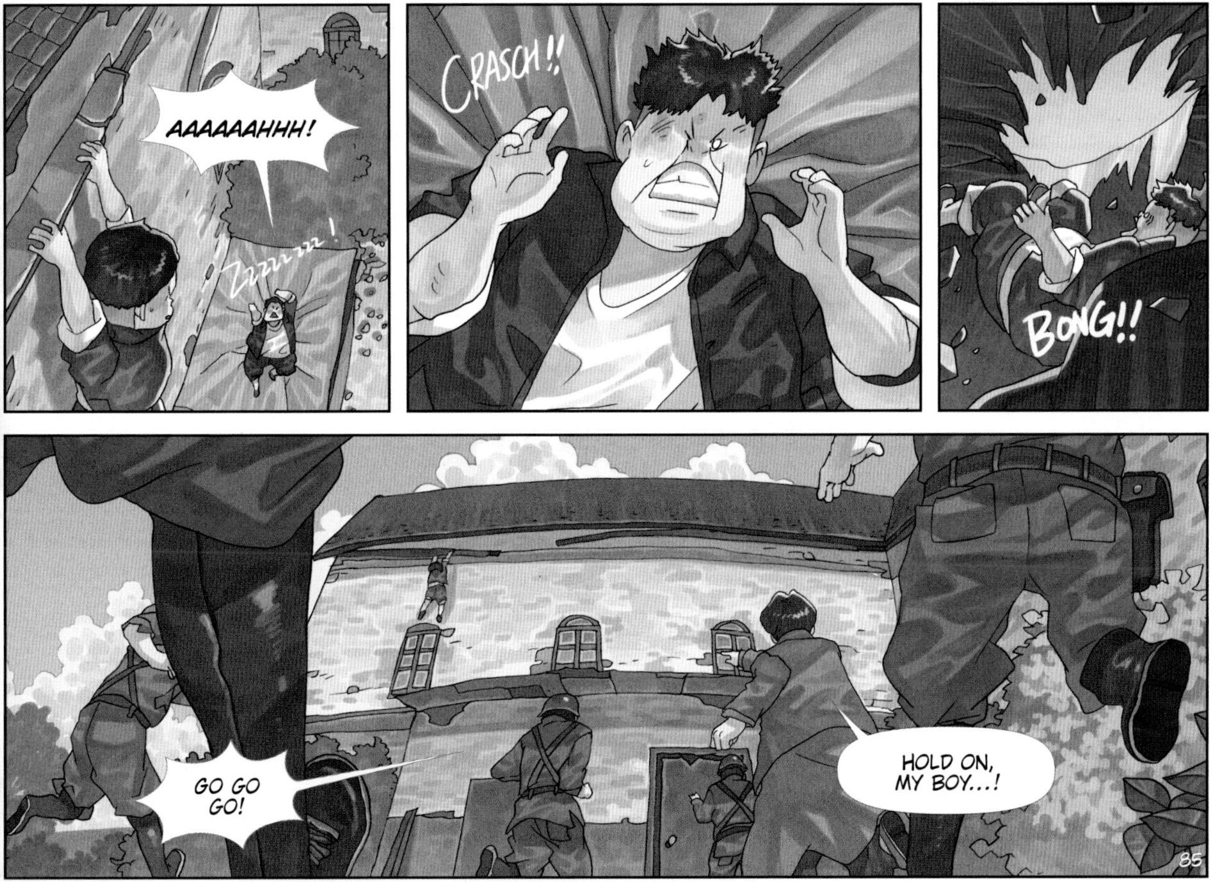
AAAAAAHHH!
Zzzzzzzz!
CRASCH!!
BONG!!
GO GO GO!
HOLD ON, MY BOY...!

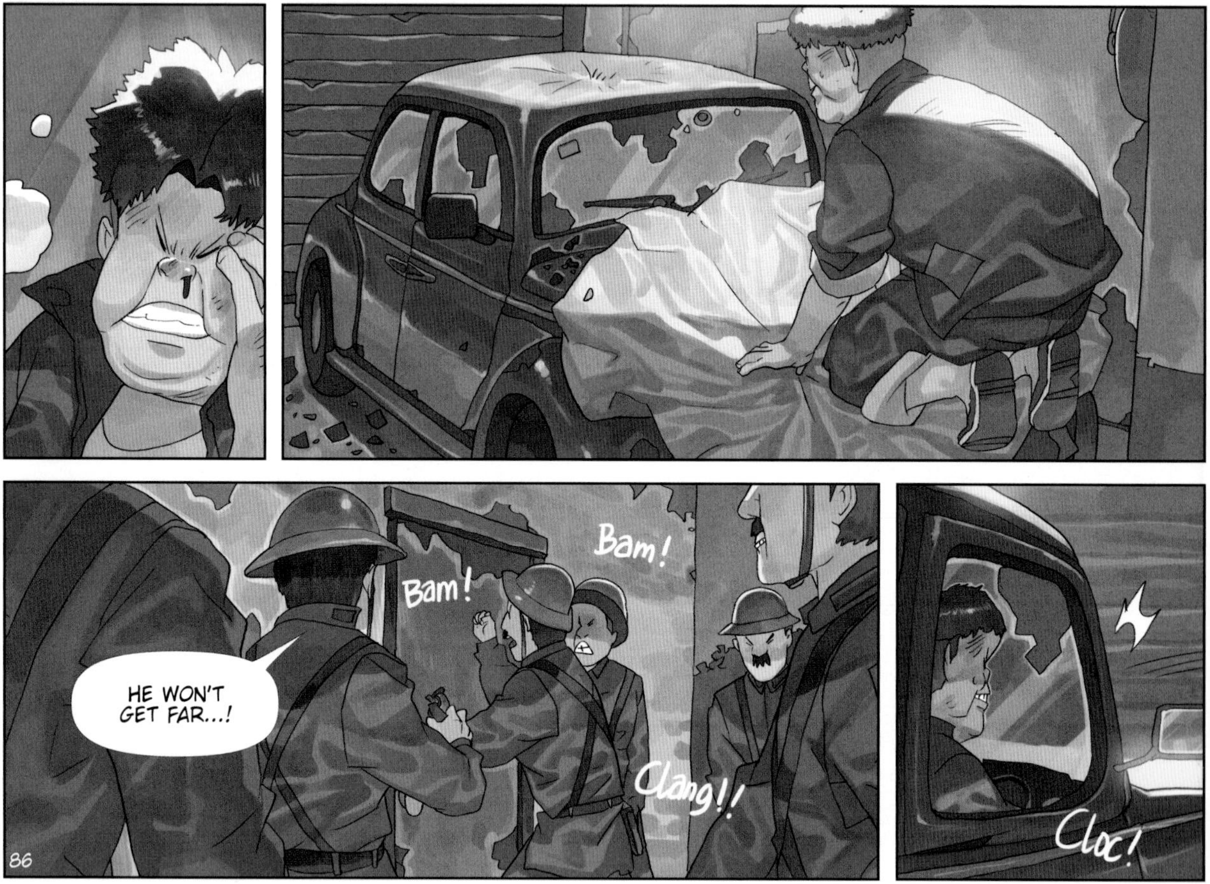
HE WON'T GET FAR...!
Bam!
Bam!
Clang!!
Cloc!

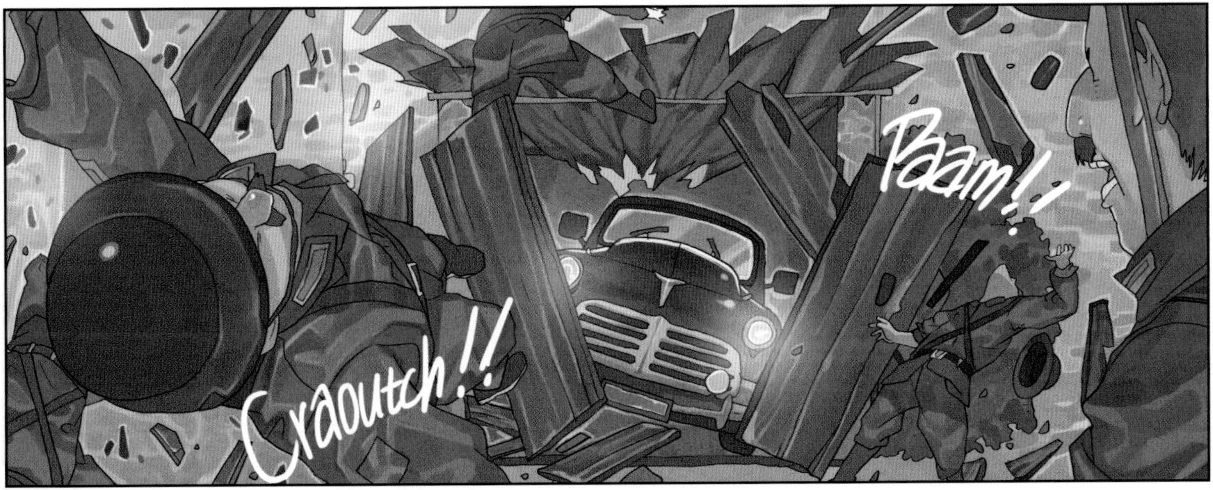
Craoutch!!
Paam!!

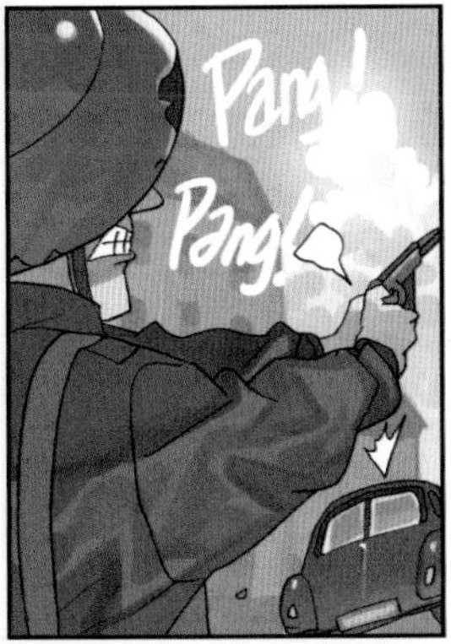
Pang!
Pang!

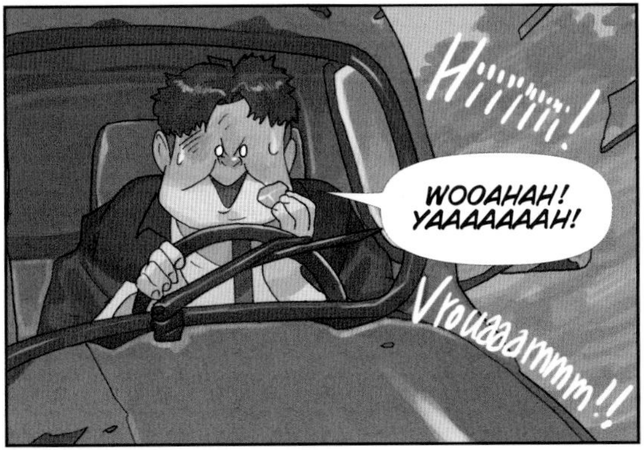
Hiiiiii!
WOOAHAH! YAAAAAAAH!
Vrouaaammmm!!

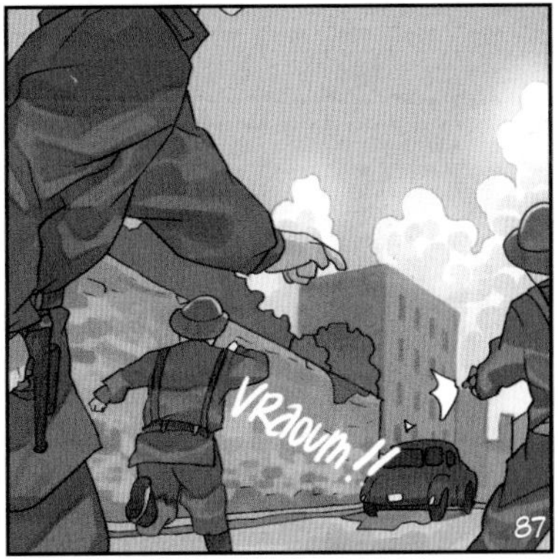
Vraoum!!

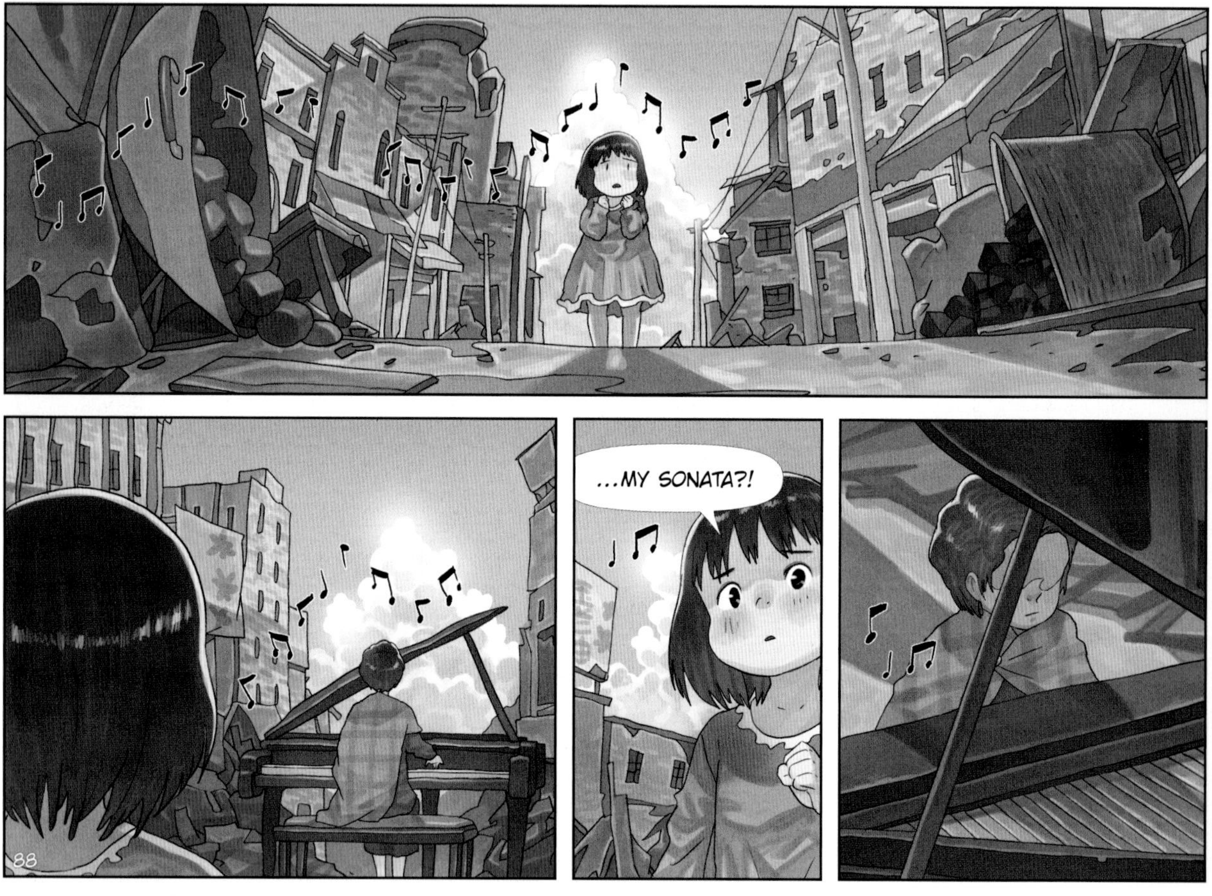
...MY SONATA?!

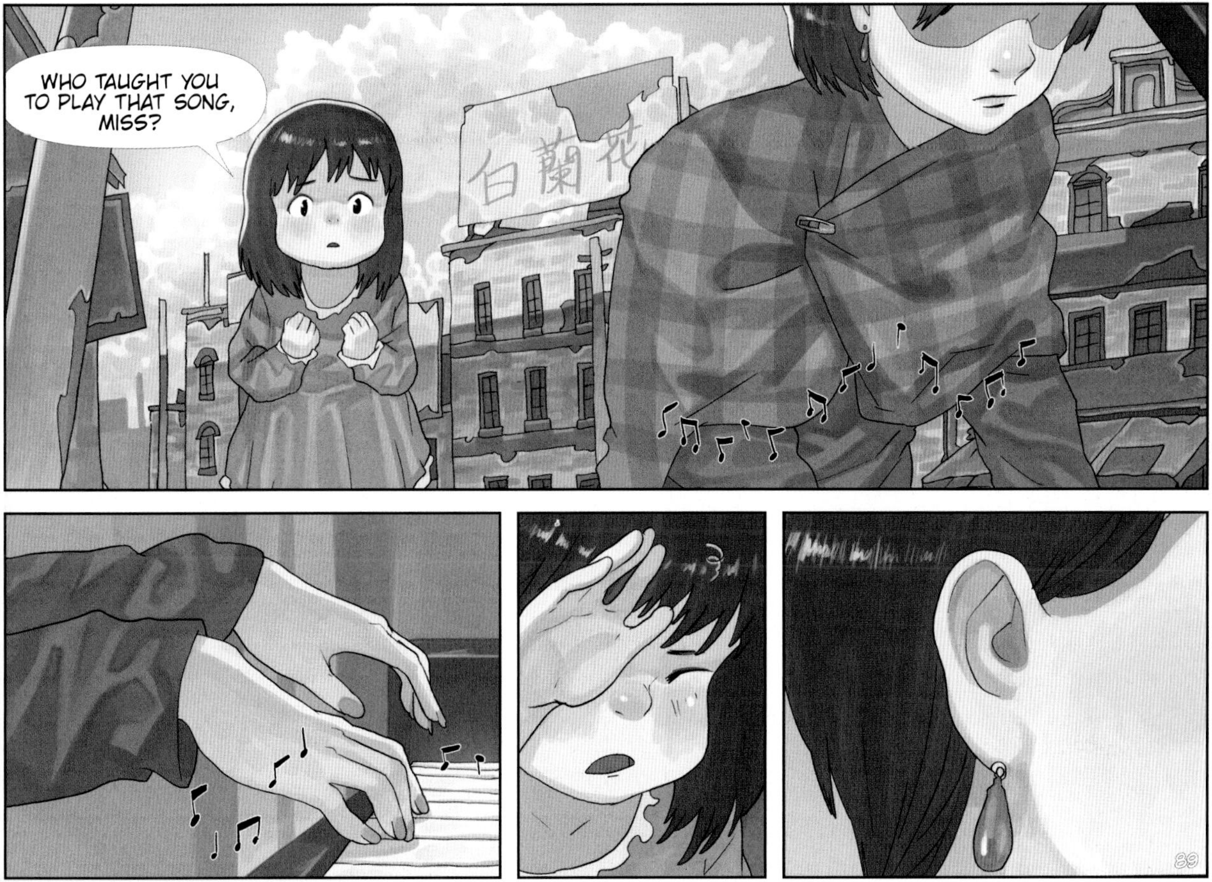
WHO TAUGHT YOU TO PLAY THAT SONG, MISS?
白蘭花

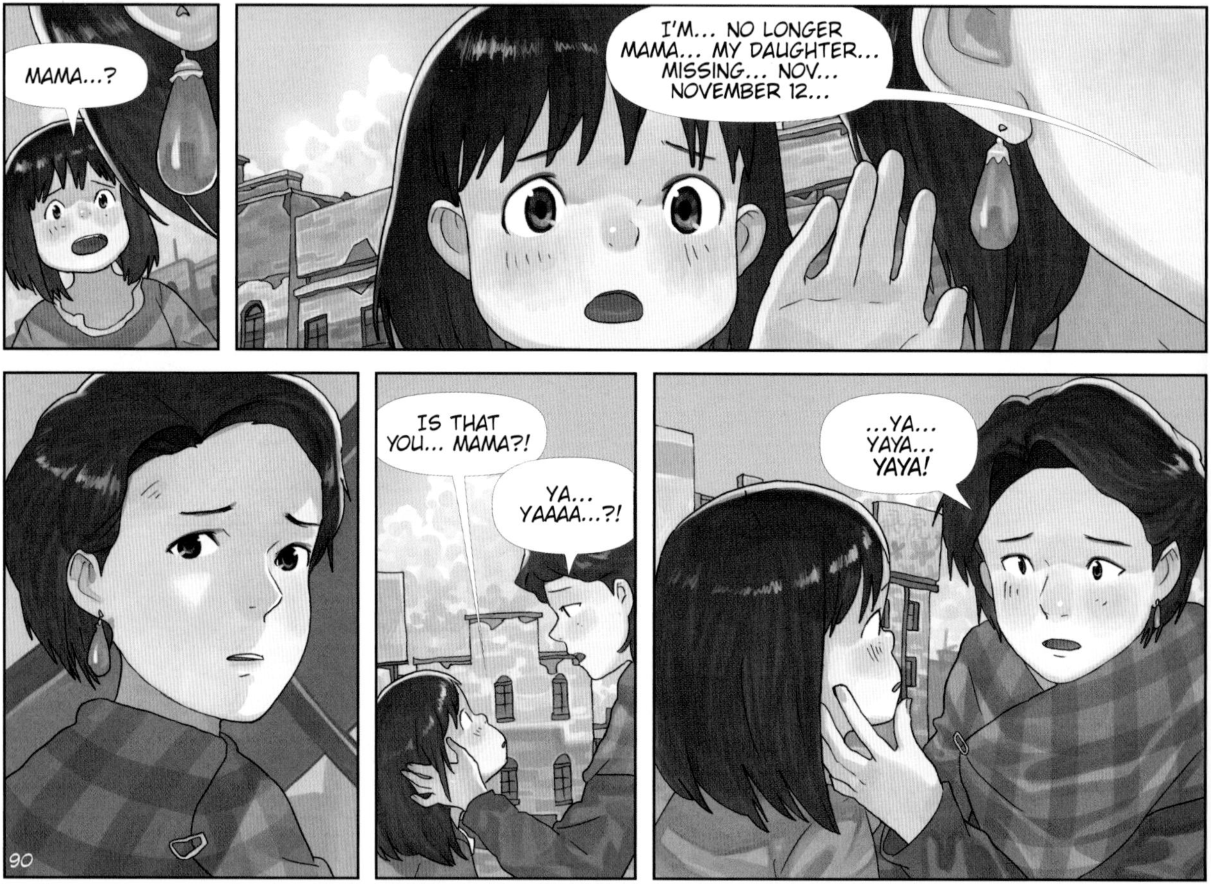
MAMA...?
I'M... NO LONGER MAMA... MY DAUGHTER... MISSING... NOV... NOVEMBER 12...
IS THAT YOU... MAMA?!
YA... YAAAA...?!
...YA... YAYA... YAYA!

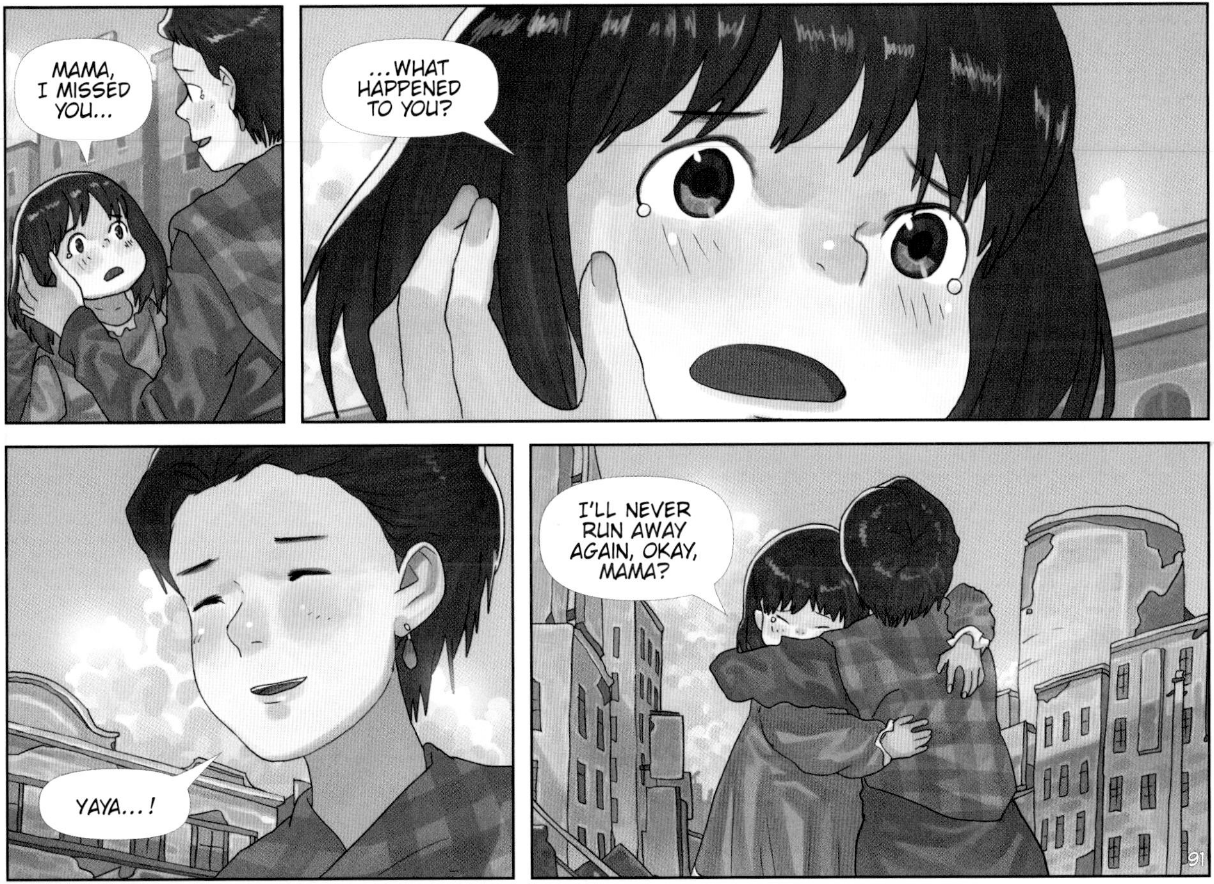
MAMA, I MISSED YOU...
...WHAT HAPPENED TO YOU?
YAYA...!
I'LL NEVER RUN AWAY AGAIN, OKAY, MAMA?

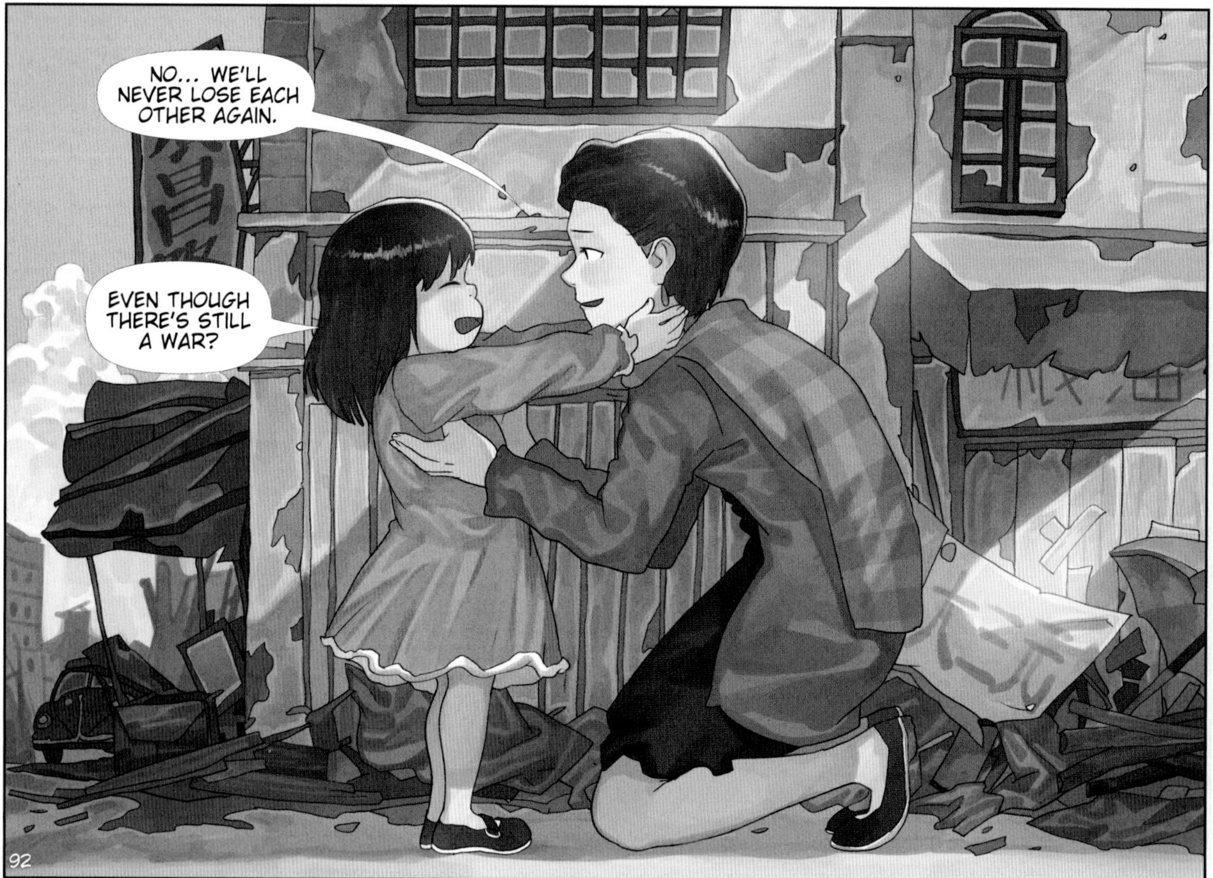
NO... WE'LL NEVER LOSE EACH OTHER AGAIN.
EVEN THOUGH THERE'S STILL A WAR?

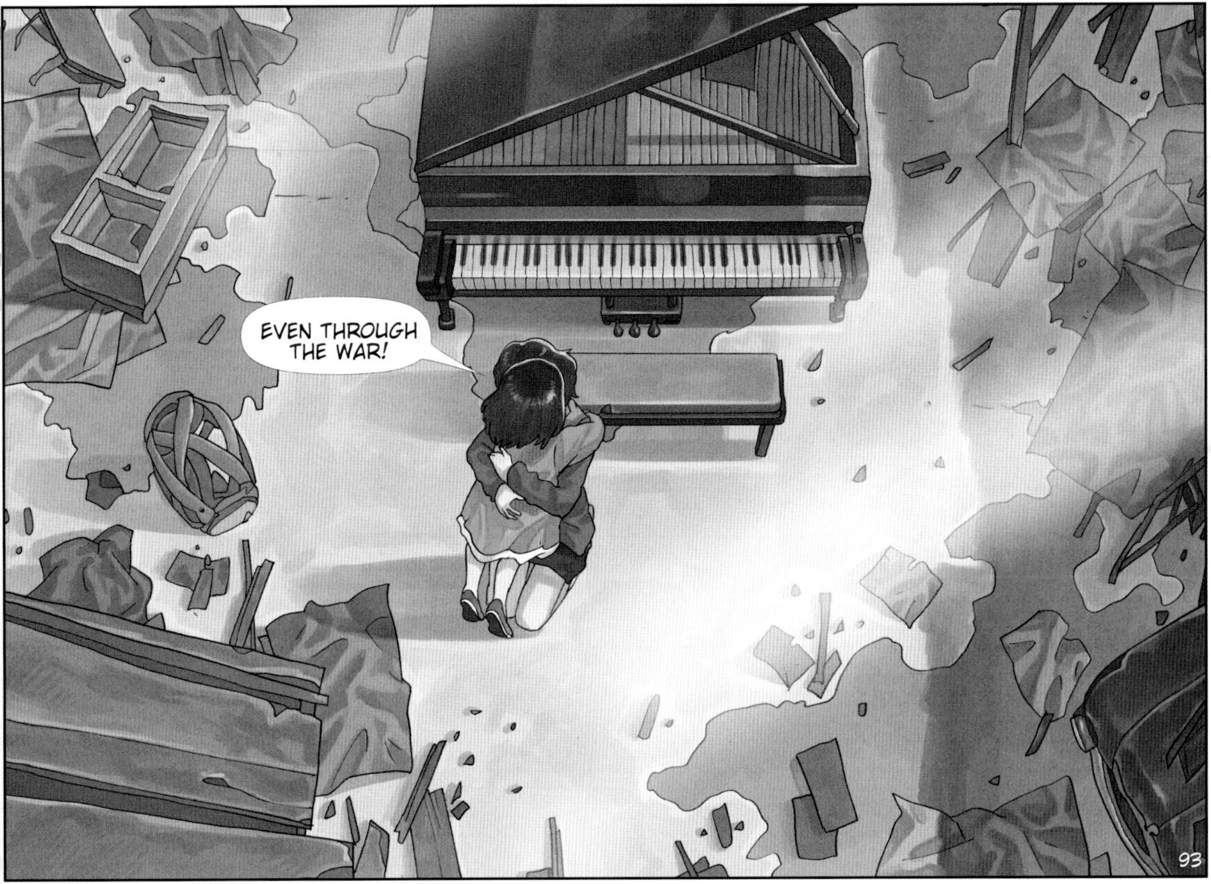
EVEN THROUGH THE WAR!

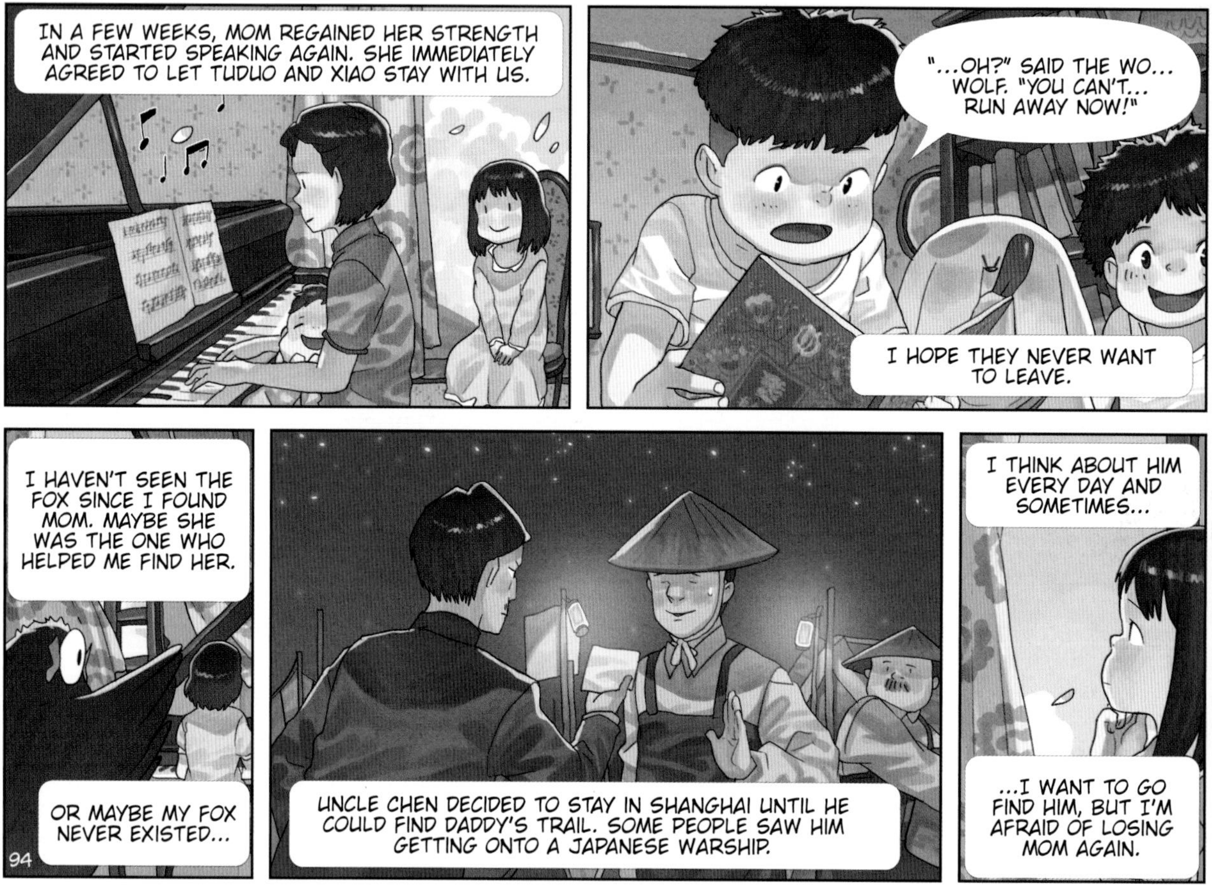
IN A FEW WEEKS, MOM REGAINED HER STRENGTH AND STARTED SPEAKING AGAIN. SHE IMMEDIATELY AGREED TO LET TUDUO AND XIAO STAY WITH US.
"...OH?" SAID THE WO... WOLF. "YOU CAN'T... RUN AWAY NOW!"
I HOPE THEY NEVER WANT TO LEAVE.
I HAVEN'T SEEN THE FOX SINCE I FOUND MOM. MAYBE SHE WAS THE ONE WHO HELPED ME FIND HER.
OR MAYBE MY FOX NEVER EXISTED...
UNCLE CHEN DECIDED TO STAY IN SHANGHAI UNTIL HE COULD FIND DADDY'S TRAIL. SOME PEOPLE SAW HIM GETTING ONTO A JAPANESE WARSHIP.
I THINK ABOUT HIM EVERY DAY AND SOMETIMES...
...I WANT TO GO FIND HIM, BUT I'M AFRAID OF LOSING MOM AGAIN.

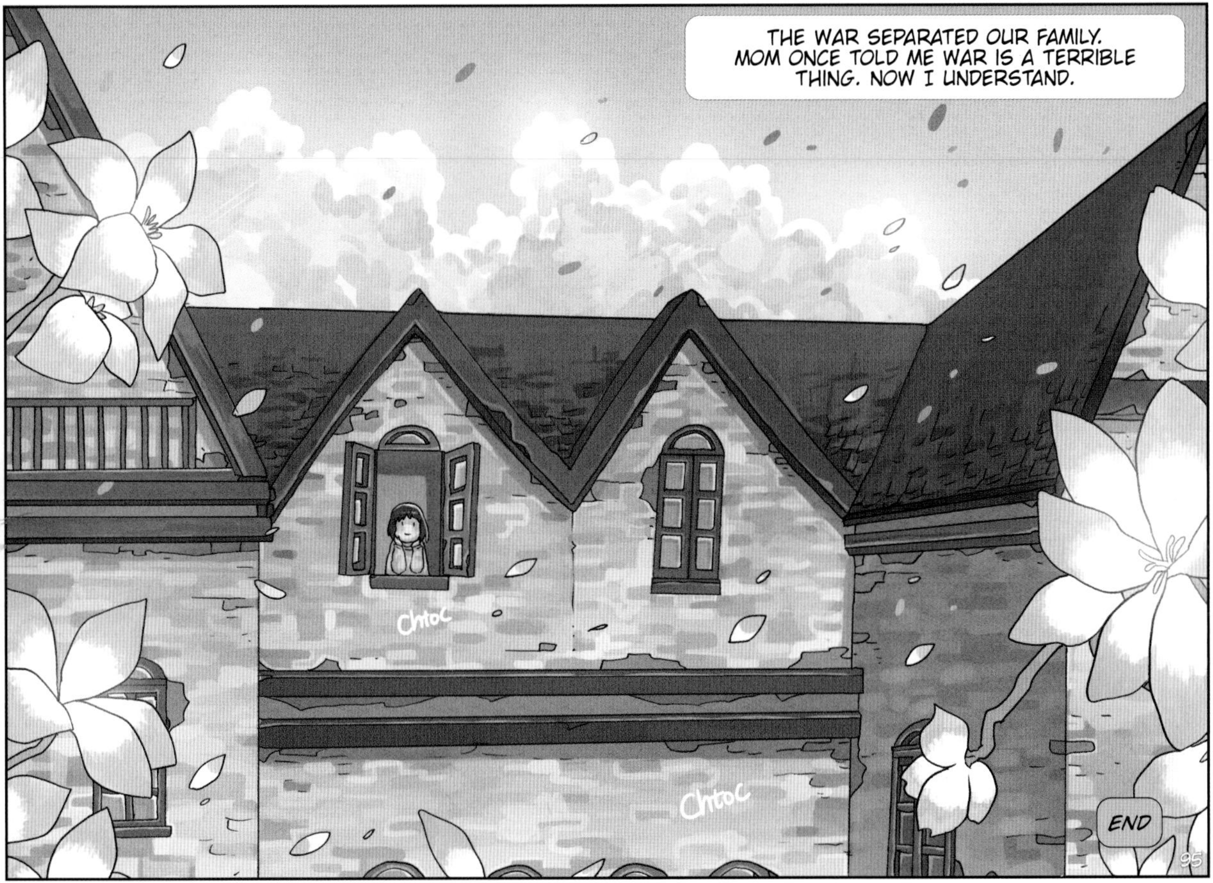
THE WAR SEPARATED OUR FAMILY. MOM ONCE TOLD ME WAR IS A TERRIBLE THING. NOW I UNDERSTAND.
Chtoc
Chtoc
END

HOW WONDERFUL IT IS TO FIND YOUR WAY HOME WITH ALL YOUR FRIENDS! I KNOW YAYA IS SAD THAT HER FATHER HASN'T COME BACK YET, BUT I ALREADY PUT THE SEAGULLS ON THE JOB TO FIND HIM!

ISBN: 978-1-951719-02-9
Library of Congress Control Number: 2020915854

The Ballad of Yaya, Vol. 9: Sonata, published 2020 by Magnetic Press, LLC.
Originally published in French under the title *La Balade de Yaya 9, La sonate* © Editions Fei 2013/Golo/Omont/Marty/Girard, in partnership with Beijing Total Vision Culture Spreads Co. Ltd. All rights reserved. MAGNETIC PRESS™, and all associated distinctive designs are trademarks of Magnetic Press, LLC. No similarity between any of the names, characters, persons, or institutions in this book with those of any living or dead person or institution is intended, and any such similarity which may exist is purely coincidental.

LES ÉDITIONS FEI

Printed in China.

10 9 8 7 6 5 4 3 2 1

TOTAL VISION
大視全景